BEHIND HER EYES

A RILEY THOMPSON THRILLER

ROBIN MAHLE

HARP HOUSE PUBLISHING, LLC.

Published by HARP House Publishing
July, 2018 (1st edition)

Cover design: Covermint Design

Editor: Hercules Editing and Consulting Services www.bzhercules.com

[1]

The patrol car rolled to a stop in front of the IGA, the main grocer in Owensville, Indiana, and the place had just been robbed. Two of the town's finest, Officer Riley Thompson and her partner, Officer Ethan Pruitt, emerged from their vehicle and headed toward the store's entrance. A few locals had gathered with growing interest in the muted light of a rising sun. Crime was a rare occurrence in this town and tongues were already wagging. Just a speck on a map, it was a town Riley Thompson knew well and had called home since birth.

"You want to talk to management, or should I?" Ethan stepped through the parting glass doors, hands on hips, scoping out the place with an eagle eye.

"Why don't you run on that. I'll have a word with the cashier who was confronted by the thief." Riley started toward the woman who'd had the misfortune of being in the wrong place at the wrong time. But on second thought, she stopped short. "Hey, Ethan?"

"Yeah?" The young officer with sharp refined features and a slender build turned back.

"On the off-chance they have video surveillance, see if you can get a copy?"

"You got it."

Riley was the senior officer, if only by a hair, which meant she gave the orders and did so with authority, minus the bravado. She'd joined the force shortly after her close friend and former Owensville officer Daniel Ward became captain of the department. That was going on six years now, when she was at the tender age of nineteen. However, Riley hadn't been a typical nineteen-year old. And now at the age of twenty-five, there was, in fact, nothing typical about her.

Riley and Daniel Ward were among those who had survived the EF4 tornado that had touched down fifteen years ago. It was a catastrophic event that changed them both.

"Good morning, ma'am. I'm Officer Thompson. You mind if I ask you some questions?" She whipped out her pad and pen.

The woman, perhaps in her late twenties, was traumatized and could only shake her head in response.

"Would you like some water?" Before the woman could answer, Riley was already on her way to the small fridge in the checkout lane that housed cold drinks, including bottled water. She retrieved one and returned to her. "Here."

"Thank you." The cashier swallowed down at least half of it.

"Can you tell me at about what time the suspect entered the store?" Riley asked.

"Um, I guess it was—I don't know exactly..."

"That's okay. Your best recollection is fine," Riley added.

"I guess about 6am. I started my shift at 2. I usually work 2 to 10." She chugged down the rest of the water.

"Okay. And was he wearing a mask?"

She nodded.

"Did you pick up on any identifying marks? Tattoos, scars, anything like that?" Riley continued taking notes.

"No. He wore a hoodie and a bandana over his mouth. But he had brown eyes, I saw that much. And he was kind of short, like maybe five-foot-five or something like that."

"That's good. Did he speak with an accent? New York, Texas, anything? Maybe a foreign accent?"

The cashier seemed to replay the terrifying exchange in her mind. "No. Just sounded like a regular guy from town."

Riley stopped writing and peered into the woman's eyes. She felt something that broke her train of thought. That was what usually happened. The feelings came first, then the images. But what Riley felt now was unrelated to the woman's recent trauma of the robbery. This person was suffering. And she was suffering from an addiction. Riley envisioned in her mind's eye the woman tying a tourniquet on her arm and flicking the needle she was about to insert in her vein.

At this point in Riley's life, she had learned to control the aftershocks the feelings and visions left in her. It had taken years, but there was a place tucked in the back of her brain where she stored these visions. A place she could call upon if needed, but that allowed her to function. Otherwise, it was likely she would end the way of her grandfather, who also had the gift. And it hadn't ended well for him.

Ethan approached with the manager. "He has video for us. It

captured the suspect, but the guy was smart enough to keep his face hidden."

"Anything outside? Do we know what kind of car he was driving?" Riley asked.

The manager was an older gentleman, fifties most likely, with kind eyes and a full head of salt and pepper hair. "I'm afraid I don't have cameras in the parking lot. Suppose I ought to consider installing them in light of what's happened."

"I saw the car," the cashier said. "It was a Chevy Malibu, I'm pretty sure. My dad had one when I was little. I remember what it looked like."

"So it was an older model?" Riley turned to her.

"Yeah, like 80s or something. It was black and had grey Bondo on one of the doors."

"That will be very helpful, thank you." Riley put away her pad and pen. "I think we've got enough to get started. Thank you both for your cooperation and we'll do everything we can to find the suspect."

"Thank you, Officer Thompson, Officer Pruitt." The manager looked to his employee. "You should go home, Brianne. Get some rest. In fact, why don't you take tonight off too?"

"But I..."

He raised his hand. "Paid, of course."

Riley waited for the manager to step away. "I'll meet you outside," she said to Ethan. When the two young women were alone, Riley began, "Brianne. That's a beautiful name. You know, you've been through a lot this morning. Your boss is right, you should try to get some rest. But if you need anything or just want to talk to someone, give her a call." Riley handed Brianne a business card. "She's a good listener. She'll be able to help you—with whatever else you're dealing with too." Riley tipped her head with gratitude and walked outside where Ethan waited. She stood next to him as they both gazed out over the parking lot. Most of the townspeople were leaving now that the show was over.

Ethan eyed her. "You must've seen something in her."

"Not much I can do about it. Just offered her an ear—and a shoulder, if she wanted one." Riley approached the patrol car and opened the door, stepping inside.

Ethan slid into the passenger seat. "I truly believe you have a gift from God, but all I can say is, I'm glad it's not me. Pretty sure I couldn't deal with that."

Riley started the engine. "You get used to it."

———

Owensville had a population of about 4,000, which was an increase from the 3,000 it had been when Riley was growing up. Many people left town after the Caterpillar plant closed when she was eight years old. However, times were better now. Jobs were coming back and the town was in the middle of a renaissance of sorts. But all this meant for Riley was that the four officers, the dispatcher, and the captain who ran the department would become increasingly busy. A side-effect of the economic growth.

Owensville still had miles to go before it could compete with nearby Terra Haute. The station house alone was in need of maintenance. Its interior lacked a certain quality, or rather, any quality. But that didn't matter much to Riley. She was working for the man who had believed in her, a man who saved her once. And had saved her entire family.

Captain Daniel Ward was at his desk at the return of half his police force. Riley and Ethan entered his office.

Ward sat back and removed his reading glasses. "How'd it go?"

"We got surveillance video, but nothing that showed the suspect's face," Ethan began. "But Riley talked to the cashier, a woman named Brianne, who'd been confronted by the robber, and lucky for us, she caught a pretty good glimpse of his car."

"Is that right?" Ward turned to Riley. "Plates?"

She shook her head. "We weren't that lucky. But we'll run a search for the vehicle and see what comes up."

"Good. Anything else?"

"Nope." Riley was quick to answer before Ethan had the chance. "We'll file the report and start searching for the vehicle."

"All right, then. Best get on it." Ward returned his glasses to his face and continued working.

As Riley and Ethan stepped back out into the bullpen, Ethan began, "Why didn't you tell him what you saw in that woman?"

"Because it has nothing to do with the investigation."

"It could. Should she be called to the stand in a trial, her credibility could be at stake."

"That's assuming we catch the thief," Riley said. "We'll cross that bridge when we come to it."

"Whatever you say." Ethan returned to his desk.

The other half of the police force worked the night shift and Riley hadn't had the opportunity to work with them much, but she liked the guys well enough. A couple of local boys who went to the same school as Riley. It seemed most people born in Owensville around the time she was couldn't figure out how to leave. Maybe that was what made small towns so great. Everyone knew everyone else. Of course, maybe that was what made small towns not so great. Everyone knew everyone else.

Riley never regretted her decision to stay. After the tornado, her folks, who had been on the verge of divorce at the time, couldn't make amends and finally divorced a few years later. She laid some of the blame at her own feet. It had been a tough time. She was just discovering her abilities and they were harder to control—damn near impossible, more like. A lot of things contributed to the end of her parents' marriage, but that was all water under the bridge now. Especially since her dad, Jack, had remarried and had moved to Indianapolis. His new wife had popped out a couple of kids, meaning Riley had more siblings, aside from her full-blooded brother and sister, not that Jack visited any of them. It lingered in the back of Riley's mind if those new siblings of hers had the same power she did. After all, it had come from Jack's father. So far as she knew, only Riley had been the chosen one. Lucky her.

Ward dashed out of his office. "A body's turned up at the plant. We need to get down there ASAP."

Riley shot up from her chair. "What? They're still refurbishing it, aren't they?"

"Yes, they are. It's one hell of a mess down there right now. Fortunately, no one's working today and it was only the project manager who showed up and spotted the body. I'll explain more in the car. We need to get down there. Pruitt, you mind holding down the fort?"

"Not at all, Captain, but if you need me..."

"Gotcha. Let's head out, Thompson." Ward pulled open the door and waited for her.

Ethan watched as the two left and the captain sped out of the parking lot. Yet another thing that rarely happened in Owensville —murder. "What in the world is going on here today?"

He was used to playing second fiddle to Riley. It was the history she had with Ward. And it was a long one at that. He knew someday he'd get his opportunity. Ward was getting up there and he figured it would be Riley who would take his place sometime in the future. Then he'd be her right-hand man. Didn't matter that he'd wanted to be more than that. Riley was closed off when it came to relationships. He suspected she knew he had feelings for her. Hell, reading minds was the least of her talents. Given that she'd never acknowledged them left the impression she didn't feel the same. But maybe someday she would.

————

RILEY SENSED WHAT HER CAPTAIN WAS FEELING THE MOMENT the plant came into view. She hadn't been back since the tornado. Ward had been, but that was for security measures the new owner wanted to put in place as the rebuilding process began. The plant had been purchased by a dog food manufacturer, of all things. Once a thriving plant that turned out heavy-duty earth moving equipment, it would now turn out organic, gluten free, dog food. Maybe she'd buy some for her dog, CJ. He was getting up there in age and could probably benefit from the healthy kibble.

"You okay?"

She was pulled back into the moment. "Huh? Oh, yeah. I'm fine."

"Cause I can go in alone, if you'd prefer," Ward added.

"No. I'm an officer of the law. Besides, I don't want this place to hold that kind of power over me any more. It's about time the two of us reconciled."

"Good. I'm glad to hear you say that. Better go see what kind of hellacious scene we've got in there." He pulled into the lot where only one other vehicle remained, and that was likely the project manager's truck.

Ward cut the engine and began to step out. When he noticed Riley hadn't moved, he leaned back in. "Riley, it's time."

"Yeah. Right." She stepped out and peered at the enormous building.

They began their approach when the manager stepped through the doors and into the light of the late afternoon sun. With his eyes squinted, he offered his hand. "Kilroy Bayliss. People call me Roy. I'm the project manager in charge of this refurb."

"Mr. Bayliss—Roy. I'm Captain Dan Ward, and this is Officer Riley Thompson. Why don't you show us what you found?"

"It's a hell of a thing, Captain. Don't know what's happening to society these days." He led the way into the building.

Riley stepped inside, and a rush of memories surfaced. "Stop," she whispered.

"What's that, Miss?" Bayliss asked.

"Nothing. Sorry."

Ward peered at her, his eyes asking the question she already knew.

She nodded in return and continued trailing the men. The building hadn't changed much. The new windows were in the process of being installed. Should help button down the place. But inside, it was just about the same, albeit the machinery that had been left behind and that had turned into deadly projectiles the night of the tornado was now gone too.

"She's just over here." Bayliss walked toward the back of the large shell of a building. "The contractor was using this as a concrete washout." He pointed to a large plastic tub, like a kiddie pool, but heavier duty and gray. "When I got here, I was just walking around, making note of what's been done and that's when I saw her. Weren't no need to check for a pulse. Looked like she'd been gone a long time. And of course, all the concrete."

Riley was no novice when it came to viewing dead bodies, and it wasn't because she was a cop. Her eyes fell upon a great many terrible things in her youth; dead bodies were but one.

"I called you all out just as soon as I saw her. I have to tell you, Captain Ward, I've never seen a dead body before and I can't say as I'd ever want to see one again."

"Do you have any idea who this is? Does she work for the company?" Ward asked.

"I don't believe so. If she does, I've never seen her before. Who would do such a thing?"

Riley examined the young woman. She looked to be in her late teens, maybe early twenties. Hard to say with the concrete someone had poured into her mouth. As it dried, it expanded and now her face was ripped open in some kind of horrific permanent smile. The rest of her hadn't fared much better. Her t-shirt was ripped, partially exposing her bra beneath. And she wore a denim mini-skirt, which, considering autumn was here, seemed an odd choice given the chilly weather.

"You guys got a forensics team or something? Like a CSI?" Bayliss asked.

"I'm afraid we are the CSI." Ward turned to Riley. "Let's start documenting the scene so we can call out the coroner and get her out of here."

Riley retrieved her cell phone and began snapping pictures of the girl. Her skin was blue, like she'd been drowned, what skin was left uncovered, anyway. Most of her body was cast in solid concrete. With a gentle touch, Riley placed her fingertips on the girl's right arm. She'd hoped something would arise in her mind. Something that might reveal who she was and what had happened to her. However, it seemed Riley was too late. The young woman was too far gone and Riley couldn't see anything inside her except a black void.

The coroner soon turned up and Ward met him at the entrance. "Doc. You're not going to believe this one." He started back toward the body where Riley stayed on watch.

The coroner peered at the victim. "How are we supposed to get her out?"

"I was kind of hoping you might have an idea," Ward replied.

He shook his head and folded his arms across his meager chest. "Lord Almighty, Dan, I don't have a clue. Guess we have no choice but to cut her out."

"I'm sure there's some equipment around here," Riley began. "Mr. Bayliss? Do you have anything that would work?"

"Well, I suppose I do, as grizzly as that sounds. Let me call in a few of my guys to help."

"I'll supervise," the doctor began. "Can't afford any mishaps."

———

WHEN BAYLISS' CREW ARRIVED WITH THE EQUIPMENT, THE men cringed at the idea.

"I'm sorry, boys. It's gotta be this way," Bayliss replied.

With saws and chisels in hand, the men began to carefully carve away the concrete around the victim's small frame.

"Please be careful," the doctor said.

"I'm sure they're doing the best they can." Riley sensed the apprehension and repulsion the men felt as they began to extract the young woman from her concrete grave.

"What about all that stuff on her face?" one of the men asked.

"Don't touch that. Just get enough off so we can haul her out of here," the coroner replied.

"How long before you'll know anything? Identity would be most useful," Ward asked.

"We have to get all the concrete off of her first. That won't be easy. And, it'll leave burn marks on most of her body, making it that much harder to determine cause of death."

"Excuse me for being naïve," Bayliss began, "but isn't cause of death all that concrete that hardened in her mouth?"

"I can understand why you'd think that, but this could've happened post-mortem. I just can't say with any certainty," the doctor replied.

"I need to know who this girl is so I can notify next of kin." Ward turned to Riley. "While the doc here is working on an ID, let's you, me, and Pruitt get to work on pulling up recent missing persons cases."

"We don't have any in Owensville that I'm aware of," Riley replied.

"No, but I'm figuring this girl isn't from around here, so we'll need to include the larger municipalities in the search."

"I can ask around too. I mean, here in town. It's possible she's a resident," Riley said.

"Sure. Can't rule out anything just yet." Ward placed his

hands on his hips as they hauled the woman still partially cast in concrete outside. "We'll have a look around. Check for prints and such."

"Beg your pardon, Captain, but this site has seen every trade and company rep inside its premises going on three weeks now. I imagine you'll pull up a whole lot of prints," Bayliss said.

"Well, you're right about that. In fact, it's best we get in touch with someone high enough on the food chain at your organization who can give us the names of those working this job. We'll have to rule out the prints we find in hopes of uncovering something useful."

"Okay. I'll get on it."

"Thank you, Mr. Bayliss. Thompson, let's go have a look-see."

[2]

The home where Riley grew up was in better shape now than when she was a child, though the memories within had been resistant to change. She and her brother, Dillon, often acted as home renovators for their mother, who now lived there alone. They helped her keep up on regular maintenance, something their father hadn't the money nor the desire to do. The recent exterior paint job and stained deck was completed this summer just in time for the inclement weather that was due to arrive any day now.

Dillon and Riley had remained close and he also still lived in Owensville with his family: wife Marjorie and their two children, baby Ella and toddler Danny. Daniel Ward was, of course, his namesake. After all, Ward helped shape Dillon, which was traditionally the job of a father.

Riley approached the front door and knocked lightly before inserting her key into the lock. Upon opening the door, she called out, "Mom? It's me." Riley continued inside in search of her mother, Ellen, and found her wrapped in a blanket curled up on the couch.

"Mom, it's freezing in here. Isn't your heat turned on?"

"It's cheaper to wrap up." Ellen's face wore all the pain and torment she'd experienced during her years with Jack. Gone were the bright eyes of the young girl who'd fallen head over heels for the high school football star. Now they stared back in a display of regret for what she'd let her life become.

Riley walked to the thermostat and kicked on the heat. "It's 55 degrees in here. No wonder you're in a blanket. You want a hot tea or coffee?"

"There's no need to fuss over me, Riley. I'm surprised to see you here. Is everything okay?"

Riley joined Ellen in the living room and sat on the chair next to her. "It's been a rough day. The IGA was robbed this morning. Ethan and I had to write the reports. Then," she hesitated, "a body was found."

At this, Ellen sat up. "A body?"

"At the old plant."

"You were at the plant today?" Ellen asked.

"I was. Some poor girl was found. We don't know who she is yet. It's been a few years since we had a homicide and Dan handled it then. But this one, the captain wanted me involved in."

"Why would he want you to go back to the plant? He should know better."

"Mom, I can't avoid the place forever. I think he knew that. He's trying to help. And I'm still a cop. It's my job. So, anyway, I thought I'd come see how you were doing. And I'm glad I did."

"Have you heard from your father lately?"

"No. Not for a few months, since my birthday. I know you don't like the fact that he's got another family, Mom, but he seems happy."

"Well, I guess you'd be the one to know." Ellen pushed the blanket from her shoulders. "I know your dad helped you get your house and I know he's tried to be a good father. But I fear for his wife—and his kids."

"I try to stay out of it, Mom. I can't let his life consume mine. I learned that a long time ago."

"I know you can't, baby. I appreciate you stopping by, but it sounds like you had a tough day. You should go home and get some rest. I'll be fine. Dillon's bringing the grandbabies over this weekend, so I have to start planning for that."

Riley stood and leaned over to kiss her mother's cheek. "Okay, Mom. I'll see you soon, then. You better call me if you need anything."

"I will. I promise."

Riley began to leave, but her mother called out again.

"Riley?"

"Yeah?"

"I know you like to show everyone how strong you are on the outside, but I also know what it must've meant for you to go back to the plant. Just remember, you can talk to me. I'm not as fragile as you think I am."

"I know, Mom. Thanks. Love you."

———

IT WAS THE MOMENT SHE'D WAITED FOR ALL DAY. RILEY WAS home and her schnauzer, CJ, was there to greet her. While she'd learned to control the influx of visions from the people she came across on a daily basis, it was her dog that gave her the much-needed break from the humanity that forced its way inside her brain. His short wagging tail, the excitement he expressed at the sight of her, and she couldn't feel anything but love. Perhaps she should've become a veterinarian.

"Hey, boy! You must be starving. Come on; let's get you some dinner." Riley walked into the kitchen and scooped the food into CJ's dish. While he scarfed it down, she began to make herself as sandwich. Riley wasn't much of a cook and it didn't make sense to cook for one anyway. Sometimes she'd get takeout, but usually a salad or soup would suffice.

After changing into her sweat pants and t-shirt, Riley plopped onto the sofa and turned on the television. The local news was airing and she immediately recognized the scene. A reporter stood outside the IGA that had been robbed and relayed the story to the viewers. Luckily, she'd left before the media arrived and now the reporter searched for someone to talk to, eventually finding a customer carrying groceries to her car.

He caught the woman off guard and hurled questions at her as to whether she felt safe now. Riley had to smile at the woman's response.

"Of course I feel safe. I have a license to carry," she'd said.

The reporter fumbled through the rest of the interview and quickly cut back to the station. At this, Riley had had enough and was ready to call it a night. As she turned off the television and walked around the house to lock up, she spotted headlights in her front window. It was 10:30 at night and this was a quiet neighbor-hood. A family neighborhood. So her cop instincts kicked into overdrive. She removed herself from view of the window and stepped into the breakfast nook, where she peered through the blinds in the dark room. The car drove down her street and slowed to a crawl in front of her house.

It finally disappeared, but the sensation lingered in her that raised the hair on the back of her neck. And Riley never dismissed her intuition. Ever.

————

EVEN IN THE LIGHT OF DAY, AFTER A FAIRLY RESTFUL NIGHT, Riley couldn't shake the impression that tickled the corner of her brain. What was it about that car she saw last night? Maybe it was best to put it aside for now because they had a murder investigation on their hands.

"Morning." Ethan held a cup of coffee as he made his way to his desk. "Can I get you one?"

"Thanks. I'll get it myself." Riley pulled off her coat and placed it over her desk chair before walking toward the coffee maker. "How was your night? You catch that interview at the IGA?"

"I did catch it. Funniest damn thing I've seen in quite a while."

"Cracked me up and put that reporter in his place, that's for sure." Riley poured the coffee and walked back to her desk. "Where's the captain? Didn't see his car outside."

"He's at the plant." Ethan sipped on his coffee.

"He is? Why?"

"Guess the big wigs over there wanted to meet with him. I don't know. I think they're looking to keep this quiet, wanting to avoid bad press."

Riley wondered if this was the nagging sensation that tugged at her. Could the car have been someone from the plant? No, of course not. That was something only a suspicious cop would think. But why hadn't Ward asked her to come along?

"Hey. You okay?" Ethan seemed to notice her sudden inattention.

"Yeah. Fine." She sat down and checked her email. "You know what? No, I'm not okay. Captain wanted me there yesterday. Why not today?"

"I wouldn't worry about it, Riley. What's going on? Something's clearly bothering you and I don't think it's about Ward."

"It's just—well, I've got one of those itches that needs to be scratched and it's bugging me is all."

"Oh yeah? What's crawled under your skin?"

"Last night. I was getting ready for bed and this car—I don't know. It was like hanging around my house or something."

"Hanging around? Like what, stalking you?" Ethan appeared concerned.

"I don't think so. It just didn't feel right, but don't worry about it. I'll keep an eye out. If I see it again, I'll make note of it."

The station house doors opened and Captain Ward entered. "Morning, guys. Sorry I'm late." He peered at Riley. "Can I talk to you for a minute?"

Riley glanced at Ethan before pushing up from her chair. "Sure." She followed him into his office, where he promptly closed the door. "Okay. What happened?"

"Sit down." Ward sat at his desk and began. "That girl—you said you didn't know her."

"I don't. I mean, it's not like I could really see her face well. It was covered in concrete. Do you know who she is now?"

"No, but I was asked to meet with one of the head honchos

from the plant. I guess they found something we missed yesterday."

His pause made Riley grow more concerned.

"They were trying to make up time because we had them shut down for so long yesterday. Anyway, they had guys in there before sun-up this morning. They found a school ID."

"*They* found a school ID? And you're telling me we missed it?"

He nodded. "Owensville High. Meaning she's a local girl. And yet nothing came up on our missing persons searches. Your brother still teaches there, right?"

"Yes." That gnawing feeling clawed its way back into her brain. "Who is she, Dan?"

"It's still undetermined because of the state of her body, but if the ID matches, and it wasn't left behind by someone else, it's likely she's Chloe Dawson. The ID was in bad shape and the year was illegible. Tough to say if it was current."

"The name doesn't ring a bell," Riley started. "I don't know the family. What concerns me is that if she is local, why hasn't anyone reported her missing?"

"Damn good question. The Dawson name doesn't ring a bell with me either. Could be some new family's just moved here. We can run a BMV search for cars registered to the Dawsons and check the other databases for the name."

"Or, the ID had already been there. You and I both know what the kids do there sometimes. But if that's the case, what was she doing there? When was she there?"

Ward leaned back in his chair. "I'd like you to take the lead on this. Get Pruitt to help you out, but whatever you find, come to me first. I don't want the press getting wind of anything until we get a positive ID on this girl. And I know what Pruitt can be like sometimes. He enjoys the attention when a reporter calls into the station."

"He'd never do anything to jeopardize an investigation."

"Not intentionally, I know that. Just keep a lid on things and get what you can. And, Riley, check with Dillon too. He might know Chloe Dawson."

She left his office and returned to her desk before reaching for her coat.

"Where are you going?" Ethan asked.

"I forgot to feed CJ this morning. I need to just run back home for a minute. I'll be back soon." She started out the door.

"Okay. Bye." He watched her pull away with doubt on his face. He approached Ward's door and knocked.

"Come in."

"Hey, Captain. Riley said she had to run home because she forgot to feed her dog. Is she okay? Ever since she got in this morning, she's been off. Got one of her feelings again."

"You know how she is, Pruitt. Just let her be. She won't be gone long, I'm sure."

"Whatever you say, boss."

———

RILEY SAT IN HER PATROL CAR OUTSIDE THE SCHOOL AND texted Dillon. Going inside would draw too many eyes and without knowing who this girl was, she didn't want the attention. It took a few minutes, but his reply appeared.

"Meet me in the courtyard in 5."

She replied with a thumbs-up emoji and waited.

A bell sounded and Riley remembered it well. It was the lunch bell and she could hear the high schoolers' voices from where she sat in the parking lot. The school had grown and had even undergone some improvements. Things had gotten better in Owensville, but they still had a long way to go.

Riley stepped out of her car and headed into the courtyard, but not before checking in with the front office. No one was allowed on school grounds without signing in. Even her. In fact, the buzzer system they'd recently installed made sure of that. "Just meeting Dillon," she'd said to the administrator.

"Go on ahead, Officer Thompson."

Riley stood near a tall oak with a bench built around it in the courtyard, when she spotted her older brother.

"Hey, sis. What's up?" Dillon had grown into a loving father, husband, and now teacher. God only knew how he managed that considering their upbringing. He leaned in to kiss her cheek.

"Hi. Listen, thanks for taking time out of your lunch break. I won't keep you."

"It's okay. I can see you're bothered by something. What is it?"

"I'll get right to the point. But hey, you can't say anything to anyone about this, okay? It's an ongoing investigation and we haven't ID'd the body yet."

"You haven't ID'd the body yet? What the hell's going on?" His face wore grave concern.

"Do you know a student named Chloe Dawson? I don't know the year."

"Oh my God, is she dead?"

"Dillon, just take a breath. We found an ID at the scene. Do you know who this girl is?" She showed him her school ID card.

Dillon examined it. "I don't know. Maybe. This school's grown a lot. Her face doesn't look familiar to me, though. It doesn't say what year she is."

"I know, which doesn't help. Can I ask you for a favor? Can you take a look inside the school's files? See if you can find this girl? We're searching other databases, and the BMV, but I want to cover every angle."

"How am I supposed to do that? I can't just rifle through things in the front office or break into the admin computer."

"Can't you make something up? If I go in there, questions will be asked. And right now, Dillon, I have no answers. I don't know if this girl is the victim or if she's..."

"The perpetrator?"

"I just—I don't know. Can you please just do this for me? And it needs to be sooner rather than later."

"Well, yeah, of course I can. Can you at least give me today? I'll find some excuse, but not until school lets out. I've got classes."

"Thank you." She cast her gaze around the school before continuing. "I saw Mom last night. She said you and Marjorie were bringing the kids by this weekend."

"Unless one of them gets sick, we should be good to go. You want to join us? Marjorie's going make dinner so Mom can relax. She's been working double shifts at the restaurant."

"I'd like that. But if this thing blows up..."

"Right. I gotta go, Riley. I'll call you later, when I know something." He turned toward the school grounds and walked away.

Upon returning to her patrol car, she stepped inside and keyed the ignition. She stared at the school for a moment, wondering if Chloe Dawson was a student or had been one. But the answer to that question would have to wait. In the meantime, Riley wanted to make a quick stop before heading back to the station. She wanted to see the only person who could help scratch that itch when it came.

———

THE INSIDE OF THE ASSISTED LIVING FACILITY REMINDED Riley of an old hotel, a grand one with sparkling chandeliers and marble floors. Except this place had a much smaller light fixture without all the grandiosity. And the marble floors were in need of buffing. Too many scratches left by walkers, wheelchairs and canes. But none of that mattered because she was only here to see one person, the one man who'd made nothing short of a colossal impact on her life.

"Well, hello, Riley. I'm surprised to see you here, and in uniform. To what do we owe the pleasure?" The kind middle-aged woman who worked behind the reception desk smiled widely at their most frequent visitor.

"I was wondering if Carl was available? I know I'm a day early, but I had a few spare minutes and I wanted to see his smiling face."

"Carl? Smile?" She pursed her lips. "Now really, I don't think that man's smiled since 1975."

Riley laughed. "You might be right, but I'd like to see him in any case."

"To each his own. He's in his room, though he's just had lunch, so he might be napping. I'll ring him and let him know you're here. You can go on up."

"Thank you." Riley walked toward the elevators and stepped inside, pressing the second-floor button. Her weekly visit was early, but all she wanted was to see him and she hoped he was in a good mood. That depended on how the Hoosiers were doing—and it was still a little too early in the season to tell.

Riley knocked on his door. "Carl, it's me, Riley."

"Come in. It's open."

She stepped inside the small apartment. Just a bedroom, bathroom, and living room with a small kitchenette. No cooking appliances, though. All the residents ate downstairs in the dining hall.

"You're early. What's wrong?" Carl sat in his recliner and peered over at her.

His hair was much greyer and thinner than when Riley met this man fifteen years ago. He'd also grown even more cantankerous, if that was possible. But she loved him with all her heart. And he felt the same.

"Nothing. I just wanted to stop in and say hello," she replied.

"You're in uniform. You don't usually come by in uniform. Means you're working."

"I am. I was actually doing some running around for the captain and thought I'd stop by on my way back."

"Uh-huh. Well, it's good to see you anyway, Riley. Sit down. If you want something to drink, you'll have go back downstairs. I just ran out of pop and those damn nurses haven't brought me any more."

"I'm okay, Carl, thanks. How are you doing?"

"Watching these damn pansies play basketball like a bunch of girls." He stopped short and turned to her. "No offense."

"None taken."

"So, what'd you see? I figure you're here because you saw something that isn't sitting right with you."

He always could tell when she was going through a difficult time.

"It's just this case. We found some poor girl in the old plant —murdered."

Carl's eyes widened. "The plant? You said they was turning it into something else. Or something."

"They are. A dog food manufacturing facility."

"And you found a girl?"

"A dead girl. Young. Don't know who she is yet."

"I see. And you can't see inside her, is that right?" Carl took a deep breath but coughed up the air quickly.

"She's been gone too long. I got nothing. Not one damn thing." Riley slumped into the chair.

"And that's what's bothering you?"

"I guess. Maybe something else too."

"I figured as much. Come on, spill it. What's really going on?" Carl raised a brow.

"I'm getting this weird feeling. I saw a strange car outside my house last night and I don't know. Just gave me the willies, I guess."

"You guess, huh? Well, I've known you long enough to know that those feelings of yours usually amount to something. Maybe you'd better keep an eye out. See if you see that car again. Do your research."

"That's what I was thinking."

"Okay then. Go on now. I need to get back to the game. Go on back to work. That's where they need you most. You don't need to keep looking after me. I got plenty of nurses here to do that."

Riley stood. "Okay, Carl. I'll leave you be. Oh, Dillon says hi. I saw him earlier."

"He's a good kid. Turned out be to a good man too."

"You had a lot to do with that. Listen, I'll check up on you again soon." She kissed his cheek. "See you later."

[3]

Intuition was a powerful thing, but for Riley Thompson, it had been known to save her life a time or two. While her current unease didn't feel life-threatening, it was disturbing nonetheless. And it was more than the death of that young woman. Putting her finger on it remained elusive.

She returned to the station house knowing Ward would want answers from Dillon, but what she didn't know was that an old friend and lover would be waiting for her.

"Riley." Jacob Biggs stood inside as she entered the station, a tender smile playing on his lips.

Her jaw fell to the floor. "Jacob. What are you doing here?"

Ethan was at his desk and witnessed the exchange with suspicion.

Everyone knew Jacob. And the relationship he had with Riley back in high school was the stuff of legend. But he broke her heart, as some boys do. And it was particularly difficult for Riley when this was the same boy she'd fallen in love with when they were only ten years old. Of course, it had been several years later before they would date, but they had been close friends until that time. Almost as close as Riley had been with Kaitlyn Ross, her best friend since birth. However, Kaitlyn left Owensville too, just like Jacob had. She hadn't blamed either of them. In those days, jobs were still scarce and they decided college was a better path for them.

Riley's path diverged. She knew her skills would be put to better use helping to keep the community safe from harm. Putting others ahead of herself was something she'd done for as long as she could remember. And squandering the gift she received from God and her grandfather was something she wouldn't dare consider. It was her purpose on this planet.

"I stopped by your house—your mom's house. She said you worked for the department now. Guess I should've figured that. It's what you always wanted."

"Yeah." She continued inside, stunned and unsure of herself for the first time in years. It was Jacob's parting gift—creating uncertainty.

"Do you think we could maybe talk? Outside?" He placed his hands in his pockets, looking as though he was seeking forgiveness for something.

Riley looked at Ethan. "Captain here?"

"In his office." Ethan kept a keen eye on Jacob. "He's been waiting on your return."

"Right. Um, okay." She walked past Jacob. "Just give me a minute, please. I need to check in with Captain Ward."

"Sure. Of course." The boy with dark, floppy hair and a gangly stance had grown into a man with a sultry gaze and a frame that had filled out nicely.

Riley walked into the captain's office. "I'm back. Dillon said he'd look into Chloe Dawson, but that he didn't recognize the name right off the bat."

"Did he say when he'd get back to you?"

"He has to find a work-around. Getting into student files isn't something he's permitted to do. He asked me to give him till the end of the day."

"Good. Good work."

She dropped her tone to just above a whisper. "How long has Jacob been here?"

"Not long. Any idea why he's here?"

"Not a clue. He wants to talk. So I guess I'll talk to him."

Ward studied her. "And you're okay with that?"

"Yes, I'll be fine." Riley began to leave.

"Hey, remember, he's the one who left. Not you," Ward was quick to remind her.

She closed the captain's door and returned to the bullpen, where Jacob still waited. "If you don't mind the chill in the air, we can talk outside." Riley continued out, but not before a final glance to Ethan, who was less than pleased by Jacob's arrival.

"Sorry for the unexpected visit." Jacob pulled his coat around him and joined her outside. "How've you been? You look good."

"Thanks. Keeping busy." She peered into the distance, avoiding him as best she could.

"You like it here? Working for the police, I mean."

"Of course I do. It's what I was meant for, just like you said." He'd caught her off guard and she didn't like the feeling. In fact, she wondered if it had been his car that passed by her house last night. "When did you get into town?"

"A couple days ago, actually. Took a while for me to muster up the courage to come see you."

"And you say you stopped by my mom's house?" She'd begun to sound as though she was interrogating him.

"Um, yeah. Yesterday. She said you'd just stopped by earlier in the day or something. And that if I'd been there a little sooner, I would've caught you. Anyway, she said you worked here."

"Did she tell you where I live now?" Riley pressed on.

"Well, yeah, she did. But I didn't want to just show up at your house."

"Right." At least she knew who the car belonged to now. That put her mind at ease. "What brings you back home?"

"I sort of broke up with my girlfriend, and I got laid off a few weeks ago. I didn't really know what was going to be next for me. So, I figured, maybe I'd take some time to sort things out."

"Your folks are living in Terra Haute now, right? You stop by there first to see them?"

"No, I came straight back here. I'll make it out to see them, though, once I figure out some stuff. They'll just grill me on what my plans are, and honestly," he peered at Riley. "I don't know what I'm going to do."

He captured her gaze and held it. She felt queasy. His head was jumbled, his thoughts incomplete. And it all hurled toward her like the debris on the night of the tornado. She finally closed her eyes.

"I'm sorry, I forgot." Jacob broke away.

"You didn't forget. And you never were very good at keeping your feelings from me."

"How could I be when you recognized them before I did?" He took in a breath of the fresh cool air. "Look, I know you need to get back to work. Do you think we could meet later? For dinner, maybe, and catch up?"

"I don't know, Jacob. We've got this big case going right now. I need to see how the rest of my day pans out."

"Sure, I understand." He retrieved his keys from his coat pocket. "Just, maybe give me a call when you can. Maybe we can set something up. I'll be in town for a while." He stepped off the curb and into the parking lot.

"Where are you staying?" she asked.

"With my cousin."

"Right. I forgot he's still here."

"Yeah. Most everyone left," Jacob said.

"Except me."

"Except you." He stepped into his car and pulled away.

———

LATE AFTERNOON BROUGHT IN THE WINDS FROM THE NORTH as the fall weather grew cooler. It also brought in the other officers who worked the nightshift. Lowell Abrams and Chris Decker had been partners for a number of years, long before Riley joined the force. And they preferred working nights because that was usually when things happened. It was also better pay.

Riley considered working nights when she was hired on, but she knew what went on in this town at night, after football games, on weekends, and she really didn't want any part in that. She preferred the days, not because they were easy, but because she didn't have to deal with teenagers. They were the ones who couldn't control their emotions. And Riley felt every last one of them. It would've been too much. Of course, she'd learned much since those early days of the gift. The voices eventually quieted. The images became fewer and she learned what to listen to and what to ignore. But teen angst, teen drama, and worst of all, seeing how so many of them despised their parents made it difficult. Most of those kids didn't know how lucky they were.

"Evening, folks." Lowell Abrams, a moderately handsome but too thin man, was pushing thirty and was still single.

Riley had no interest in him. He was brash and oozed machismo to the point that it could be misconstrued as sexist to anyone else. It was like he grew up watching a bunch of cop shows and figured that was how the cool ones behaved.

Chris Decker was almost the polar opposite. In fact, it seemed implausible the two could remain partners. He was cool, calm, and collected. Average looks. Nothing special. But he had a big heart and that went farther, in Riley's eyes, than looks did any day of the week.

"How's the homicide investigation going?" Abrams sat down across from Riley and stretched his legs out. "Can't believe you were lucky enough to get in on that one. It ain't like we get a lot of murders in Owensville."

"I wouldn't say I was lucky that a girl is dead, Lowell," Riley replied.

"Ah, you're right. I didn't mean it that way."

"And no, nothing new yet. But it'd be helpful if you two kept an eye out for anyone coming or going from the direction of the plant. No one but the company and the contractors should be in that area."

"Ten-four. We'll keep our eyes peeled," Abrams replied.

"I heard Jacob Biggs rolled into town," Decker began. "Didn't you two have a thing going on back in the day?"

Riley wanted to roll her eyes because he knew they'd dated. Everyone knew. Even though he was three years her senior, he'd been around town. He also remembered the tornado.

"Yeah. He stopped in here to see her a few hours ago, didn't he, Riley?" Ethan looked at her with some irritation.

"He did."

"Great. College boy decided he needed to come home, eh?" Abrams added sardonically.

"He's been out of college for a few years now, Lowell. He was working for an architecture firm in Indianapolis. There's nothing wrong with that," she replied.

"I'm just pulling your chain, Riley. Geez. No need to get your panties in a bunch."

Captain Ward appeared from his office. "Hey. We don't need talk like that around here, Lowell."

"Sorry, Cap." He looked at Riley. "Sorry, Riley. No offense."

"Don't worry about it, Lowell. You couldn't cause my panties to bunch no matter how hard you tried."

Ethan and Chris Decker chuckled, though it seemed Ward didn't find the humor in it.

"You hear from your brother yet?" Ward asked.

"No, sir. Not yet. I'd like to give him just a while longer, if that's all right. He's risking a lot by doing this."

"Sure, course he is. But we still got us a dead Jane Doe," Ward replied.

"I'll call him if I don't hear from him in the next hour," Riley said.

"I finished the BMV search," Ethan added. "Nothing popped

up on the girl's name. So I figure she didn't have a license. Maybe she's not of age yet."

"We still need to track down any Dawsons we do find here and in the vicinity. If we can find the girl's parents, that'll go a long way to identifying the body," Riley said.

"Agreed." Ward turned to the other officers. "In the interim, you boys have arrived just in time. I got off the horn with a lady who says she knows who robbed the IGA."

Riley and the other officers showed renewed interest. She was the first to speak. "Who was the lady? And how does she know?"

"She's the suspect's mom apparently. Turned in her own son," Ward said.

"Frosty," Abrams replied.

"He broke the law. It's what any good parent would do." Riley pulled on her jacket and strapped her holster around her waist. "Are we going now to bring him in or did she convince him to come down to the station?"

"Oh, we aren't that lucky. She gave us an address and guaranteed he'd be there. I think we should all head out. We don't know if he's alone, but we do know he's armed."

———

THE APARTMENT BUILDING WAS NOTHING MORE THAN A concrete tower with small square windows and black security bars. A fire escape snaked down the side of it. It was in a poorer area of town, which was saying something for Owensville, and had been built in the early 1980s. Its original intent was to become a dormitory for a satellite branch of the University of Indianapolis. But money ran dry when the Savings and Loan crisis hit because the lender was one of the institutions that closed. It was soon converted to apartments with small kitchenettes and was now Section 8 housing.

"What's the apartment number again?" Ethan asked Riley as they pulled into the parking lot.

"218. Second floor on the west side." Riley raised the captain on the radio. "Where are you, Cap?"

"Pulling up behind you now."

"We're outside the building," Riley continued. "Abrams, Decker, you copy?"

"Heading to the south end of the lot," Decker replied on the radio.

Ward called in. "Okay. I want Pruitt and Thompson to head in from the front, Abrams and Decker flank them on the right, and I'll flank them on the left. It's getting dark out there, so keep your eyes open."

"Copy that, Cap," Abrams replied.

"Let's go." Riley stepped out of the car into the dusky light. She double-checked her weapon while she waited for Ethan to join her. "Let's get in there and pray he's alone."

"I'm with you."

She spotted the other officers and Captain Ward in their designated positions, each team ready to converge, but keeping an eye out in case the thief decided to bolt or someone gave him a heads up. But in this light, it was tough to see much. Trees surrounded the first floor of the building, making it difficult to notice anyone hiding near. "Stay alert," Riley said.

Ward used hand signals to coordinate their approach. The teams drew nearer, and so far, no one was outside or appeared to notice them from a window. This was a good sign. The quieter, the better. No one wanted any trouble.

The four officers and their captain started up the stairs to the second floor where the man known as Ainsley Nolen was about to be taken into custody. They reached the corridor and Ward was the first to knock.

"Ainsley Nolen. This is Captain Ward of the Owensville PD. I need you to open the door." Ward shook his head and knocked again. "Mr. Nolen, we need to speak with you. Open the door. Don't make this harder than it has to be, son."

A blast of fear shot through Riley's body and she rushed to the end of the hall. "He's taking off!" She started back toward the others. "We need to catch him!"

"You sure it was Nolen?" Ward asked.

All she had to do was give him the look and Ward picked up on it immediately. "Let's go. Now!"

The officers ran down the steps and returned to their patrol cars. Riley kicked on the lights and sirens.

Ethan grabbed the radio. "Suspect is headed northbound on Stanfield Rd. Unit 1-8-9 in pursuit." He turned to Riley. "You'd better haul ass."

She spun the tires and smoke billowed around them before she made it onto the road, heading toward Nolen in his old Chevy Malibu with Bondo on the doors, just like the cashier said. When they arrived earlier, she hadn't seen the car, meaning she'd missed it or it wasn't there. "He must've known we were coming. Did you see his car?"

"No. He could've parked around the back of the building. But yeah, like you said, he would've had to know we were coming." Ethan peered at her again. "You felt him, didn't you?"

She nodded. "He was scared. Must've been some kind of fear for me to pick it up from outside his apartment. Especially since he must've already been at his car."

Ethan returned his sights to the road. "He's pulling ahead. You'd better put your foot down."

Their cohorts and Captain Ward roared onward. She was losing ground from distraction. "Damn it."

Ward was out front and Abrams pushed his way between them.

"Why is he such a jerk?" Riley slammed her foot down again and gripped the wheel tighter.

"Because he can be." Ethan grabbed hold of the safety handle above the window.

"He's pulling over! Captain's got him." Riley slowed as the Chevy moved toward the shoulder of the road. "Ward's pissed. I need to get up there before he yanks that guy out of his car." Riley stopped behind him, jumped out and raced toward the captain.

Abrams and Decker were only steps ahead, but Riley blew by them.

"Hey," Abrams said.

"Leave her. She needs to get to the captain." Ethan followed her as she continued toward the captain, who was approaching the . suspect's vehicle.

"Captain!" Riley reached for his shoulder. "Hang on."

"That son of a bitch is going to jail. Let go of me, Riley."

"Captain, please. Hold up. He's not who you think he is."

"What the hell does that mean? Is this the guy or isn't it?" Ward stopped cold.

"It is, but he's not a thief."

"Riley, what are you talking about? Is he the guy who robbed

37

the IGA? Because I'm looking at a car that matches the description the cashier gave you. Am I right or am I wrong?"

"You're right. but he's scared. He might do something stupid. Let me talk to him first."

"No way. Not a chance." He drew his weapon. "Stand down, Thompson. Let me handle this."

"Captain, I can't let you do that."

"Damn it, Riley."

"Please!"

"Fine. I'll approach the passenger side. You take the driver's side. Pruitt, stand at the rear and if this guy makes a single wrong move, shoot him!"

Riley drew her gun and cautiously approached the car. As she reached the window, the man had his hands up but looked straight ahead. "Sir, step out of the vehicle with your hands up." Riley eyed Ward at the passenger window and Pruitt at the back.

She stepped back as the suspect opened the door, her weapon trained on his head. "Carefully." It was then that he looked at her, and she saw it, the reason why he robbed the store, the reason he was in this situation right now.

"It's okay, Mr. Nolen, just relax. Everything will be fine. I'm going to need you to get on your knees and put your hands behind your back."

Ward stepped around the vehicle toward Riley to address the suspect. "What the hell is wrong with you? Why'd you run? I was about to shoot your damn head off!"

"I'm sorry, officers," Nolen replied.

Ward placed the cuffs on his wrists and pulled him up. Nolen eyed Riley again.

"I'll make sure your kids are okay," she replied.

His brow furrowed. "I never said I had kids."

"I know that's why you did what you did. Doesn't make it right."

"No, ma'am. It doesn't."

Ward's eyes softened and his shoulders dropped. "I'm taking you to the station. Where are your kids now?"

"In the apartment."

"And how old are they?"

"My boy's six. His name's Zack. My girl's ten. She's Holly."

"Is there anyone with them or another family member we can call to pick them up?"

"No, sir, it's just me. Their mom died last year."

"I'll go pick them up, Captain." Riley started back to the patrol car and eyed Ethan. "You coming with?"

"Go with her," Ward said.

"You got it, Captain." Ethan returned to the car and waited for Riley to step inside. "You okay?"

"Me? I'm fine. Not so sure about those kids, though. God knows what'll happen to them now."

[4]

The green door of Dillon's humble home swung open and Riley cast her sights down to see her four-year-old nephew, Danny. "Aunt Riley!" He lunged at her and wrapped his small arms around her slim waist. Riley had grown out of her chubby pre-teen figure and into a strong, fit young woman.

"Danny!" She kissed his head. "Where's your daddy?"

"He's in the kitchen with Mommy. Come on, I'll show you." He took her hand and pulled her inside.

Riley closed the door and followed the little boy, but before they made it to the kitchen, Dillon appeared.

"Hey, we're just cooking dinner. You plan on staying?" Dillon wiped his hands on a dish towel and greeted his sister.

"Depends on what you're having. Is that meatloaf I smell?"

"It is."

"Then I'd love to stay."

"I figured as much. Come on in and say hi to Marjorie." He started toward the kitchen.

"Where's Ella?" Riley asked.

"Sleeping. She had Marjorie up most of the night. Poor kid's been colicky lately."

"Sounds like Marjorie's the one who needs the sympathy." She spotted her sister-in-law. "Hey, there."

"Riley." Marjorie set down the spoon in her hand and approached for an embrace. "How are you?"

"I'm fine, but I hear you're not getting much sleep lately."

"Oh, I know. Can you believe it? This one over here." She pointed to Danny. "Never had a problem. But Ella, she's a whole other story. Hey, you want a glass of wine or something? You're staying for dinner, right? Got plenty of food."

"I'll pass on the wine, but I'm all in for your meatloaf." Riley had made the decision some time ago that drinking alcohol caused the gift to go a little haywire and so she abstained for the most part. The occasional drink, if she was really stressed and was at home. But never in public or at anyone's house. Too much could go wrong.

"Great. Well, dinner's going to be ready in about ten minutes. Why don't you catch up with your big brother while I finish things here?"

"You don't need any help?" Riley asked.

"No, ma'am. I have it under control."

Riley was grateful for the dismissal. There were things to which she needed answers and looked to Dillon for them. "You have a minute?" she asked him.

"Sure. Let's go talk in the living room." Dillon led the way to the small, informal space where the family curled up on the sectional sofa and watched television. "Have a seat."

"Thanks. Listen, I know I asked a lot of you today..."

"I got into the files." Dillon retrieved his cell phone and opened the images. "Take a look here."

Riley reached for his phone and viewed the pictures. "So she was a student."

"Was. Yes. Graduated two years ago."

Riley continued to peruse the photos of Chloe Dawson's student file. "Looks like she was an average student. Nothing stands out as unique. Did you happen to find any request for transcripts? Like if she applied to colleges or something?"

"No, I didn't find anything like that. But I did get an address and name of her parents. I couldn't tell you if they still lived in that house or not, but thought it could be useful for you."

"Very, thank you."

"So, you think this is the victim?"

"I don't know yet. She was..." Riley turned away for a moment. "She was in pretty bad shape, but at least we have a name. Can't figure out why she's not in any databases. No BMV records either. We need the coroner to get dental records or something like that. Then we'll know for sure if she's our victim."

"And if she is? Where does that lead your investigation?"

"Honestly, Dillon. I have no idea."

"Dinner!" Marjorie shouted from the kitchen.

"I'm sorry I couldn't get you more." Dillon stood up.

"This is a huge help. And I know it was risky. I appreciate it."

"Come on, let's get something to eat. I'm starved."

"I haven't had a good home cooked meal in a long time, Marjorie. Thank you." Riley sat at the table. "It looks delicious."

Marjorie placed Danny in a booster seat and served him a plate. "You don't do much cooking?"

"For myself? No, not really. Not unless you count grilled cheese sandwiches as cooking. Maybe a frozen dinner or two."

"Well, I'm sure that will change once you get married."

"Do you know something I don't?" Riley sliced into her meatloaf.

"Well, no. I'm just saying."

"I'm only teasing, Marjorie. I know what you meant." She turned to Dillon. "Hey, have you heard from Gracie lately? I haven't talked to her in a couple of weeks."

"As a matter of fact, she sent me a paper she wanted me to take a look at. It was for her psych class."

"Oh yeah? How'd she do?"

"Better than anything I could've done. Turns out, she's the smart one," Dillon finished a bite. "I hope she sticks it out up there."

"Well, she owes you a world of thanks for what you're doing for her," Riley said. "Helping pay for school and all."

"It's not like our parents were gonna pitch in. Besides, you do your part on that end too."

"Not much. But still, neither of us is swimming in money. I'm just saying it's really kind of you to help her."

Marjorie reached for Dillon's hand. "We do what we can. Gracie had a hard time of it."

"That she did. Probably harder than either of us, eh, Riley?"

"I suppose so."

———

RILEY PULLED OUT OF THE DRIVEWAY AND WAVED GOODBYE TO Danny and Dillon as they stood at the door. The confirmation Chloe Dawson was a former student at the high school needed to be relayed to the captain. It was still early enough in the evening to make the call.

"Captain? It's me. I just left Dillon's. He said Chloe Dawson graduated from the high school two years ago, but that he didn't know if she'd gone on to college or where she went after that. Her records didn't indicate anything else. Oh, and I have her parents' address." Riley's cell phone rested in her center console with the blue tooth activated and Ward's voice sounded over the car speakers.

"That's good news. Are you headed home?"

"I am. Just finished up dinner. Unless you need me to come back to the station? You want me to run the address and see what we can find?"

"No. Go home and get some rest. We'll tackle it in the a.m. I think I'll call in the address to the boys and have them run it. Last I heard, it was pretty quiet at the station house. They're probably looking for something to do."

"Okay, if you're sure. Because I can run back down..."

"Riley, go home. I'll take care of it from here and we'll talk in the morning."

"Okay, Captain. Oh, and Dillon says hi."

"That's nice. And how's my namesake?"

"That boy is a handful," Riley said.

"Yep, just like his aunt, I expect. Good night. Get some rest." Ward ended the call.

Riley turned the corner and drove along her street, where her home was about halfway down and on the right. Her headlights shone down the quiet road of the modest home she'd bought a few years ago at auction, with some help from Jack. Captain Ward helped her with some of the improvements because it had been vacant for a long time. And now it was hers. No one could take it away or could threaten to make her leave. It was the only place she could really call home. The house she grew up in, where her grandfather had committed suicide and her father drowned himself in booze, never felt like home.

Jack had stopped drinking after that night he decided he was going to let the tornado take him and Riley stopped him. Her gift made him come inside for shelter, and while he had been struck and almost killed by debris, he had survived, and it changed him. But it was hard to erase the past, no matter how much Riley tried to forget.

Dillon never did forgive Jack for what he'd done to their mother. Riley supposed, deep down, she hadn't either but did her best to put the past behind her and move on. It was the only way she could focus on her future. A future that now seemed in flux thanks to Jacob's return.

As she approached her house, she saw a car was parked in front of it. It was the same car from the night before. Only now that she'd talked to Jacob and had seen his car, it occurred to her this definitely wasn't him.

The car's lights flicked on and pulled away from the curb as she neared. "What the hell?" Riley considered following it, but it would be too obvious now. Whoever it was had seen her approach. And in the dark, it was nearly impossible to determine the make and model.

CARL NARROWED HIS AGED EYES, PRODUCING EVEN DEEPER wrinkles. "Someone's trying to scare you, but the question is why?"

"I don't know. I think it has something to do with the plant and Chloe Dawson." Riley sat next to Carl in his room and peered at the rising sun. "We don't even know if the body is this girl or not. It'll take days for a positive ID. What do I do?"

"Riley, you know better than most, maybe even better than me, what you need to do. But I would say put a camera on your front porch. It'll pick up whoever comes by your place when you're not home. Or if you're home and you're asleep."

"Then I could get a plate, if I'm lucky."

"Who the hell knows? Dumbass who's doing this could show his face. And then there you go."

"Yeah, you're right," Riley replied.

"Okay, then. You'd best get on into work. Don't want Ward to write you up for being late."

"He would never do that."

"Yeah, well, maybe he should once in a while, keep you on the straight and narrow."

Riley smiled. "Thanks, Carl. You need me to bring you any supplies tomorrow?"

"Wouldn't mind a six-pack."

"You know the nurses don't want you drinking beer. They say it messes with the meds."

"Fine. Don't know why the hell I'm asking a cop to bring me booze."

Riley kissed his cheek and started to leave. "Don't cause too much trouble when I'm gone." She closed the door and headed down the corridor to the elevators.

Surveillance was a good plan. Carl, a Vietnam Veteran, was still sharp as a tack. The nightmares he'd had that brought them together were long gone, luckily. But he was still a combat veteran, and as such, had been well versed in the tactics of his enemies. And anyone who tried to harm Riley would be a guaranteed enemy of Carl's. It was a designation one should try hard to avoid.

Riley pulled into the parking lot of the station and made her way inside. It was just before eight a.m. when her shift officially started. "Morning."

"Hey, Riley." Ethan turned away from his computer screen. "Captain wants to see you."

"Thanks." She approached Ward's office door and knocked. "It's Thompson."

"Come in," the voice beyond the door replied.

"Pruitt said you wanted to see me?"

"Close the door and have a seat." Ward removed his reading glasses.

"This have something to do with the address Decker and Abrams ran last night?"

"I actually came in and did it myself. I figure, until we know more about this Chloe Dawson, best not to get too many fingers in the pie, especially Abrams. He's cocky with something to prove. A hell of a cop, but the kid uses an axe when the job requires a scalpel."

"Got it. So what did you come up with?" She sat down.

"Well, if that was Chloe's folk's house when she was in school, it isn't anymore. In fact, no one lives there."

"When did they sell it?"

"Doesn't look like they ever owned it. It was a rental for some time. Now it's just empty. The owner is someone out of Ohio. I'll keep working that angle, but I can't say if it helps us now, in our present situation."

"Nothing back from the coroner for an ID?" she asked

"Afraid not. Poor girl's body was so disfigured. Hell, he says they just got all the concrete off her. He doesn't know if he can pull prints. Her fingers suffered pretty bad chemical burns. Damn near bare bones now."

"For God's sake," Riley replied. "There has to be something more we can do, Captain."

Ward pulled up and leaned over his desk, arms folded atop it. "Look, you know I hate asking you this kind of stuff, but a case like this...I'm starting to feel a little desperate for answers."

"You want me to go to the rental house and see if I pick up anything?"

"Damn if I hate asking, but—yeah, that's what I'm asking."

"If it helps us to figure out who this girl is, then I'll do it. I don't have a problem with that and I wouldn't expect for you to either."

"It's just. I know how it can—get to you sometimes."

"Well, I'll deal with that. I want to know who our victim is and who would've wanted her dead."

"The house is vacant."

"You want me to go now?"

"Take Pruitt with you. Bayliss is coming here for an update. Unless you want me to put him off and I can go with you?"

"No, but I'd rather go by myself."

Ward regarded her. "Out of the question. I won't have one of my officers out there alone. No, you go with Pruitt and let me know what you find."

Riley nodded and returned to the bull pen, looking to Pruitt. "We're heading out."

"Wait? What?"

"Captain wants us to check out an address. He thinks it might have something to do with the Jane Doe."

"Oh, okay. I'm ready. Let's roll."

———

THE HOUSE WAS BURIED BEHIND OVERGROWN TREES AND shrubs, but it was a house Riley recognized almost immediately.

"Oh my gosh." She put the patrol car into park and stared at the house.

"What? You get something already?"

"No, it's not that. I recognize this house from when I was a kid. I didn't pick up on the address. I guess it hadn't occurred to me, but seeing it now..."

"So, what is this place to you?" Pruitt asked.

"After that night. You know..."

"The F4," he added.

"Yeah. Well, my parents started sending me to a shrink. They thought it would help me cope with the gift. It had gotten really bad there for a while and it caused a lot of pain. Not just for me, but for a lot of people. Anyway, the doctor; she lived here, worked out of her house. I came here a couple of times a week for therapy. Wow. That was a long time ago."

"And did it help?"

Riley looked at him. "Not really." She pulled the keys from the ignition and started out the door. "Let's check it out."

Ethan joined her on the pathway toward the front door. "Um, not to state the obvious here, but how do we plan on getting in?"

"Ward said the current owners, who live in Ohio, had their management company drop off a key and leave it under the mat for us. So it should be," she checked under the mat, "right here." Riley retrieved the key and inserted it into the lock.

Upon opening the door, a waft of penned-up musty odor spilled out.

"Geez, this place reeks." Ethan crinkled his nose as he followed Riley inside.

"Captain said it's been empty for a long time. Don't know why the owners haven't been able to re-rent it or sell it. It's just sitting here rotting away."

"Well, just do your thing so we can get the hell out of here. I don't want my uniform smelling like this crap shack."

Riley pursed her lips. "It's not that bad. Just start looking. I don't know if I'll get anything, but it's better if you leave me alone for a few minutes."

"Okay. I'll start at the back and work my way up. You—just do your thing." Ethan started down the hall toward the bedrooms.

Riley looked around. She remembered the office was on the right, next to the family room. It wasn't a particularly large home, but at the time, when she was just a kid, it seemed pretty big. Bigger than hers anyway. She walked through to the family room. The place was completely empty—no furniture, no pictures, utterly void. This wasn't going to be helpful. It was always easier if she had something personal to look at, to touch. But as she continued through the vacant home, it was starting to feel as though she wasn't going to get anything and that they would be back at Square One.

It appeared as though the office had been used for another purpose by the last family who lived here. Could've been a game room or a rec room of some sort. It was definitely not an office anymore. Riley remembered built-in bookcases with tons of books on the shelves. All that was gone now. And she was getting absolutely nothing. Zilch. "Damn it. Come on. Chloe, you gotta help me here. I can't find out what happened to you unless you can show me something."

"You say something?" Ethan peeked his head through the arched opening.

Riley spun around "Huh? Good Lord, you scared me. Don't sneak up on me like that."

"Sorry. Just thought you'd be interested in something I found."

"Oh yeah?"

"Come on back, I'll show you." Ethan started back into the hall toward the bedrooms.

Riley followed closely behind.

"It's in here." He entered one of the rooms. "The master is that one down there. This looks to be a secondary room."

"A kid's room," she said.

"Yeah. I was searching for something, but as you can see, the place is empty."

"Right, that's what I'm seeing too."

"Except for this." He pulled open the closet door. "I don't know if this'll spark anything for you, but I thought you should come take a look for yourself."

Riley peeked inside the small walk-in closet. "What am I looking at?"

"Behind the door."

She pushed the door to reveal the backside. "Posters."

"Yep. Looks like whoever lived here liked Ed Sheeran."

Riley studied the poster of the young British singer who peered longingly at the camera to melt the heart of any teenage girl who hung it in her room. "Well, I can see how this was missed when the movers came."

"That's what I figured, behind the door and all. So, you getting anything from it?"

"Just give me a second. It's not like it just happens."

"I know. I'm sorry. I'll give you some space." Ethan stepped out of the room.

Riley continued to peer at it. "Was this yours?" she whispered. "I like his music too. And he's not bad-looking. Not exactly my type, but handsome enough."

She placed her hand on the poster and closed her eyes. Scenes flashed in her mind's eye. Two girls sitting on a bed in this very room, laughing, giggling, doing what young girls do. Teenage girls. But Riley couldn't tell if one of them was Chloe Dawson. Even from the school photo, these girls just didn't seem to match.

"Come on, Chloe, help me out," Riley pleaded.

The scene changed. A girl stood at the closet, staring at the clothes, wondering what to wear. It was her. It was Chloe. Riley knew this without a doubt.

The girl turned to Riley, as though she saw her clear as day standing in the room. Riley flinched.

"You have to stop him," the girl said.

"Who? Are you Chloe?"

"Stop him before he hurts anyone else." The girl began to fade from view.

"No. Wait. Chloe. Who hurt you? What happened?" But the

image was gone. Riley opened her eyes and stepped out of the closet. She turned to see Ethan reappear in the doorway.

"What happened? I heard you talking."

"It was her. I'm sure of it. I saw other girls, but then her. Maybe the others lived here after she did, I don't know. But that was Chloe Dawson. And she's the victim."

"How can you be sure?"

"I just am."

[5]

Inside Captain Ward's office, Riley and Ethan waited for a response from their superior as he studied the images of the house from which the two had just returned.

"And you're sure it's her? Chloe Dawson?"

"I saw her, Captain," Riley said. "As plain as I see you now. It was her. And she saw me. She told me I needed to stop him."

"Stop who is the question," Ward continued.

"Yes, sir. But now we can go back to the coroner and have him compare Chloe's records against the Jane Doe. There's no doubt in my mind that it will be a match."

"What do you think, Pruitt? Do you agree with Riley?"

"I don't have what she has, sir. But I'll tell you one thing, when I see her confidence is unshakable, I don't question it further."

"I suppose not." Ward pulled up in his chair. "I'll make the call to the coroner. The question now is, given that she'd been away from Owensville for two years, why come back to town and who did she come back for?"

"If we find that out, Captain, then we'll most likely know who the killer is," Riley replied.

"Let's keep doing the legwork on Chloe Dawson then," Ward added, dismissing the two officers.

Riley and Ethan returned to the bullpen when Ethan asked, "how do you want to plan this out?"

"Once we get confirmation of her identity from the coroner, we'll want to make contact with her parents. Now that we have the old lease agreement, tracking them down should be pretty straightforward. " Riley returned to her desk. "I'm going back to the high school."

"What for?" Ethan asked.

"To get copies of the yearbooks for the years Chloe attended. I want to know who her friends were and if any of them are still in Owensville. If they are, she might've come to see one of them." She grabbed her things. "I'll be back soon. Do me a favor and let the captain know?"

"Will do."

Riley was out the door, once again, and headed back to the school, her second visit in as many days. Only this time, she wasn't going to see her brother. No more favors could be asked of him. She'd relied on Dillon far too often in the past. Maybe that was the job of the older brother, or maybe she'd taken him for granted. Either way, Riley needed to take charge of this investigation. The question of the identity of the dead girl had been resolved, at least in her mind, the formalities still being worked out. But that wasn't going to stop her from getting to know Chloe better. Someone in town had to know her, and Riley needed names.

The school was just ahead and Riley pulled into the student drop-off area. She parked her patrol car and stepped out, heading toward the administration office. While on-duty, she kept her hair pulled back in a short ponytail. Her uniform rested on her frame in a rather bulky manner, which was enhanced by the holster belt. But unlike her younger years, Riley no longer felt uncomfortable in her skin. She'd long ago stopped worrying that she wasn't thin enough or pretty enough, because in light of what she'd seen in her few years on this planet, and especially the last fifteen, it was completely inconsequential.

The secretary behind the desk buzzed Riley in as she waited at the doors. "Well hello again, Officer Thompson. Are you here to see Mr. Thompson?"

"Afternoon. No, ma'am. I'm here for another reason."

"Oh. I see. Well, what is it that I can do for you today?"

"I was wondering if the school retained copies of old yearbooks. Specifically, within say the past five to seven years?"

"As a matter of fact, we do keep copies of the previous ten years in the library. Anything older than that would be in the archives at the district office."

"Don't suppose I could go take a look at them?" Riley asked.

"I don't see why not. You remember where the library is?"

"I sure do. Thanks very much." Riley left the main office and walked through the halls of her former high school. It hadn't changed much since she graduated some seven years ago. And she remembered exactly where the library was located. She'd spent a lot of time there. After learning to control her gift, she started to read books about telepathy, clairvoyance, which in this library was limited, but it was all she had access to at the time. Of course, now she just ordered books off of Amazon if she wanted to read something. Not that she had much time for that anymore.

Inside the library, everything was as she remembered it. In fact, the computers still looked to be the same as they were seven years ago—yikes. Maybe once this new plant came online and added lots of jobs, tax revenues would help improve the school. If not, perhaps she should help host a fundraiser to get these kids some decent learning tools.

"Good afternoon, officer. Can I help you with something?" The school's librarian was new. The lady Riley remembered had passed away a few years ago. This woman was much younger, perhaps only in her thirties.

"Yes, I'm Officer Riley Thompson. I was just in the front office and inquired about yearbook copies."

"Certainly. They're just over there along the back wall, second shelf from the bottom."

"Thank you." Riley made her way to the back of the room and spotted the books. She retrieved the years in question and made her way to a nearby table.

The books were laden with dust, and as she opened what would have been Chloe Dawson's senior yearbook, Riley blew off the grime and combed through the pages for the girl's name inside.

The senior photos were in alphabetical order, which made the search easy. Riley picked out Chloe's picture almost immediately, but that wouldn't tell her the whole story. She needed to know what clubs the girl belonged to, what groups of friends she sat with in the cafeteria. These were the things she needed to unearth in order to know more about this girl who turned up dead, forced to eat liquid concrete.

Riley continued to peruse the pages of the yearbook. She

checked the drama club. No luck. The varsity cheerleaders. Still no luck. It wasn't until she spotted the girl standing behind a table displaying homemade baked goods that she figured out Chloe's interests. It was the Glee Club. Chloe was a singer and they'd been raising money with a bake sale. The idea made Riley feel somehow worse. That the girl perhaps aspired to be a singer someday and now that day would never come.

With her phone, Riley snapped pictures of the pages in the yearbook along with whoever was with Chloe at that bake sale. A few other random pictures had been taken around the school grounds where the kids hung out before or after class: the lockers, the common areas. And she jotted down the names of the students who appeared to be her friends.

In the earlier yearbooks, only a few images of Chloe appeared. None included any extracurricular activities. Maybe she joined Glee Club in her senior year. A question to raise to Pruitt. When had Chloe's family moved to Owensville? Why had they rented? Riley couldn't ignore a possible family connection to Chloe's death either. Right now, they couldn't afford to overlook anything.

———

WHEN RILEY ARRIVED BACK AT THE STATION, SHE NOTICED Jacob's car. "Damn." He always had a way of taking Riley by surprise. And while that was endearing when they were younger— and dating—it was not the case now. Especially when she was working a homicide investigation and was vulnerable to his presence.

She pushed open the door and stepped out of her car. There he was, smiling sheepishly, knowing he shouldn't keep showing up at her place of employment, dragging along the baggage he brought with him. As she approached the entrance, she began, "Hey, you're back."

Jacob held the door for her as they entered the station. "I was hoping we could grab some lunch? Is this a bad time?"

Riley caught Ethan rolling his eyes as they walked inside. "We are pretty busy right now, Jacob."

"Right. Yeah. Well, how about dinner? I'd really like to talk to you, Riley—please."

She caved in to his will, as usual. "Sure. Dinner would be fine."

Jacob's spirits appeared raised by the acceptance of his invitation. "Great. Okay. I can pick you up at your place around seven?"

"Sure. I really need to get back to work, but I'll see you tonight, seven o'clock."

"Great. I'll see you then." He turned to Ethan. "See you later, Ethan."

"See ya, sport."

After Jacob left, Riley looked at Ethan. "Sport?"

"After what that guy did to you, you're going to have dinner with him?"

"He left town, like most everyone else. Can't blame him for trying to better himself." She was convincing herself of this, more than anything. "Besides, it's just dinner. Calm down, I'm not marrying him."

"Not yet," he muttered.

"Anyway, on to more important things. I have the names of the kids who I think hung around with Chloe Dawson back in school. I found them in a lot of the yearbook photos together. We should see if any of them still live in town. How'd you fare with the background check?"

"Prior to their move to Owensville, the parents lived in Indianapolis. Her father, David, and mother, Elizabeth, both worked in the medical fields. I don't know why they moved around or came to Owensville, for that matter. I did find what I believe is a current address. They live in Muncie. That's all I have right now."

"Did you let the captain know you found her parents?"

"He's not here. Went to see the coroner about what you said earlier, about the girl being Chloe Dawson."

"Good. We need him to confirm it's her before we call up her parents. I'd also like to find out if her friends from school still live here. Can you run a search on a kid named Justin Rehnquist and a girl called Heather Gallagher? They seem to be in most of the pictures with Chloe."

"Will do." Ethan paused a moment before continuing. "Why are you having dinner with him, Riley?"

"I already told you, it's only dinner, okay? He wants to talk about something. Whatever it is, he'll get off his chest and that'll be that. I have to give him the opportunity."

"Maybe he joined some twelve-step program and he's going around apologizing to everyone he screwed over."

"He wasn't a drunk, Ethan."

"Not that you know of." He returned to his computer. "Better get back to work."

———

THE BEST RESTAURANT IN TOWN WASN'T SOME FANCY PLACE that served tiny food on a plate drizzled in colorful sauces. In fact, a place like that didn't exist in Owensville. They'd only just recently opened a Chili's. But Riley wasn't much for that place either. No. Her favorite restaurant was the place she used to visit every Sunday after church, a small diner that by the grace of God had survived both the recession and the tornado and was now a thriving local joint owned by local citizens.

"Thanks for agreeing to come to dinner. I haven't been here in years." Jacob sipped on his bottle of beer.

"That's because you've been gone for years. I still come here on Sundays, even bring my mom once in a while."

"Just like when you were a kid."

"Yep." Riley took a drink of her Pepsi.

"Still don't drink, huh?"

"Not usually." Sometimes Riley wondered if she blamed her gift or her alcoholic father for her abstinence. "Why are you here, Jacob? Why now?" She took a bite of her top sirloin drenched in mushroom gravy.

"After I was laid off at the firm and broke up with my girl-friend, I wandered aimlessly for several days. Checked the ads for work, but it didn't feel right. I was missing something. So, with what little money I'd saved up, I decided to come here, to see you."

"You came here specifically to see me?" She'd realized his story from earlier had been slightly modified.

"I did. I wanted to know how you were doing."

"As you can see, I'm doing fine," she continued. "I'm happy with my work. I have my own house."

"How's Carl? Is he doing all right? He must be what, like in his eighties now?"

"He's fine. Mean as hell, but he's family—to me, anyway."

"I know he is. He's always meant a lot to you. Look, Riley, I don't know how long I'll be here, or even if I'm staying. I need to figure out some things, you know?"

"No, I don't. I figured out my life a long time ago. You were always the one who was never happy with what you had."

"That's not true. I was happy with you."

"And yet you still left." She immediately regretted the remark.

"Well, I can see you're in no mood for forgiveness. I was stupid to think you'd ever forgive me for leaving. Even if I was trying to make a better life."

"Jacob, I'm proud of what you've accomplished. And it wouldn't have been possible here, I realize that. We just wanted different things. It was no one's fault. I'm happy in Owensville. I have a purpose here."

"I can see that," Jacob replied.

"But the fact remains, you broke my heart, regardless of your reasons. And I never thought you were ever capable of doing that." She wiped her lips with a napkin. "Why don't we just talk about something else? So, how are your parents?"

———

THE DRIVE BACK TO RILEY'S HOUSE WAS QUIET. SHE'D SAID what she'd wanted to say to Jacob and he had nothing to offer in reply. They'd gone their separate ways and that had become painfully obvious at dinner.

"Thanks for the ride." Riley placed her hand on the door handle when Jacob pulled into her driveway. For a moment, she considered inviting him in, but what would be the point? And it wasn't until she held his gaze that she again caved in to his will. "You want to come in for a coffee?"

"Sure." Jacob pulled the key from the ignition and stepped out. "Nice night."

"It is." She walked past him to her front door where CJ could be heard barking inside.

"You have a dog?"

"Yeah, his name is CJ."

"Carl's son's name."

"That's right." She stepped inside and found the light switch. "Hey, buddy!" Riley leaned down to greet her dog. "Calm down. I know, I know." She looked to Jacob. "He's friendly, he won't bite. Might jump up on you, but that's all."

"Hey, CJ. How's it going, dude?" Jacob scratched behind CJ's ears and the dog rolled onto his back.

"CJ! Go on now, you're embarrassing yourself." Riley started into the kitchen and put on a pot of coffee. "Cream and one sugar, if I recall."

"You recall correctly, thanks." Jacob joined her inside the small kitchen. "Nice place."

"Been fixing it up here and there. Did all this tile work myself."

"No shit?"

"No shit." Riley smiled at her handiwork.

"You've managed pretty well without me around," Jacob surveyed the home.

She handed him the mug and skirted his remark. "Let's go sit in the living room." Riley led the way to the sofa and sat down. "I know I've been—irritable—tonight. And I'm sorry for that. You came to visit me and I've given you grief the entire time."

"You have every right, Riley, and I honestly expected worse. You've been extraordinarily kind to me tonight, all things considered. I would like us to be friends. We grew up together. We've been through a lot."

"That we have." She sipped on her coffee.

"And when I figure out what the hell I'm going to do with the rest of my life, I'd really appreciate your support. You've always been supportive of everything I've done."

"Well, not everything." A light from a car passing in front of the window caught her attention. Riley set the mug down and raised up, peering over Jacob's head to see.

"What is it? What's wrong?" He tossed a glance over his shoulder.

Riley moved closer to the window as the car slowly passed. "Nothing. It's just…"

"What? Is everything okay? Is that someone you know?"

"No, it isn't. But I've seen that car a few times now on my street. I thought it was you at first. And every time, it slows down in front of my house."

"Jesus." Jacob stood and joined Riley at the window. "Who the hell is it?"

"I wish I knew."

[6]

September was a traditionally low risk month for tornados in Indiana. Spring and summer offered the greatest threats. So when Ethan Pruitt gazed through his kitchen window at the grey fall sky, the idea of a looming tornado didn't cross his mind. Instead, his thoughts were on Riley and how her date with Jacob Biggs went. Here they were, trying to track down the person who'd taken the life of Chloe Dawson in a most horrific manner, and while he was ready to get back to work and tackle that enormous task, he was also concerned about Riley. He detested Jacob for what he had done to her. But it was her life and he had to let her live it, even if it meant letting her make a mistake with that man again.

Ethan poured coffee from the carafe into a travel mug, pulled on his uniform jacket, and started out the door. A final check that he'd turned off the coffee pot and he left his one-bedroom condo.

Their department was small and Captain Ward was lax on the

policy regarding driving home patrol cars, so Ethan unlocked his police vehicle and stepped into the driver's seat. He still needed to run the names of Chloe Dawson's friends that Riley had discovered. And hopefully, get out to talk to them today, assuming they still lived in Owensville.

The short drive to the station ended and Ethan parked his car next to the captain's, who'd arrived early, as usual. Sometimes Ethan wondered if Ward slept at all.

"Morning." He entered the station to find Decker and Abrams heading out. "How'd it go last night?"

"No problems," Decker replied. "Pretty quiet. Not like what you guys got going on. You sure you don't need help with that investigation?"

"I guess that'd be Ward's call. Right now, we're still waiting for a positive ID on the girl." Ethan placed his mug on his desk and sat down. "You all get some sleep."

"Nighty night," Abrams said as he walked out the door.

"See you, man." Decker followed him out.

Ethan had hardly a chance to boot up his computer when the captain stepped out of his office.

"Is Riley in yet?"

"No, sir."

"Okay. Listen, I'm going to need you to do something for me."

"Sure. What is it?"

"I'll need the contact info on Chloe's parents. They're going to want to get down here asap."

"We have a positive ID?" Ethan asked.

"Yes. It is, without a doubt, Chloe Dawson, just like Riley said it would be. We need to get down to the business of letting her next of kin know."

"I'll get right on it, Captain." Ethan caught sight of Riley pulling into the parking lot. "Looks like she's here."

Captain Ward started toward the door and held it open for her. "Morning."

"Morning, Captain." Riley walked inside. "What'd I miss?"

"I have confirmation on the victim's identity. It's Chloe. I've asked Pruitt to get me her parents' info."

Riley continued inside to her desk. "It's better to know so we can move the investigation forward."

"Hey, Riley, I haven't had a chance to run those other names yet. Chloe's friends?" Ethan said.

"No problem. I'll run the names."

"Her friends?" Ward asked.

"Yes. I found what appeared to be a few of her friends when I searched the old yearbooks yesterday."

"That's great. I'll let you get on that then. The more we know about why she was here and who she was with, the better off we'll be." Ward started back toward his office. "Pruitt, get me the parents' number asap."

"I'm on it, Captain." Ethan watched as Riley settled in and got to work. "So are you going to tell me how it went last night or do I have to guess?"

"What? Oh, it was fine."

"Fine? That's all you have to say after having dinner with your ex?"

"What do you want me to say, Ethan? The dinner was fine. The food was good. We went back to my house and had a coffee. And that was it; he left."

"I see. Is he staying in town long?"

"I really don't know. Look, Ethan, I get why you're asking the questions. And I do appreciate your concern. But right now, we have much bigger fish to fry, so I'd really like to just get to work."

"Sorry I asked." Ethan returned to his monitor hurt but trying to hide it.

She eyed him with a hint of regret for her curt tone before returning to work. However, it wasn't long before she stopped and turned to Ethan again. "I'm sorry. I guess I'm just on edge with Jacob in town. Chloe Dawson. Seems like everything's piling on at once."

"It's okay, Riley. I get it. It's my fault for prying." Ethan pulled up the information on Chloe's parents. "Better get the contact info to Ward." He started toward the captain's office and knocked.

"It's open." Ward's voice sounded through the door.

"Hey, Captain. Here's the number of Chloe Dawson's folks. Should I make the call?"

Ward inhaled a deep breath. "No. Let me do it. Something like this should come from me."

Ethan handed him the slip of paper and shut the door, returning to his desk. "I don't envy him."

"Neither do I," Riley said. "Her parents could shine light on why she was here, but until then, I want to keep looking into her friends."

———

JACOB PULLED INTO THE PARKING LOT OF THE DINER WHERE he'd had dinner with Riley the night before. His cousin hadn't been much for grocery shopping and had nothing in his house to eat, and he was starving. This place held a lot of memories for him and it felt good to be back home. It felt good to see Riley again.

Inside, the smell of pancakes and bacon brought a smile to his face. He sat down at one of the booths and peered into the parking lot.

"Morning." A waitress who had seen her better years pass stood in front of him with pad and paper. "What can I get for you?"

"Coffee and I'll take a short stack with a side of bacon." He handed her the menu.

"You want cream with that?"

"Yes, please. Thanks."

As she walked away, Jacob gazed through the window again of the sleepy town in which he was raised. The trees were just starting to change color. The skies had cleared from earlier. Things had made a turn for the better since he'd been away. A few more people walked the streets, entering shops and coming out with bags of goodies. People seemed just that little bit more pleasant. Gainful employment tended to do that to people.

"Here's your coffee, son." The waitress placed the mug in front of him and set down the small porcelain pot filled with Half and Half. "Haven't seen you around here before. You just move into town?"

"Just visiting. I grew up here, actually. Left after high school."

"And you're back? Good on you. Don't think I'd be much for coming back here. Course my roots are too deep now. Anyways, you enjoy."

Jacob nodded and sipped on the coffee. It was a tasty brew. He continued to gaze outside, wondering where he would go next. Riley had made it pretty clear she was finished with him. Could he blame her? He'd burned that bridge a long time ago and it was a surprise she'd even agreed to dinner. Maybe it was best. Let the past be. How many times had he told her that very thing?

He stood by her as she struggled to come to terms when her parents finally decided to throw in the towel. But watching Riley go through that and try to learn to control her gift was draining on both of them. And in the end, it was he who couldn't take the strain. He was the weak one, not her. Not by a long shot.

It wasn't until Melissa died that a switch in Riley finally flipped. Captain Ward—Daniel, as he recalled—ended up marrying Melissa, the woman who paid a price for something Carl's son had brought on. Riley had seen it in her visions when she was a child. She told Jacob that Melissa and Dan would marry, but never told either one of them. So when Melissa contracted ALS at a much younger than average age, Riley was angry with herself for not seeing what would happen earlier. She couldn't save Melissa, and after a few years, the young vibrant woman succumbed to the disease. And this left Dan Ward devastated. So much so, Riley could hardly stand to be around him. His pain was so deep. It was like she could see his heart breaking inside of him. That was when she closed herself off to her feelings. And Jacob was the one on whom the door had been slammed.

As he tucked into his pancakes, drenched in syrup, Jacob's attention was caught by a passing car. In the back of his mind, he recalled a similar car at Riley's last night. But it was dark, he couldn't be sure. It was traveling along the main street slowly and its occupants seemed to be on the lookout.

Jacob set his fork down and retrieved his cell phone. He took pictures of the passing car. Maybe with the pictures, Riley could determine if this was the same one. And if it was, who was driving?

THE MAN BEHIND THE WHEEL CONTINUED AHEAD. "I'm telling you, he's wrong about this. The kid is here and all this sneaking around isn't helping us get the money." He scratched his stubbly beard and pressed on the gas, gaining speed of another mile or two.

"We're here to send a message, that's all." The man in the passenger seat continued to survey the streets of the small town. "This place is a real shithole. I'd never live in a dump like this."

"So how long's it going to take to get our message across?" The driver, who went by the name Eddie Costa, turned right toward the highway.

"We're just waiting for Virgil to make contact. Put the kid on edge and hope that'll be enough."

"What if it ain't enough?" Eddie asked.

"It will be. Eddie, you missed the turnoff."

"Oh, right. It's only cause you're distracting me."

"Just get back to the hotel so we can report back to Virgil."

Costa turned the car around and headed back toward the highway. "Whatever you say."

RILEY SAT BACK FROM HER COMPUTER AND FURROWED HER brow. "Hey, I picked up something on Justin Rehnquist. You want to come take a look?"

Ethan made his way toward her. "Something useful?"

"I don't know; you tell me." She waited while he read the information on the screen. "Well?"

71

"We should go talk to this guy."

"Yeah. That's what I was thinking." She stood and reached for her jacket. "He's not far from here. I'll let Ward know." Riley walked into the captain's office. "Hey, Cap. How'd the call go?"

"Her parents will be here tonight. I'm going to meet them at the morgue. In fact, it would be a good idea if you came with me, if you're available."

"Of course I am. Definitely. Listen, Pruitt and I were going to head out and talk to a guy who I believe knew Chloe. He lives in town and works at the Auto Zone."

"And what about him makes him of interest?"

"He recently posted on Instagram a picture of Chloe and him at a club in Terra Haute. It was dated last week. For all we know, he might've been one of the last people to see her alive."

"I'd say that's compelling enough to have a chat with him."

"That's what I thought. We'll see you later, Captain." She returned to the bullpen.

Ethan grabbed his keys. "I'll drive."

"Let's go talk to Justin." She continued outside and made her way to the passenger door of Ethan's patrol car. As the locks clicked open, they both stepped in, and when he turned the engine, she continued. "She was in Terra Haute only a week ago and then came here at some point after that. Who was she coming to see?"

"I don't know. Makes no sense the girl would go to the plant. Unless it was a bunch of them and people were messing around and some God-awful accident happened."

"Hard to say. You'd think if it was something like that, we'd have heard about it. Someone would've made a call. And even if it was an accident, who the hell would think to pour concrete into her mouth? I think this was intentional."

"Well, if someone's trying to make a point, seems like they did." He continued to drive south toward the center of town where the Auto Zone was located. "Are we sure this kid's working right now?"

"Middle of the day, during the week? I hope so. I'd rather hit his workplace before going to his home. I have no idea if he has roommates and I don't want anyone else to know about what happened, at least not until Captain talks to the girl's parents."

"Sure. This is it up ahead." Ethan pulled onto the lot and cut the engine.

Riley started to get out but stopped short. "Hey, let's do our best to pull him aside and talk to him. I don't want customers listening in."

"Right." Ethan followed her to the door and pulled it open. The bell at the top chimed as they entered.

All eyes turned to the officers. And by all, it was really only three people.

"Hey, Riley! Good to see you. What are you two doing here? What, did the place get robbed or something?"

"Mr. Bernhard, nice to see you too. No, everything's fine. Just here for a quick visit." She felt his eyes continue to follow her as they walked toward the counter. It was exactly what she had wanted to avoid, but in a small town like Owensville, it was to be expected. "Morning," she said to the man at the counter.

"Well, hey there, Officer Thompson. What can I do for you both today?"

"Hi, Mr. Hughes," Ethan started. "We were wanting to know if Justin Rehnquist was working today?"

"As a matter of fact, he is. Everything all right? He's not in any trouble now, is he?"

"No, sir. We're just wanting to have a quick word with him is all," Ethan replied.

"I'll go get him." Mr. Hughes walked back into the storage area of the store, and a moment later, returned with the kid. "Justin, these fine officers want to have a word with you."

The kid looked to be around twenty, same age as Chloe, which made sense if they were in school together. Riley smiled at him to put him at ease because right away she felt his anxiety level rise. No one wanted to talk to the cops, least of all a young kid who probably liked to get himself into trouble once in a while.

"Justin, I'm Officer Thompson, and this is Officer Pruitt. Could we talk to you—outside?"

"What'd I do?"

"You haven't done anything. We just need to ask you about something," she added.

"Um, yeah, okay." A gangly kid, a little gaunt and dirty from whatever work he'd been doing, followed them out to the front of the store. "What is it you wanted to talk about?"

"Do you know a girl named Chloe Dawson?" Riley asked.

"Yeah. Course I do. She's a friend of mine."

"And when was the last time you saw her?" she continued.

"Oh, I don't know, last week. Why? Is she okay?"

"We're just wanting to find out a little more about her." Ethan peered at Riley, noting the kid's obvious anxiety.

"Such as?" Rehnquist folded his arms across his chest and widened his stance.

"We were hoping you could tell us about the last time you saw her. Where, when, things like that," Riley said.

"Look, if something's wrong, then please tell me. She's one of my best friends. Is Chloe all right?"

Riley felt his emotions grow erratic. Telling this kid Chloe was dead before her parents were notified was against protocol, but sometimes, she'd learned she had to break the rules. A quick glance to Ethan and she knew he didn't want her to say more. But she had no choice. It wasn't fair to him. "Listen, Justin. I'm really sorry, but Chloe's dead."

[7]

With nothing more to do other than drive aimlessly, that was exactly what Jacob did. He was caught somewhere between his old life and a new life he'd desperately wanted to start. But what to do in the meantime? How was he supposed to make that leap? First of all, he had to tie up loose ends back in Indianapolis. Things were said, things were left behind, and if he wanted to start anew, he couldn't have those strings pulling him back.

Jacob stopped at a traffic light and picked up his cell phone. He pressed the contact button that had been at the top of his favorites list for the past three years. Hardly seemed fathomable they'd been together for that long, but time flew when one was busy trying to climb the ladder of success. And Jacob had already slipped a rung or two.

The line rang through on his Bluetooth and the traffic lights changed. He drove head-on into the intersection of uncertainty and resolution. She answered.

"Hey, it's me."

"Jacob? Where are you?"

"I had to get away. I'm sorry I left the way I did. But I wanted to talk to you about..."

"Look. You have to come back, you hear me? You have to come back now!"

"What? Why? Rachel, what's going on? Are you okay?" He heard the line crack and static come through as though she'd dropped the phone. "Rachel? Rachel? Hello?"

"Jacob Biggs. How are you?"

A voice he didn't recognize sounded on the line. "Who is this? Where's Rachel?"

"Lucky you called when you did. Your girlfriend here wasn't answering our questions, so we're hopeful you can."

"What questions? Who the hell are you? I swear, you'd better not hurt her." Jacob hadn't realized it, but his foot pressed down harder on the gas and his speed picked up along the lonely road.

"Where's the money, Jacob?"

"What the hell are you talking about? What money?" His foot pressed down harder.

"Rachel really needs you now, Jacob. You don't want to let her down. Where is the goddam money?"

"I promise you, I have no idea what you're talking about."

"Maybe this will jog your memory."

Screams sounded through the speaker.

"Rachel! Rachel! Stop! Don't hurt her. Please!"

Another crackle of the line and the man was back. "Then you'd better speak up, kid."

"Okay. Okay. I don't know where it is—right now. But I can get it to you. I swear it."

"You better not be lying because if you are..."

"I'm not. I'm not lying. I—I just need some time. A day or two, that's all. Please don't hurt her. I'll get you the money."

"Suppose I'll have to give you the benefit of the doubt, Jacob. This time. You have forty-eight hours."

"How do I..." But the line went dead before he could finish. And as he stared at his phone, wondering what had just happened, the car veered right and smashed into a sign post. "Shit!" He slammed on the brakes, but the sign folded like a deck of cards.

Jacob turned off the engine and stepped out, walking toward the sign post. "Son of a bitch." He looked around for anyone who could help, but the road was empty. He'd just passed through most of the town and was on the outskirts, not realizing he'd gone that far out of the way. His cousin lived two miles back. "Damn it." Not only did he have no idea what money he owed these people, or who they were, but he didn't know how much, how to get it, and was now staring at a public property damage charge. Worst of all, Rachel was in danger.

The last person he wanted to ask for help from was Riley. But this was something bad—really bad—and he was going to need help. He knew she was already dealing with a homicide. Her hands were full. But what would happen if he didn't come up with this money this guy said he owes? Would they hurt Rachel? Or would they kill her?

"Damn it!" he yelled at the top of his lungs. Jacob truly had no idea what was happening. But before he went to Riley, there was someone he could call first who just might know what was going on.

Jacob pulled his cell phone from his pocket and pressed the button. "Hey, look, man. I need your help. And I need you to be honest with me." He started back toward the driver's side of the car. "I just got a call from some scary-ass dude who says I owe him money." He sat down inside. "I have no idea who the hell he was, but I'm guessing you might. Dude, they've got Rachel. They're going to hurt her. So you'd better tell me what the hell is going on and I mean now."

———

RILEY LISTENED AS JUSTIN REHNQUIST RELAYED HIS FINAL exchange with Chloe Dawson. She sensed he'd begun to calm down, although his eyes were still clearly pained. "And you hadn't heard from her at all after that night?"

"No, ma'am. Since she and her folks moved away after we graduated, we don't get to see each other as much. And so when she's nearby, we do our best to meet up."

"Her parents live in Muncie now, isn't that right?" Ethan asked.

"Yes, sir. Muncie. It's not too far a drive to meet in Terra Haute. There's plenty to do there and we always have—had lots of fun."

"What about another girl, um, Heather Gallagher?" Riley continued.

"We were all friends, but I haven't seen her in a long time. She went off to Kansas State. I think her parents still live here, though."

"I'm so sorry to have to give you this news, but I have to ask, because Chloe's parents are going to be here in a few hours to ID the body. Technically, I wasn't supposed to tell you what happened, so I'm going to ask that you please not say anything to anyone. At least give us tonight so her parents can have some privacy."

"I won't say anything. Can I see her too?" Rehnquist's eyes pleaded with hers.

"It's usually just family, but I can pass along your contact information so the family can get the funeral arrangements to you."

"Okay. I understand."

"Thank you, Justin. Again, I'm so sorry. Chloe seemed like a really great girl," Riley said.

"She was the best."

Riley placed her hand on the young man's shoulders. A man who really wasn't much younger than she was, but Riley was an old soul in any case. "Thank you for your help."

They began to walk away when Riley stopped and turned back. "One last thing, you and Chloe were just friends, right?"

"Yes, ma'am, since we were kids."

"In that Instagram post of you two in Terra Haute, there was a man in the background. Did either of you know him?"

"He dated Chloe on and off. Mostly off."

"Do you know his name?"

Justin replied with certainty. "Blake Rhodes."

"Did he go to school with you guys too?" she asked.

"No, ma'am. He's a little older. I don't really know him. He was kind of tagging along that night. Just wanted to get into her pants, as usual."

"Okay. Thank you, Justin." Riley continued to the patrol car and waited for Ethan to unlock the door.

"I know that look." Ethan stepped inside. "You want to do some digging on this Blake Rhodes guy."

"Yeah, I think we should. But there was something else. I couldn't quite see it. His grief overwhelmed his state of mind."

"Like what?" Ethan started the engine and pulled away.

"I'm not sure. I'll give it a few days. He might settle down enough for me to see what else he knows because I'm pretty sure he knows more."

Within minutes, Ethan turned the corner and the station house came into view. "Looks like your ex is back."

"Huh?" Riley looked up from her phone. "Oh, geez. What's he doing here again?"

"Probably wants to ask you to dinner. I mean, he got a yes the first time. Might as well give it another shot."

"Okay, okay. Look, you've made your feelings about Jacob pretty clear. Feel free to let it go now."

"Sorry. Just don't know why he keeps showing up."

"Yeah, well, neither do I. Guess we'll find out when we get inside." Riley stepped out of the car and started toward the door. She noticed his car had some damage on the front bumper, something she was sure wasn't there before.

"Well, this should be interesting," Ethan said as he opened the door.

Jacob and Ward turned at the sight of the officers' arrival.

"Good. You're back," Ward began. "Jacob here was just confessing to a crime."

"What?" Riley asked.

"I ran over a stop sign. Figured I should come here and let you all know. Wouldn't want it to be down for long and cause an accident."

"How did you manage that?" Ethan asked.

"Guess I wasn't paying attention."

"Good thing you didn't hurt anyone." Ethan made his way to his desk. "So, Cap, are we taking down a report?"

Ward eyed Riley. "No. Just call street maintenance and put in an emergency order for a new sign."

"Sure. We'll cut the tourist some slack." Ethan started on the order.

"I thought I spotted damage to your car," she said.

"A couple of scratches on the front bumper. No biggie."

"Good. Well, we've got a lot going on here, so if you don't mind, I need to have a word with the captain."

"Oh, sure. Yeah. I'll um, I guess I'll just head out then."

"I wouldn't leave town anytime soon," Ward added. "Not until we get you the bill for the new stop sign."

"Sure. I'll get it taken care of. Thank you, Mr. Ward—Captain." Jacob started out the door.

"So what'd you find?" Ward stood with his hands on his hips. "That friend of hers have any info?"

"Yes and no," Riley started.

"How about we start with the 'yes' portion of your story, then?"

"Justin Rehnquist had been with Chloe at a bar in Terra Haute last Wednesday night. He said he didn't see Chloe all that often, but the two made the trip. Anyway, he said there was a guy there."

"What guy?" Ward pressed on.

"Sounds like he was her on and off boyfriend, by all accounts," Ethan replied.

"That's a start. Did he give you a name?"

"Blake Rhodes. That's all he knew. Didn't know where the guy lived or where he worked, just that he saw him sometimes with Chloe," Riley said. "I think he was hiding something too, but I couldn't pick it up. I would like to revisit that soon, though."

"Okay. Start looking into Rhodes until then. No luck with the other friend?"

"Not really. She went off to college in Kansas or something. He said they hadn't spoken in a long time and didn't think she talked to Chloe much either," Riley added.

"Okay. You two get to work on finding Blake Rhodes." Ward checked his watch. "Chloe's parents are due here in another hour. Riley, you'll be okay to come with?"

"I will. No problem."

"Thanks." Ward returned to his office.

"Your boy is still out there," Ethan said.

"What? Jacob?"

"Who else? Follows you around more than CJ, by the looks of it."

"Give me a minute. I'll go tell him we've got too much happening right now and I can't waste any time." Riley continued outside and approached Jacob. "Hey, you're still here?"

His face wore a concerned expression. "Look, I know how busy you are with this investigation. It's just. Well, I guess I wanted to show you something. It's about that car you saw at your house last night."

"Did you see it again?" She expressed renewed interest.

"I think it was the same one." He retrieved his cell phone and opened the images. "Looks like it to me anyway. I was at the diner this morning having breakfast when I saw it driving by. It was going slowly and that's what really drew my attention. Then I started looking and thought..."

"That's the same car. Please tell me you got a plate?" Riley pleaded.

"Not from where I was. I'm sorry." He swiped through a couple of images. "When it had gone past, I couldn't zoom in enough to see the plates clearly."

"Looks like Indiana plates though, but tough to make out the numbers. You mind texting that to me?"

"Um, I don't have your number anymore."

She relayed the information. "Thanks. Look, I need to get back inside. We've got a lead and I need to jump on it."

"Sure. Okay."

"Is there something else on your mind, Jacob?" She sensed his apprehension.

"What's that? Oh, no, nothing else."

"Okay. Thanks for coming in and confessing to the damage. Most people would've just taken off if no one had seen them."

"You know I'm not like most people. I'll see you around, Riley." Jacob made it back to his car and slipped into the driver's seat.

She watched him pull away, feeling there was something else but again unable to decipher it. Maybe she was losing her touch. The stress of the investigation and Jacob in town weighed on her. Could it have been throwing her off her game too? She walked back inside. "He's gone."

"For good, I hope," Ethan replied.

———

Jacob drove for over an hour before reaching his destination. He would be meeting with the man who had to know what that frightening call was all about. Keeping it from Riley about killed him. He didn't want to bring any more problems for her than she was already facing. And if he hadn't distracted her thoughts with the pictures of the car, she'd have seen his turmoil. Jacob had learned, to a certain extent, how to hide his feelings from her. It wasn't easy having a woman like her in his life, knowing his every emotion.

He sat in the bar and downed his second Blue Ribbon. He was being thrifty with what little cash stores that remained.

"Jacob. Hey, man. You all right?" Blake Rhodes pulled up a stool next to him at the bar.

"I didn't think you were going to show," Jacob replied.

"I got caught up is all. What's going on?"

"I was hoping you could answer that. Someone's threatening to hurt Rachel. And this someone wants money. Only problem is, I don't know who, what, or how much. So can you shed some light on this? Because I got two days before they do something to her."

"Jesus. Are you serious?" Blake replied.

"Come on, man. Don't screw around with me. You know who it is, don't you? Dude. They might kill her."

"They aren't going to kill her." Blake waved to the bartender.

"So you do know? You'd better tell me, like now."

The bartender approached.

"I'll have a Bud Light, thanks." Blake pulled out his wallet and dropped a five. "Okay, look, I can't say for sure, but someone might've found your name and might've tracked down Rachel to get to you."

"What? Are you serious? Who?"

"I'll handle it, okay? This is just a big misunderstanding."

"You think?" Jacob grew angry from his friend, who seemed incredibly blasé, all things considered.

"Relax, Jake, just calm down."

"I will when you tell me who's making the threats. What are we talking about here, Blake? Who do you owe money to?"

"Okay, here's the deal. You remember that project we were working on? That manufacturing plant conversion?"

"Of course I do."

"Yeah, well, you left before we got the final approvals. And, well, let's just say that those approvals cost the boss a hefty chunk of change."

"First of all, I didn't leave. I was fired. And what do you mean? Like a bribe?"

"Something like that."

"What the...? Since when do we bribe council members to approve a project?"

"Since the name attached to the funding was a name no one wanted to be associated with. A name people around here are scared of." Blake tossed back a swig of beer.

"So, what, George bribed an official to move the project along? Okay. If that's true, why is this person asking for money? And why the hell is he asking me?"

"George might've said he needed more than was actually required. Jake, you know how much we lost on that design. We were about to the lose the whole deal until strings were pulled and they got the funding in place. George was just trying to make up for lost earnings."

"I can't believe I'm hearing this. Seriously? The firm took money from some shady person or group to bribe officials, then kept some of it? And this involves me how? Cause right now, I'm crapping my pants, wondering if they're going to hurt Rachel."

"It's not just some shady dude. Like I said, I'll take care of this." Blake took another drink. "I just need to get them to understand that the money is gone."

"The money's gone? This extra money George kept is gone? And these guys think I have it?"

"I thought you disappeared, man. I hadn't heard from you and I needed to buy time. How did I know they'd find you?"

"Oh my God. You did this? You told them I had the money? How long did you think it'd take them to find Rachel? She works for the damn county." Jacob tried to steady his nerves. "How much, huh? How much money are they looking for, Blake?"

"Sixty thousand. I can fix this, man, I swear it."

"Holy mother of God. I have to get to Rachel. I have to get her out of here." He ripped his wallet from his pocket and dropped a ten on the bar top.

"I wouldn't do that. If you go there, they'll be watching you. They'll follow you wherever you go. Hell, they could be following me, which is why I had someone drop me off here."

"What am I supposed to do then, Blake? How do I get sixty grand I don't have? Where's George?"

"I don't know. He took off when shit went south. He's got the money."

"These people can track me down through Rachel, but not George?"

"That's because they think you have the money," Blake replied.

"Well, tell them I don't. That I don't have a damn clue what they're talking about."

"Look, let me smooth this over. It should've never gotten this far. I'm seriously sorry they got you and Rachel involved. Where are you staying? You want to crash with me while we sort this crazy shit out?"

Jacob eyed his former colleague, who he'd thought was his friend. "I'll find a way to get Rachel out of here. You just get those assholes off my back."

[8]

The only hospital in Owensville also housed the morgue, which was where Chloe Dawson's body had remained for the past three days, waiting to be claimed, waiting to be laid to rest. Although that wasn't likely to happen until the case was solved, which Riley felt was still well out of reach.

Her search into the boyfriend, Blake Rhodes, hadn't led her far yet, and upon Chloe's parents' arrival, she had to turn over the duties to Ethan, who was still at the station working on it. Right now, she waited with Captain Ward to speak to the girl's family.

"You're sure you're okay to do this?" Ward asked.

"I'm fine. It might help the investigation if I can talk to them. And now that we know who she was dating, we can ask them what they know about Rhodes."

"I expect them here any minute. You want a coffee or something?"

"Sure. Thanks." Riley watched him head toward the café

while she remained in the lobby. She began to consider the likelihood that this man, Blake Rhodes, was Chloe's killer. Seemed he would've had plenty of opportunity to do the deed elsewhere. Why come back to Owensville to do it? And why at the plant? These were questions that haunted her. And of course, her vision. What did Chloe mean by saying she had to stop him? Stop who?

As the parents entered the hospital, Riley immediately picked up on their debilitating grief. That was the worst part of her gift. Sometimes the emotions were so strong, she couldn't help but shed tears as well. And for those who didn't know about her gift, of which there were many, her emotional expressions came off as insincere and patronizing, when in fact, it was the complete opposite.

She started toward them. "Mr. and Mrs. Dawson?"

"Yes, I'm David Dawson and this is my wife, Elizabeth." He offered his hand.

"I'm Officer Riley Thompson. Captain Ward should be back in just a moment." And as if she could foresee the future—sometimes she could—Ward approached.

"Here you go." He handed her the paper cup and turned his attention to the parents. "Evening, I'm Captain Ward."

"David and Elizabeth Dawson," the father replied. "Can we see our daughter, please?"

"Yes, of course. Follow me." Ward started back toward the corridor that led to the morgue.

Riley had been here before and not just as an officer of the law. She'd been here with Carl to see his son, CJ, shortly after he'd been shot dead. But that was fifteen years ago.

"Dr. Trent," Ward began. "This is Mr. & Mrs. Dawson."

"Oh, yes. Hello, my condolences." The doctor offered a greeting. "Right over here." He directed them toward the chest where Chloe was put on ice.

She was inside a body bag, mostly because her skin was so damaged from the concrete that the raw exposed areas needed to be contained. Chloe was horribly disfigured from the incident.

"I must warn you, she is not in good condition," the doctor said.

"I filled them in on what happened," Ward replied.

Elizabeth Dawson moved closer. "Please, just let me see my little girl."

"Very well." Dr. Trent unzipped the bag and pulled it open, revealing Chloe's face. "I'm so very sorry. She is virtually unrecognizable."

Elizabeth Dawson clamped her mouth shut with her hand. She buried her head into her husband's chest and sobbed.

David tried to soothe her but struggled to keep himself together. And Riley felt every agonizing emotion they were feeling. Her heart ached and felt like it was crumbling into bits on the floor. She became overheated, and her face grew red.

"I just need a minute, Captain. I'll be right back." Riley had to excuse herself because she would not intrude further on their pain. It was too deep, too personal. She felt like a thief.

Just outside the door, she took a calming breath. It was one of the ways she had learned to block the feelings, refocusing on her breathing, calming her pulse. This was how she maintained composure in times like these. It had taken years to master the technique and she had—mostly. When she returned to the others, the heat in her face subsided. "Please excuse my absence."

"Officer Thompson has been working on this investigation with me directly," Ward began. "And we'd like to ask, when you're ready, if you wouldn't mind answering some questions for us? We can do it here, in the hospital. Dr. Trent has an office. There's no need for you to go to the station."

"Who would do this to her? She was just a child, barely an adult." David approached Chloe. "I don't understand. Why was she here in Owensville? We moved more than two years ago from this place."

"That's one of the things we'd like to talk to you about, Mr. Dawson," Riley said.

Elizabeth touched Chloe's hair. "When can we take her home?"

"Not until all the forensics come back, Mrs. Dawson. I'm sorry. I wish it didn't have to be that way," Ward replied. "I'd like to think it would be in another week or so."

"My God. My daughter has to stay here in this horrible place for another week?" Elizabeth looked to David. "No, we can't let that happen. We have to make arrangements to get her home."

"Beth, they have to do this. I know we both want her home, but they need to find who did this to her. And if they need to keep her in order to do that, then that's the way it has to be." He looked to the captain. "I've seen enough. We can go answer whatever questions you have now."

Ward nodded and started out the door, holding it open for the others. "Dr. Trent? May we use your office?"

"Of course." The doctor zipped up the bag again and placed Chloe back inside the chest.

Ward led them to the doctor's office and closed the door behind them. "We appreciate your willingness to talk to us at what I know must be a very difficult time."

"You have no idea, Captain," Elizabeth began. "Do you have children?"

"No, ma'am, I don't."

"Then I don't really think you can come close to understanding what it is we're going through right now."

"Of course not." He eyed Riley for a moment before returning his attention to the Dawsons. "So you weren't aware that Chloe was here in town?"

"No. She moved out last year, got an apartment. We didn't get to see her as much as we'd have liked. But from what she said, she was going for a weekend in Terra Haute. I guess to see some friends. And honestly, we hadn't heard from her since then and that was, oh I guess about a week or so ago." David looked to Elizabeth. "Isn't that about right?"

"Yes. She was always on the go, as most young people are." She wiped away her tears.

"Do you know if she was dating anyone?" Riley asked.

"Nothing serious, from what she's said, but there was a young man. A few years older than her. I think she was seeing him on occasion. Chloe was a free spirit, not the type to settle down, at least, not at her age," Elizabeth replied.

"Do you know this man's name?" Riley had learned not to offer up information, but rather wait for confirmation that what she knew was accurate. And what she wanted to know right now was whether this young man the Dawsons knew about was Blake Rhodes.

"Blake something or other," David replied. "Did she give you any details on this boy, Beth?"

"Um, yes. I believe it was Blake Reynolds. No. Blake Rhodes. That's right. It was Blake Rhodes. We never got a chance to meet him. He worked in Indianapolis at an architecture firm, so we figured he must be okay."

"He was an architect?" Riley asked.

"Yes. I'm sorry, I can't recall if she ever mentioned the name of the firm he worked for," Elizabeth said.

"But you say it was in Indianapolis?" Riley pressed on.

"That's right."

"Well, we can probably whittle that down and see if we can find out where he works. Might be the best way to track down his whereabouts, unless you know where he lives?" Ward jumped in.

"I'm afraid not. As I said, she wasn't forthcoming with a lot of information. I assume he must've been working on something in Muncie because I don't know how else they would've met," Elizabeth added.

"Chloe did go to the city quite often," David said. "There was always something going on there, big city and all. She could've met him there, I suppose."

"Anyone else we should know about? Other friends she spent time with?" Ward asked.

"Not that I can recall off the top of my head. Oh, except Justin Rehnquist. They stayed in touch after school, from what I gathered. But we have a key to her apartment. I suppose you might ought to come take a look," David replied.

"That could be very helpful, thank you." Ward turned to Riley. "In fact, we might want to talk to the Muncie police while we're there, just so we don't step on toes. And they might have something useful."

"I agree. I know it's late, and it wouldn't take but a couple hours. Would it be okay if we went there tonight?" Riley asked.

"Of course. We want to do everything in our power to help you find our daughter's killer," Elizabeth said.

———

Jacob drove frantically to Rachel's apartment, his eyes continuing to peer through the rear-view window for any tails. So far, so good. But that didn't mean no one would be waiting for him at her place. It was a risk to go there, but what choice did he have? They'd threatened her. And no matter that they were no longer together, he couldn't let this happen to her. She had nothing to do with any of it. Neither did he, but Blake had been his friend and colleague and had now tangled up both of them in this dangerous web.

Her turn-off was just ahead. Jacob veered onto her street and drove slowly along with the dark skies hindering his vision. There would be no way of knowing if these people were holding her right at this very moment. But he would see her car in her parking spot of the apartment building.

His car rolled over the speed bumps as he entered the large complex. Eyes peeled, he drove until arriving in front of her build-ing. Jacob's heart pounded. What if they were just sitting there, waiting for him? They'd answered the call only hours ago. Perhaps they knew this was where he'd be right at this moment. Blake could have warned them too. He didn't want to believe it, but this person he used to call friend had framed him for stealing money.

Her red Pontiac Grand Am was parked in the spot. Rachel was here. Well, her car was. "They're going to know I'm here. They're probably waiting for me." Jacob slowed to a stop just behind her car. He feared calling the police, confident they would hurt her if he did. He didn't know what to do.

Jacob peered at his cell phone and pulled up Rachel's contact information. "No. They'll be listening." There was never a more appropriate time to call Riley than this. She was a cop. She would know what to do. But this was Indianapolis, not Owensville. This city reeked of crime, drugs, and the mafia. "Just go."

He opened his car door and stepped outside, and as he continued toward the pathway to her building, he peered over his shoulder, wondering if he was being followed. Maybe it would've been better if he'd at least been armed. But coming here today, to see his so-called friend, he didn't think he would end up needing a gun.

The staircase was just ahead and he now stood on the bottom rung. "What the hell am I doing?" But he had to protect her. This was on him, no matter what really happened, and he couldn't let her suffer for it.

He reached for the iron handrail and started up the steps quietly. It was almost midnight and it appeared most of the residents were sleeping. No lights were on in the windows, not even Rachel's. This was what really concerned him. If she wasn't there, then where? Could he call her cell? Would she answer, or would they answer again?

Jacob reached the landing. Twenty paces and he would be standing at her door. But could he continue? He always believed himself to be a brave man, but one never really knew how one would act in situations like this. Would he rise to the occasion? Or would he end up being another Blake Rhodes?

With his shoulders thrust back and his chest puffed, Jacob knocked. He stood waiting, unable to let go the breath in his lungs.

No answer. He tried again. One leg was poised behind the other, a stance that would offer some protection should anyone attack. But so far, no one had. And after another minute, it appeared no one would. "Shit." Rachel wasn't there, meaning he didn't know where she was and was helpless to come to her rescue.

He suddenly recalled the key. Jacob still had a key, and by some miracle, it still worked. He walked inside the dark apartment. The light from his phone shining inside, he continued toward the wall to flip the light switch. The kitchen nook lit up. Stunned, Jacob surveyed the damage. They'd destroyed her apartment. Sofas upturned, tables smashed, papers strewn on the floor. "Oh my God."

The phone call he'd received earlier today frightened him. That was why he met with Blake. But being here now, seeing what they'd done, his fear for her safety intensified. With his phone still in his hand, he called Blake. "Where is she? Where the hell did they take her, Blake?"

"Dude, where are you?"

"Where is Rachel? Just tell me. Now!"

"I warned you not to go looking. We need to sit down and figure this shit out. I don't know where she is. I told you that already. If you're at her place, you're crazier than I thought. They could be there, watching you."

"I swear to God, if they hurt her, they won't survive and neither will you." Jacob ended the call. There was only one thing left for him to do. He was going to have to find his old boss, George Hammond.

The head of the architecture firm where Jacob was employed until very recently owned a lavish home. And now he knew why. The firm had only been three years old, and when George hired him, he felt like the luckiest man on earth. Fresh out of architecture school and two semesters of internships, and he had been hired on after everyone, including his professors, told him it would probably take another year to land such a lucrative position. Perhaps he should have seen the red flag, but the money and the job were too good to pass up.

Now he found himself sitting in his car in front of George's large and ornate home with gates at the driveway to keep out the riff-raff, which apparently included him. He pressed the contact button on his phone. "You'd better answer, you son of a bitch." The line went straight to voicemail. "Damn it!" He peered again at the closed gates. "Screw it." Jacob jumped out of his car and walked toward the gate, looking for a way to hop over. A column on the left side. That was where he would go. A small electrical transformer that controlled the gate might give him the height he needed to make it over.

With one foot, he stepped up and tried to grasp at the brick column. Missing by a hair, Jacob slipped but regained his footing. He again surveyed the area. "I'm getting in there one way or another." This time, he gripped it with his fingertips. Luck must've been working in his favor because the shoes he chose to wear today just happened to be hiking boots. He could use his legs to climb farther, and it worked. He gained just enough height to wrap his arm over the top edge of the column. Now he had a good hold of it and continued to climb higher until reaching the top of the fence. However, he hadn't considered what was on the other side. And from where he sat, it looked to be a fairly substantial drop. One that could, at best, twist his ankle upon landing, at worst, break his leg. "Just do it, you wuss." With a deep breath, he leapt. And with a resounding thud, he smacked hard against the ground. At least it was grass and it had rained fairly recently. Still, he grabbed his right foot, which had taken the brunt of the landing, and cringed. The good news was there was no blood. No bones protruding. It looked like he'd twisted it pretty good, maybe a small fracture, but he would manage. As pissed as he was, he would push through the pain to find George.

Jacob began to hobble, trying to walk it off as best he could. He reached the front door and peered through the large glass insert. It was dark as hell inside and out. If George was here, he was either asleep or his camera caught Jacob rolling up to his house and now he was hiding. He pounded on the door. "George!" It felt as though the pane of glass would give way to his aggressions, but Jacob didn't care. "Where is she? Where's Rachel?" he shouted.

He knew the house had a security system and that thought probably should have occurred to him before getting to this point. Because if George wasn't here, and it was looking that way, he wasn't going to break in. Not unless he wanted to get arrested. And then any chance of saving Rachel would fly right out the window. "Damn it!" He turned away from the door and considered what he would do next. That was when the door opened. He whipped around, only it wasn't George who answered. It was George's wife.

"Kelly. Oh my God, Kelly. Where's George? I have to see him."

"He's gone, Jake. I'm sorry. He took off several days ago."

"You gotta help me. I'm in serious trouble if I don't find him. Where did he go? Please. Someone's life is at stake, Kelly. Please help me."

"I wish I could. He emptied our bank account and took off. The kids and I are staying somewhere else. I just came back to get some clothes. I must've fallen asleep. Who's in danger?"

He believed she was telling the truth, but feared revealing too much about the situation. "Just someone I care about. Kelly, I don't know what to do."

"I think they got to him and that's why he's gone," she said. "I knew it was a bad deal. I should've said something. Is that why you're here? Is that why you're in trouble?"

"Yes, and I can't get out of it without his help. I need money, a lot of it."

"So do I. Like I said, he cleaned us out. Took everything of value in the house. There's nothing left, Jake."

———

It was almost midnight when Riley and Captain Ward arrived in Muncie to check out Chloe's apartment.

"This is it." David Dawson retrieved his key and opened Chloe's apartment door. "I think I've only ever used this key twice. Glad to know it still works."

"Thank you, Mr. Dawson," Ward said. "Maybe it's best if Officer Thompson and I go on in first."

"Sure, I understand."

Riley followed Ward inside. "Just give us a minute to give the 'all-clear,'" Ward continued. "Well, are you picking up anything?"

"I need more than thirty seconds," Riley replied.

Ward shrank back. "Right, sorry."

Riley continued to study the small one-bedroom apartment of the dead girl who used to live in Owensville and somehow found her demise to be in the very same place, despite her living a couple hundred miles away. Riley had picked up on Chloe back in the parents' rental home, which was frightening that she was capable of reaching that far into the past. Something that hadn't happened since she met Carl in his awful dreams about the war. But now, seeing Chloe's personal belongings here, it did bring with it a certain urgency. Perhaps there was more at stake and she was the one to have to find the answers. What she needed to find was a way to track down Blake Rhodes. If there was any place that would happen, it would be here.

"Riley, can I give them the okay to come inside?" Ward asked.

"Just let me take a look in her bedroom. Give me one minute." Riley walked along the hall and toward the only bedroom. Inside, the room was pretty typical of a young woman just starting out in life. The bed was made. The floor was clean. That alone suggested she was a fairly organized woman and unlikely to succumb to chaos brought to her by a close friend or loved one. "Jackpot." Riley spotted a laptop on the dresser. "Captain?" She started back out toward the living room. "We need to take this."

He eyed the computer. "Absolutely. Anything else strike you as odd in there?"

"Not really. It feels like she's fading away. I thought the energy in here would be substantial, but it isn't. Like maybe she hadn't been here in a while."

"A long while?"

"It's possible."

"Okay. We need to let those folks inside now."

"Yeah, okay."

———

THE LONG DRIVE BACK TO OWENSVILLE HAD TAKEN ITS TOLL on both of them. Ward spotted the station ahead and pulled into the lot. He stepped out and waited for Riley to join him. "Why don't you get that laptop checked into evidence and go on home. It's damn near 2am and I'm sure you're exhausted." He continued inside. "Looks like I need to light a fire under Abrams and Decker. They should be out patrolling, not sitting in there yakking."

Riley continued behind him and entered the station.

"Evening, Abrams, Decker," Ward began. "Why aren't you two out hitting the streets? Dispatch can hold down the fort."

"We were just about to head out," Decker began. "We got a call about some kids vandalizing the park."

"Better get on out there, then." Ward continued into his office but stopped short and turned to Riley. "Thompson, get that logged in and go home. That's an order."

"But, Captain, if I could just take a look now."

"Riley, there's nothing more you can do tonight. We'll hit it first thing in the morning. Go home. Get some sleep."

She was reluctant because she felt that something would turn up on that laptop. Did six hours of sleep really matter? To her it did. That meant six more hours Chloe Dawson's killer was on the streets. And she couldn't stand that idea. "Fine. I'll get this logged into Evidence and then I'll leave, if that'll make you happy."

"It will." Ward closed his door.

Riley walked to her desk and waited for the other officers as they started out the door.

"Hey, Thompson," Abrams began. "Better do what Daddy says." He laughed. She didn't. "I'm just busting your balls. Geez. Decker, let's get the hell out of here and pick up those little shits."

"Night, Thompson," Decker said.

"Night." She peered through the window and watched as Decker pulled out of the parking lot. She eyed Ward's office and the laptop. "No one will miss it." She snatched her car keys and walked out the door.

———

RILEY PULLED ONTO HER DRIVEWAY AND TURNED OFF THE engine of her patrol car. She usually parked it inside her single-car garage, but with an unknown vehicle driving slowly in her neighborhood, newly installed cameras, and Jacob, who'd taken pictures of said vehicle, Riley thought it best to make it clear she was a cop.

One of the cameras was tucked beneath the front porch in the left-hand corner and could capture anyone approaching the home. Another camera was positioned on the right side of her garage and could spot vehicles passing by. The system would alert her to movement and send a notification to her cell phone, neither of which she'd received today. Although she would check the website anyway because perhaps, having traveled out of town, a notification hadn't made it through.

And there was still the issue of Chloe Dawson's laptop, which Riley had tucked under her arm as she approached her front door. Inside, her schnauzer jumped with excitement on her legs. "Get down, CJ! I'll get you some dinner. You must be starving." She placed the laptop on her kitchen table and poured a bowl of food. "Here you go, boy."

Riley opened her own laptop and viewed the website for footage that might reveal who it was trying to intimidate her. That was what this felt like, intimidation, likely for the homicide investigation, but at this point, she wouldn't rule out any scenario.

The website loaded and she keyed in her username and password. She could search for times the cameras had been activated from movement, which would speed up the process. Riley watched the footage. Nothing that resembled the car she'd seen and Jacob had photographed. "Damn."

CJ nudged her arm. "Okay, okay, I'll let you out." Riley walked to the sliding glass door leading to the backyard and opened it. It was in that moment she recalled missing her visit with Carl. "Oh no." She'd promised to bring him sodas and snacks and it was the first time she'd ever missed a visit. She would have to stop by in the morning and make amends, not that he would hold it against her. He knew she was working a case, but it would not relieve her own guilt.

CJ began barking in the yard, but Riley couldn't see the reason for the disturbance. "CJ! Come!" She stepped onto the patio and called out for him again. "CJ, get over here, boy!" It was late and her neighbors would be awakened if he kept this up much longer.

When he still hadn't returned, a wave of emotion surged through her. Unable to identify the source, fear coursed through her veins. "CJ! Where are you, boy?"

The dog emerged from the darkness, gleeful and oblivious. "Geez, you scared me. What the heck is out there?" He rushed back inside. Riley placed her hand on the butt of her gun, which was still strapped to her waist. Something felt off and her stomach turned. She continued into the yard, along a flagstone path she'd installed herself, which led to a small fire pit. As she reached the pit, she spotted embers burning. Someone had been here. It was warm, but not hot, like it had been a few hours since something was set ablaze.

Riley drew her weapon and aimed it at the shadowy trees that lined her rear fence. "Is someone here? I'm an armed officer." No one answered. No one emerged from the shadows. The silence filled her ears. There were no crickets, no leaves rustling. Nothing but utter silence. She collapsed to the ground and her gun discharged.

Time stood still and in her mind's eye, Riley was back at the plant, standing in front of Chloe Dawson's body encased in concrete. Only she was still alive, gurgling, trying to speak, the concrete oozing from her mouth. She'd seen Riley and reached out to her.

Riley tried to grab her hand, but her fingers kept slipping, unable to get hold of them. "Chloe!" It was as though her own legs were cast in the concrete because she couldn't move them. She couldn't get closer to the girl, who was dying in front of her, begging for help. "Who did this to you? What happened?" Riley's head spun at the sound of people nearby. Her eyes frantically searched for where the voices were coming from, but she could see no one. "Who's there? Help me! She's dying!"

———

"Riley? Riley?" Ethan jostled her as she lay on the ground. "Come on, wake up!"

Her eyes finally clicked open and Riley saw a hazy vision of Ethan hunched over her.

"Jesus, Riley! What the hell happened? Are you okay?" Ethan helped her to sit upright.

"What are you doing here?" Riley's vision gradually returned to normal.

"Your gun." He pointed to her weapon that lay inches from her hands. "You fired your weapon. One of your neighbors called the station, said they heard a gunshot. Decker called me to check on you. He knew I could get to you before he could. We're all freaking out, Riley."

"I'm fine." She began to rise. "I don't know how my gun discharged. I—I don't know."

"You'd better figure it out because Ward's going to have a shit fit about this. You can't just fire your weapon with no reason."

"I know that. Don't you think I know that?" She pushed him away.

"I'm sorry. I was just scared, scared out of my mind. Come on, let's get you inside." Ethan helped her back into the house and closed the glass door, ensuring it was locked.

"Where's CJ?" she asked.

"Right here." Ethan pointed to the dog as he ran toward her. "He'd been barking the whole time, according to the neighbor. My God, Riley, I thought you'd been shot." He ushered her to the sofa. "Let me get you some water."

Riley searched for answers. Why had she been taken back to the plant only to watch Chloe die? And who were those voices coming from? It had been years since she'd found herself in this situation, having been whisked away by someone else's powers. Only this time, that person was dead, which made this all the more confusing.

"Here, drink this." He handed her the glass and sat down. "Now, do you want to tell me what happened?"

———

IT WAS 2 AM AND JACOB HAD RETURNED TO THE ROAD. WITH no answers from George's wife, he didn't know how he was going to help Rachel. But it seemed he was running out of options. Betrayed, framed, and on the run was a place he never believed he would find himself. But more importantly, what would happen to her? Come tomorrow afternoon, they wanted to collect, and the odds of him getting his hands on sixty grand were astronomical.

Blake said they could work through it together. Maybe this wasn't his fault. Maybe George was really to blame for all of it. As much as he hated to admit it, Jacob would have to return to see his former colleague. If he stood a chance in hell of getting Rachel out of this, who else could he turn to? Bringing this back to Owensville didn't seem like a good plan. Riley would want to help and what if something happened to her? It was a thought he had to banish from his mind because it would be unbearable were it to come to fruition.

Jacob turned around and headed back, back to the city and to Blake Rhodes' apartment. As he saw it, there was no other choice.

———

WITHIN ABOUT AN HOUR, JACOB HAD RETURNED. HE WAS exhausted, frightened beyond anything he'd ever experienced before, and was about to ask for help from someone he no longer knew if he could trust and suspected he couldn't.

Jacob knocked on the door. Blake opened it. "Well, you look like shit. Come in."

"I need you to help me find her." Jacob shed his coat and fell onto the couch.

"I told you we could work through this together. You're not in this alone. This is George's fault and maybe mine too. But I'm sure we can convince these guys neither one of us had a part in it. Look, man, I know you want to get Rachel back. Hell, I do too. This shit shouldn't have landed in her lap, but the first thing we need to do is cooperate."

"How am I supposed to do that? I don't have sixty grand and you know it."

"I do know that, but your folks could help."

"Oh no. Not a chance. I am not getting my parents involved in this. Besides, they'd have to put up the house or something. No. There has to be another way."

"Then we're going to have to hold them off until we can find George and the money he stole."

"How are we going to do that? Do you know where he is, Blake? Because if you do..."

"I don't know where he is. I guess I thought, in the end, maybe you did. But I can see I was wrong. We're going to need help, brother," Blake said. "Whatever help we can get."

———

"I still can't figure out how your weapon discharged," Ethan said. "I'm just glad you're okay and no one got hurt."

"What do you think the captain's going to do?" Riley asked as she sat on the edge of her sofa.

"I don't think he'll do anything. Look, no one was hurt. It was an accident."

"Ethan, I'm a cop. This isn't the kind of accident that's okay. You know that."

"Ward knows you, Riley. He knows what happens sometimes and I don't think he'll hold you accountable for that."

"He would if I'd injured someone, or myself."

"Well, we can't think about that. Let's just focus on the fact that you're okay. And, I'd like to know why you have that laptop on your kitchen table?"

"It's mine."

"Riley, it's not yours. It has stickers all over it. Come on, how long have we been partners? I don't deserve to be lied to. That's Chloe Dawson's, isn't it? Last you said when you guys were driving back was that you'd found her laptop. Why isn't it in Evidence? You know you can't bring stuff like that home. At least not before they've pulled prints."

"You're right. I shouldn't lie to you and I'm sorry. It is Chloe's.

Captain wanted me to log it in and wait until morning to look at it."

"Let me guess, you didn't agree?"

She cast away her gaze sheepishly. "Not exactly."

Ethan rose from the sofa and made his way to the kitchen. "Since it's here, might as well take a look." He grabbed it and returned to the living room. "You planning on using your Jedi mind tricks to unlock it?"

"Something like that. I thought I'd give it a shot anyway," she replied.

"You know, we can get people for this. They're called Computer Forensics. They know how to do this sort of thing without the risk of damaging files or anything like that."

"Yeah, I know, but I wanted to take a crack at it."

Ethan pulled back and folded his arms. "Have at it."

Riley opened the lid and booted up the computer. A login screen appeared. "She's shown me things and I think I know what this could be." She began typing in a username.

"If you can do this, you might be in the wrong line of work. You should be working for the NSA or something."

Riley laughed. "That's it." She sat back and admired her hand-iwork. "I knew there was a reason." She looked at Ethan. "I can see the confusion on your face. Suffice it to say, when we were at her apartment earlier tonight, I noticed several things. First of all, she's obsessed with Ed Sheeran. The poster in the rental place, and then the playlist on her Amazon Echo. I asked Alexa to play 'my favorites.' It was in her bedroom, and the first song was an Ed Sheeran song. Then I noticed a ticket stub in a drawer. Again, a Sheeran concert."

"Okay, so what, her password was Sheeran?"

"No. It was the first word in the title of the song that played. And as far as the username, well, I didn't pick up on that until just now. Luckily, my hunch was right."

"I will never question your abilities again, Riley Thompson. The stuff you do is beyond me, so I'll just go with it. Let's see what we can find in her emails first."

Riley opened the email provider and waited for it to download. "It looks as though it hasn't been updated since the day before she was found in the plant."

"Meaning no one else appears to have access to it. And that does prove she returned to Muncie only the day before she was murdered," Ethan replied.

"Let's take a look." Riley began scrolling through the unopened mail. "We should be looking for something from Blake Rhodes so we can track him down."

"We can always run a BMV check. Get his social and go from there," Ethan said.

"Yes, but I'm hoping we'll find something more current. Relevant. Something that will tell us where he is right at this moment." She continued to scroll through, opening the messages that appeared important. Nothing yet.

"Hang on." Ethan pointed to the screen. "Open that one there. The one dated four days ago."

"Okay." Riley clicked on the message and began to read it. "Oh no."

"Are you seeing what I'm seeing?" Ethan's face masked in surprise. "What the hell? Riley, this guy knows Jacob."

She continued to read as panic set in. "What does he have to do with this?"

"I don't know. But I'll tell you what, according to this, these two worked together. This email says Jacob was fired and that Blake was going to have to lay low. What is that supposed to mean?"

She turned to Ethan. "What if Jacob's in trouble?"

"In trouble? Are you kidding me? What if he's involved in Chloe's death?"

[10]

With a bag of groceries in her hand, Riley stepped off the elevator and headed toward Carl's apartment. Her thoughts, however, continued to dwell on the connection between Chloe Dawson and Jacob. She knocked on Carl's door. "It's me, Riley."

"Of course it's you. Come in." Carl's voice traveled through the door.

He was disappointed; she sensed it the moment she entered. But it seemed the reason was because he'd felt left out, not that she hadn't come by. "I'm so sorry I didn't make it over yesterday like I said I would, but I come bearing gifts."

Carl sat in his recliner, the news on the TV, but the volume turned down. "Set it on the counter." He hadn't looked at her. "It's common courtesy to call when someone expects your visit. You know, just to say you ain't coming."

"I'm really sorry, Carl. A lot has happened." Riley set down the bag and approached him, kissing his cheek. "I don't have long, but I wanted to stop by since I missed yesterday."

"Well, sit down, then. I can't keep craning my neck up at you."

Riley sat down on the edge of the chair. "How are you feeling?"

"Me? I'm fine. You on the other hand—don't take this the wrong way—but you look like hell, Riley."

She chuckled. Carl never pulled any punches. "I feel like hell. Rough night."

"So I heard." He did little to hide his discontent.

And now the truth was revealed. She hadn't filled him in on what happened and he heard it second-hand. Carl didn't like being left out when it came to Riley. "How's that?" she asked.

"Got me one of them police scanners. You know, since Owensville got a murderer on the loose. Thought I'd keep up to date on how you all were doing. By the way, appears as though not much, if you don't mind me saying."

"How did you get a police scanner?"

"It's called online shopping. You should check it out some-time." Carl flaunted a haughty smile.

"Right. You must've heard the call that came in regarding the gunshot."

"That I did. I got a feeling it had something to do with you. Ever since the old days, I can pick up on a thing or two where you're concerned. That connection never really went away."

"I know. I feel it sometimes too, but not like before," she added.

"No, not like before. I don't have those awful dreams any longer, thank the Lord. But I knew it was you. You mind telling me what happened?"

Riley was hesitant to worry him like this. "It's a long story."

"Well then, I might just have to cancel my breakfast at the country club this morning. Where the hell you think I'm going, Riley? Now are you going to tell me what happened or am I going to have to call Ward and find out from him?"

"Fine. I got home late after working on that case. And anyway, CJ was acting up in the back yard. I went outside to check it out and I saw embers in my fire pit. That was when something came over me and I thought I could be in danger, so I pulled my weapon. But I passed out, and my weapon discharged."

"You passed out? Like you used to do when you were a kid?" Carl asked.

"Yeah."

"And what'd you see this time?"

"The girl who was murdered. She was asking for help, only I had none to offer. I couldn't do a damn thing and I watched her die."

"For Pete's sake, Riley, I can scarcely imagine some of the things you go through at times. I'm sorry that happened to you. But what concerns me more is that it happened at all. That's not a good sign; means something's coming."

"I know. That's what scares me too. And I found out last night that Jacob is somehow involved, but I don't know how or why or anything."

Carl shook his head. "Never did like that kid."

"Yes, you did. You just didn't like it when he left."

"That's because he broke your heart. Pissed me off is what it did."

"Carl, I have to get to the station. I have to know how this tracks back to Jacob and why. I wish I could stay. Sometimes it feels like talking to you is my only release. The only therapy I need. And it helps me." She stood up. "Look, with things the way they are right now, I can't say when I'll be back, but I'll do my best to come check on you as often as I can."

"I know you will. Don't you worry about ol' Carl Boyd. You go on and take care of yourself. You worry about me way too much anyway. I'll be fine here."

"I'll see you soon." She began to leave.

"Hey, kiddo?"

"Yeah?"

"Don't let it get out of control. You remember what you need to do to keep it in check?"

"I remember. It won't be like last time. I won't let it." She closed the door behind her, and with a deep breath, Riley found the strength to go on. She continued toward the elevators and stepped inside, waiting to return to the lobby. Carl had been there for her for the past fifteen years and she loved him like a father. Probably even more than her own father. But she knew there would come a time when he wouldn't be there. It was just nature's way and she had no control over that. And when that day came, Riley's world would fall apart. It would be then that she would try to remember his words. He taught her to control her gift, but it was much stronger now than when she was a child. And much more dangerous.

———

WITH THE EVIDENCE TUCKED BENEATH HER ARM, RILEY arrived at the station, and upon entering, suffered the glaring eyes of her captain.

"I suggest you put your things down and come into my office. Now." Ward turned on his heel and marched back.

Riley eyed Ethan, both knowing the degree to which she screwed up. She placed Chloe Dawson's laptop on his desk. "You mind logging this in for me? I might not be employed in another five minutes."

"It's you. He'll understand," Ethan replied.

"I'm not going to hold my breath." She made her way to his office.

"Sit down." Ward kept his eyes on his computer screen and waited for her to sit before diverting his attention. "After all we've been through? You're going to start disobeying my orders? Is that how this is going to work now?"

"No, sir. I—I just felt as though I needed to keep digging."

"Yeah, well, you dug yourself into a pretty big hole there, didn't you?"

"I guess I did."

"And you discharged your weapon. I mean, for the love of God, Riley. What the hell went on last night? You have any idea how much trouble you're in? You think I can just ignore what happened?"

"No, sir. It was an accident."

"No shit it was an accident. You know I have to write this up, don't you?"

"Yes, sir, I do know that. It's the right thing to do. I was just outside, in my backyard. It was an accident."

"According to Pruitt, it was more than that, wasn't it?"

Exasperation masked her face. "He shouldn't have said anything."

117

"He was doing his job, Riley. And, to be honest, I have a right to know. You and I both know that while your gift can be valuable, it can also be dangerous. Come on, I've been around you long enough to have seen what you're capable of. Now I don't know what's triggered this most recent episode, except for the fact that we're working a murder case and that in and of itself is unusual for us here. But you have to be honest with me, Riley. When this stuff happens, I need to know. You could have injured yourself or someone else last night. I can't take that chance, you understand me?"

"Yes, sir." She hesitated to mention the embers because she'd already begun to doubt their legitimacy, figuring it could have been part of her vision.

"Now, as for your complete disregard of my orders about logging the laptop into Evidence, well, that's a whole other can of worms. I'm going to have to write you up for that one too. I'm sorry. There's no two ways about it. You took evidence home before it was cataloged and you contaminated it. And I don't even want to ask how the hell you managed to get into that computer. Pruitt said you found something, but he wanted to let you present it."

"First of all, I just want to say that I'm sorry. I understand the write-ups. I deserve it. But what I found on that laptop makes me very afraid for Jacob."

"Jacob Biggs? Your Jacob?"

"Yes. He knows Chloe's boyfriend, Blake Rhodes. His name was mentioned in one of the emails. I need to know why."

"Did you find out where we can locate Rhodes? We need to talk to him."

"I got the name of the firm, which was also Jacob's firm. I called them on my way in, but the line was disconnected."

"And an address?"

"Indianapolis, but if the line's dead, I imagine the place is shut down. That must've been the reason Jacob was let go. They were closing up shop."

"Okay, look, here's what we're going to do. You and Pruitt pull employer records for this company. Blake Rhodes' name should be included, and Jacob's. Their addresses should also be listed. If Rhodes lives in Indianapolis, you'll need to make contact with the PD there and have them go to his place."

"You want me to tell them he's a person of interest?" Riley asked.

"Yes. A person of interest in a murder investigation. If they find him, we'll have him transported here so we can talk to him."

"What about Jacob?"

Ward rubbed his smooth chin. "Hell, I don't know. He was just here. Is he gone or what?"

"I'll check with his cousin. He was staying there. I'll find out where he is."

"Good. Then you'd better get to it."

Riley pushed up from her chair and started toward the door, but stopped short. "There's one more thing. Carl bought himself a police scanner."

"Why?"

"He thinks danger's coming and he wants to try to protect me."

Ward held her gaze. "He'll never let go of the guilt."

"I just wish he knew that I've never blamed him for what happened that night. Neither him or CJ." Riley walked out and returned to the bullpen.

"You look like you still got an ass," Ethan said.

"Yeah. He didn't bite off too much, I guess. I'm getting written up, though."

"Worse things could happen."

Riley walked toward him. "Tell me about it. He wants us to pull up employer records on Rhodes and get an address."

"He lives in Indy, I thought."

"I think he does. If that's the case, Captain wants us to work with IMPD to bring him in."

———

BLAKE HELD UP A COFFEE MUG WITH STEAMING BREW TO Jacob's face while he still slept. "Wakey, wakey, eggs and bakey."

Jacob lurched and almost knocked the mug from his hands.

"Dude!" Blake pulled back. "Chill. I was just bringing you coffee."

"Sorry. You startled me. And it took me a minute to remember where I was. Thanks." He took the mug and sipped on it. "What time is it?" He reached for his phone and pressed the home button. "Shit. We're wasting time, man. What are we going to do? They'll be calling in eight hours."

"I have a plan." Blake waited for Jacob to sit up on the sofa that had been his bed for the night and sat down next to him. "We rob a bank."

"Are you being serious right now? Rachel's in danger and you're making jokes."

"I'm sorry, man, you're right. I was just trying to lighten the mood."

"Yeah, well don't, okay? Shit's about as bad as it's going to get and we need a solution."

"Okay, I got it. No more jokes. Look, here's what I think we should do. We know George is in the wind. No way we're going to find him. So what can we do to get these assholes off our backs?"

"You mean my back? They aren't after you. You pointed them right at me. And they don't have your girlfriend."

"You're not going to let that one go, are you? Here's what we do. How much cash can you come up with right now? Like liquid, this very moment?"

"I don't know. Five grand, maybe six, mostly from my credit cards," Jacob said.

"I can muster up another four, at least. That'll give us ten percent of what they say you owe."

"Dude, that's like 17 percent. You're a structural engineer, man. Besides, George owes it, not me."

"Oh, right. So we give them the 17 percent and ask for another few days so we can track down George and get the rest. And when we find the son of a bitch, we'll get our ten grand back too."

"You just said he was in the wind. How are we going to find him?"

"Your ex. She's a cop, right?"

"No way am I involving her. Not a chance in hell."

"Dude, from where I'm sitting, you don't have a choice. You want Rachel to be safe? I don't see another way."

"What makes you think they'll let her go without getting all the money?"

"Because we know that they know how to get to us. If they found Rachel, they'll find your parents, my parents, friends, siblings. They'll find everyone in our families. So if they want this money that we don't owe them, this is how they're going to get it back. We'll do an exchange. Rachel for the ten grand."

"Then I can send her as far away from here as possible." Jacob considered the plan. "You know, yesterday, when we met at the bar and you said you told them I had the money, I wanted to punch you in the face. You put Rachel's life in danger and mine too. I don't know if I can forgive you for that. But I'll work with you on this so I can get her back. After that, we're done, you understand?"

"I understand and I don't blame you. I was shitting bricks when they came to me and I shouldn't have given you up like that. George put us in this shit mess. And when we find him, he'll pay for it." Blake slapped Jacob on the knee. "Finish that up and let's get down to business."

Jacob tossed back the rest of his coffee and grabbed his cell phone. "I got to take a leak." He made his way to the bathroom and closed the door. With his phone in his hand, he pulled up Riley's contact information. He had a nagging feeling Blake was going to stab him in the back again and felt as though he and George could be in on this together. But with Rachel's life at stake, he couldn't afford to let Blake see his distrust. And no matter how much he wanted to avoid getting Riley involved, he'd begun to feel he'd waded too deep and soon typed a message to her.

"In the city. It's not safe here. Don't call. I'll call when I can." He pressed the send button. That message was going to scare the hell out of her, but he didn't know what else to say. Right now, he had to get to the bank and withdraw every dime he had.

Blake waited for him to return. "Dude, thought you flushed yourself down the toilet. Come on. We need to get out of here and take care of this shit."

Jacob followed him out the door. "Look, why don't I run down to my bank and get the cash. I can do the credit card withdrawal at the ATM too. We can meet up in about an hour?"

"Sure. Yeah. That sounds good. Let's meet at the office."

"The office? You have a key? Because I don't."

"I got a key. I thought we might take a look around for any clues Georgie boy might have left behind."

"Okay. I'll see you there in an hour." Jacob walked to his car and slipped inside, keying the ignition. He waited for Blake to pull out of the parking lot first, ensuring he wouldn't be followed. Now to make the call to Riley.

ETHAN PRINTED THE EMPLOYER RECORDS FROM THE architectural firm as well as Blake Rhodes' employers for the past five years. "Riley, I got the records." He approached her desk. "According to his most recent employer, Rhodes lives in Indianapolis. You want me to reach out to IMPD and give them a download?"

Riley's phone vibrated on her desk. She peered at the screen and creased her brow. "Hang on." She picked up the cell and swiped to read the incoming text message from Jacob. "Oh my God."

"What is it? Please don't tell me there's another dead body somewhere."

"No, it's Jacob."

"Oh, so it's important police work."

"Ethan, he's in trouble. Look." She held the phone so he could read the message.

"Damn. We need to call IMPD about this," he replied.

"No, just wait. I mean, yes, call them about Rhodes, not about this."

"What if it involves some of the same people? We can't ignore a plea for help."

"Just give him a minute. He'll call me. He'll tell me what's going on." Riley's phone rang, and with a grin, she again held up the phone. "See? There he is." She answered the call. "Jacob, what is going on? How do you know Blake Rhodes?"

"What? How do you know Blake Rhodes?" he replied.

"Chloe Dawson, the murder victim. Jacob, Rhodes is—was her boyfriend."

"Oh. That's not good."

"You'd better tell me what's going on right now. Your message said you aren't safe. Where are you, Jacob?"

"I'm sitting in the parking lot of Rhodes' apartment building. He just left. Riley, I have to get $10,000 to a couple of what I believe are probably mafia thugs so they don't hurt my ex-girlfriend."

"You're being extorted?" Riley eyed Ethan anxiously.

"It's more than that. Look, I didn't know about any of this until yesterday. I started to leave Owensville and I called Rachel, only this guy answered and started threatening her—and me. He wants sixty grand, which apparently is exactly how much money my boss stole from him."

"Your girlfriend's being held for ransom? My God, Jacob."

Ethan turned toward Ward's office, but Riley held up a preemptive hand and shook her head.

"I'm in some seriously deep shit right now, Riley. I don't know what the hell to do. I stayed with Rhodes last night. He came up with some half-cocked plan that I know won't fly. And I don't know what his motives are, which is why I'm calling you now. I think he's setting me up to turn me over to these guys."

"Did Rhodes kill Chloe Dawson?" Riley asked.

"Honestly, he hasn't said one word about his girl. I've never met her."

"Then maybe he doesn't know." She looked at Pruitt and returned her attention to the phone conversation. "Look, Jacob. IMPD is going to Rhodes' apartment. They're going to bring him in as a person of interest in our case, sending him here for questioning."

"You can't. I'm telling you, I think he's setting me up. I think he's the one really responsible for this money. I know my boss took off. I saw his wife last night. She says he cleaned them out. So I don't know what exactly he's done. Blake could be blowing smoke just to keep me near."

"I can't sit back and let you deal with this, Jacob. You need help."

Ethan leaned over Riley's desk and whispered, "Have him come here."

Riley nodded. "Come here—as soon as you can. You need to drive back to Owensville."

"What about Rachel? I can't leave her. They might kill her." He paused a moment. "Okay, here's the deal. I'll bring the money Blake asked for. I'm supposed to meet him at the office in an hour. He says he wants to look for clues as to where our boss went. I bet he won't find any. But I just need to stay until those guys call me, which should be in about six hours. If Blake is in on this, like I think he is, he'll want to get the money. And then he'll want to get the rest of it too. I need to convince them to let her go, Riley. I won't go back to Owensville until I know she's safe."

"What if you're putting yourself in danger just by showing up there?"

"I have to try. I know Blake. He's a greedy son of a bitch. I think if he believes I can get the money, he'll do what it takes to keep me hanging on and that'll mean letting Rachel go."

"Ward wants me to get IMPD out there to bring Rhodes in. What am I supposed to tell him?" Riley asked.

"The truth. He's always been on your side, Riley. I have no reason to believe this time would be any different."

"Fine. For God's sake, Jacob, just call me when you can. Text me after the meeting. Whatever you gotta do to make contact with me. If I don't hear from you in six hours and ten minutes, I'm sending in IMPD."

[11]

The small architecture firm was just ahead. Jacob pulled into the empty parking lot, meaning his so-called friend hadn't yet arrived. However, he wasn't out of the woods because the men after the money could easily be lying in wait.

Jacob pulled the keys from the ignition and grabbed the envelope stuffed with $6,000. He'd cleaned out his bank account and maxed out his credit cards. After this, he wouldn't have a penny to his name. He'd have no place to stay and didn't know how he was going to get to Rachel either. The screws were tightening.

The glass building reflected the mid-morning sun as he made his way to the entrance. Blake had the keys, or so he said, so all Jacob could do was stand there and wait, a wad of cash shoved in his coat pocket. He checked his phone. No missed calls. "Come on, man, just be on time for once in your life."

He surveyed the roads bordering the parking lot. This wasn't a well-traveled business district, but rather clung to the outskirts of mid-town where the rent was cheaper. He wished he could go back in time and pay closer attention to what was happening. Perhaps a part of him knew but refused to admit it. George Hammond wanted nothing more than to make a name for himself and the firm. But projects were tough to get, so when the plant gig came along, he saw dollar signs and ignored the fact that the company who let out the contract had a reputation and was likely associated with the mafia. The fact that the plant resided in Owensville hadn't fazed Jacob. It was the second largest plant in the state and it had been abandoned. It was a lucrative contract.

A glimmer of light caught his eye. It was Blake's car in the distance and it had just turned into the lot. Jacob's heart jumped into his throat. "Calm yourself, man. Don't screw this up." As the car approached, he bore a measured smile.

Blake parked next to Jacob's car, which made him even more nervous. It was as though Blake was preparing for the idea that Jacob might flee, which had crossed his mind, but quickly vanished with recollection that Rachel's life hung in the balance.

"Good, you're here." Blake said on approach. "You get the money?"

"I did."

"I had some trouble on my end. We might have to re-think the 17 percent idea and shoot for less." Blake retrieved the keys and unlocked the front door. He continued inside and turned on the lights.

Why did this not come as a surprise to Jacob? "You didn't get any money? So, we're only giving them my six grand? At least it's still 10 percent, if my math is right."

"Funny, man, but don't sweat it. The fact that we're here and working this out with them will hold water."

Jacob grappled with suppressing his anger and felt the door closing on this plan. But he would have to carry on. He didn't think Blake would cut off the gravy train just yet, not as long as he thought Jacob could come through.

The lobby illuminated with LEDs in the ceiling that shone down on the marble floor. George was all about appearances and he believed if a client was impressed with the office, then said client would be impressed with their work. It was probably a load of crap, but Jacob never questioned anything George did, something that had clearly bitten him in the ass as he stood here now. He followed Blake inside, still poised, although he was terrified down to his bones. "So what are we going to do now? Just sit here and wait for half the day?"

"No, man. I told you. We're going to stick to the plan and look for any signs of where George might've gone or what he did with the money. We need to check the books."

"I don't have access to the books; that was accounting's job. And I can wager no one from accounting is coming in today —or ever."

"George had me examine and print up the monthly statements for his review. I have a username and password," Blake replied.

This was a curious development. So far as Jacob knew, no one but Lisa Ortiz had access to the accounting software and he had no idea where she was. For all he knew, she could be in danger too, but what seemed more likely was that Blake was lying. He might've had access, but not because George wanted him to review the books. Blake didn't know anything about numbers, except when it came to structural engineering. No, this was another ploy, but to what end?

"Maybe we'll get lucky and you'll find the money hidden in

some secret bank account." Jacob played along because there was no other choice. He needed to know more about this situation with Blake and find out if he knew about Chloe Dawson's death. Or if he killed her himself. Even Jacob didn't think that was likely, but right now, he didn't know what to believe. He would have to wait for the day to unfold and make a determination before Riley had the Indianapolis Police storming the building.

Blake started down the hall and walked inside George's office, which looked exactly how Jacob remembered. In fact, it could have been any other day, under any other circumstance, and it would still appear completely normal.

"Why don't you have a look around here?" Blake started. "And I'll log into the system from my desk and see what I can find. We only have a few hours. Balls to the wall, my friend."

Jacob headed toward the lateral file cabinet behind George's desk. He sat down in his boss' chair and pulled open the top drawer. It was the personnel files, where he didn't expect to find anything, but he wanted to keep Blake appeased, so he searched.

Blake soon disappeared and Jacob sat there, alone. He wasn't going to find anything. It was obvious now that Blake had failed to come up with his share of the cash. Jacob was being played and all he could do was play along. Meanwhile, Riley was back in Owensville, waiting for him to tell her everything was fine. He didn't have the conviction to believe that right now.

———

THE TIME ON RILEY'S COMPUTER SHOWED 10:12AM AND ALL she could do was stare at it as if she could will it to move faster. "He's there. He's at the office and I have no idea if he's safe."

"Captain's going to ask you why you haven't called IMPD yet," Ethan began. "What are you going to tell him?"

"I know I can't keep this from him. And the longer I do, the angrier he'll be." Riley glanced toward Ward's office but then returned her attention to Ethan. "You know what I don't get?"

"You mean besides the fact that this whole situation is seriously messed up?"

"Besides that. I don't get why whoever killed Chloe, whether it was Blake Rhodes or not, why leave her ID? It's like we were supposed to find it."

"What are you saying?"

Riley pondered the idea forming in her mind. "I can't be sure, but what if it wasn't the boyfriend, Rhodes, but was made to look like it was?"

"At this point, anything's possible. Jacob said the guy didn't seem to be aware of what happened. Did you tell him to say something about it?"

"No. I don't know what Rhodes' angle is and neither does Jacob. I told him to keep quiet about it until after he gets his girlfriend free."

"You really think his plan is going to work?"

"I'm not feeling anything to the contrary. But then again, I've never met her, so maybe I'm only sensing Jacob's desire to free her."

Ethan appeared overwrought. "Riley, you have to tell Ward. Just rip off the Band-Aid. He might have a solution."

"Maybe you're right. Maybe he can figure a way out of this." She headed toward Ward's office and knocked.

"Come in," he replied on the other side of the door.

She entered. "Hey, Cap. I've got a problem and I know I should've said something before, but I'm saying something now."

"Not a good way to start off a conversation, Riley. What is it?" Ward laced his fingers behind his head as she sat down. "By the way, I'm sorry about jumping down your throat earlier."

"Don't be. I disobeyed an order."

"You did. Now, with that out of the way—go on."

For the first time, Riley truly believed Jacob's life could be in danger and like she had so many times before, she turned to her mentor for a solution. "I need to talk to you about Jacob and his involvement in the Dawson case."

"The email you found. I'm listening."

"I talked to Jacob this morning and asked him about it. Captain, he's in trouble. He believes he's being extorted and so do I. There's already one life at stake." Riley continued to reveal the whole sordid mess and how she ended the conversation with Jacob.

"For crying out loud, Riley. You've been sitting on this for over an hour?"

"I had to let Jacob do what he needed to do."

"And you don't expect to hear from him again until what, 6pm?"

"That's when he said the men would make contact. But that he still had to convince them to give him time to get the rest of the money. And Blake Rhodes is behind this somehow. He just doesn't know to what degree yet."

"I can see why this is a problem."

"Yeah. Captain, I still think there could be more to this that ties to Chloe. I was just telling Pruitt, finding Chloe's school ID? That seemed—too easy."

"Like we were meant to find it."

"Exactly. What do we know about Roy Bayliss, the project manager? We searched that place thoroughly. No way we would've missed that."

"Do you think he could be tied in with the men Jacob's tangled with?"

"It would make sense. I just can't figure out why here? Why Owensville? Where's the connection?"

"And why that plant, of all places?" Ward considered Riley's point. "Let's do some legwork on our end into Bayliss and the company he represents. We'll find out if they're on the up and up. In the meantime, Riley, I'll trust that you know what you're doing with regard to Jacob's situation. But if something starts to smell bad, you'd better let me in on it. I won't let anything happen to that kid if I can help it."

"Thank you, Captain. I'll research the company and Bayliss and see what I can come up with." She walked back into the bullpen.

"What'd he say?" Ethan asked.

"You want to take a trip with me?" She grabbed her jacket and keys.

"Where to?"

"The plant."

Ethan stood up and pulled his jacket off the back of his chair. "I'm in."

———

JACOB STEPPED INTO THE HALL AND MADE HIS WAY TOWARD Blake's office. It had been almost an hour and no sign of him.

George had left nothing behind by all accounts, and if he had, it was very well hidden. "Hey, you have any luck?" He entered the office where Blake remained seated behind the desk.

"Nothing yet. You?"

"Nah. He's gone, man, just like you said. Took the money and ran. I can't believe he left us like this," Jacob said.

The idea that he was about to be handed over on a silver platter to these men consumed him. It felt like Blake was killing time, preparing to make the deal. Jacob needed a plan B, and considered mentioning Chloe Dawson. Riley had advised him against it, fearing it would place him in greater danger. But what if that was the ace up his sleeve? Assuming Blake had feelings for Chloe, could there be a way to bring Blake back into the fold?

"Hey, um, listen." Jacob shoved his hands in his pockets. "You know I was back home earlier in the week?"

"Course. You were right to take off, man. No one blames you. I mean, what was the point of staying here, until all this shit happened." Blake continued to view his monitor.

"Right. I met up with my high school girlfriend."

"The cop—right. What about her? You think she can help after all?"

"Well, look, man. I didn't know what do to with this information, but truthfully, I think you should know."

Blake pushed back in his chair with sudden attention. "Know what?"

"She's worried about me being here, leaving Owensville so quickly."

"Why is she worried? Look, I know I initially thought we should turn to her, but now that the deal's done, if you said something, bro, it would be bad."

"I didn't say anything, but she's very intuitive."

"Oh. Well, you'll be able to alleviate her stress after we get this taken care of. What's the time anyway?"

"Noon."

"Let me make a call. Maybe I can speed these assholes along and convince them we have a plan in place to get them their money. Maybe we can get you back to Owensville yet tonight."

"I still won't have the other 54 grand they want."

"We'll cross that bridge when we get there." Blake stood from his desk. "I'll see if I can make contact and get this ball rolling. I'm telling you, dude, it's a good plan. They'll go for it if they want to see any money at all."

"Guess I'll have to trust you." Jacob stood in the hall and watched Blake head down to the lobby again. Why he felt the need to make the call in private was yet another red flag. Still, it didn't seem like he knew about Chloe Dawson. In fact, it didn't seem like he cared much about what Riley did for a living. Either he was playing it off exceptionally well, to which Jacob would have to give credit, or he really didn't know, which made this a whole lot more troubling.

Jacob walked to the breakroom and grabbed a Red Bull from the fridge. He popped open the can and chugged it down in one fell swoop. He was tired, hungry, and anxious.

Footsteps sounded in the hall and Blake entered the breakroom. Jacob noted the look on his face. "What is it? You get hold of them or what?"

"Yeah, man, I did." Blake started inside.

Jacob's pulse quickened. "They aren't going to go for it, are they? Did they tell you where she was? Is Rachel safe?"

"Relax, dude. They agreed to come here for the exchange. The six grand for Rachel. And the promise that we'll deliver the rest of the money by the end of the week."

"End of the week." Jacob sighed. "And if we can't come through?"

"I don't know, man. But it won't be just Rachel's life on the line. It'll be ours too."

———

THE PLANT WAS ALWAYS A PLACE THAT HELD MYSTERY FOR Riley since she was trapped here during the night of the EF4. She'd had a connection with the storm, driven by something that she never could explain. A strange connection that frightened her and everyone around her, which included Daniel Ward, her captain. Even now as she and Ethan arrived in Riley's patrol car, she cast her eyes upon it and saw a dark nature behind the building. It was just a building, she reminded herself. But now, with the murder of Chloe Dawson, it was again more than just a building. It was a place that held dark secrets within it and when it chose to reveal them to her, as it had when the storm came, she would learn of its purpose.

"Riley, what are you waiting for? Let's go," Ethan said. "Unless you're getting a bad vibe?"

"No. No, it's fine. Come on." She opened her door and stepped outside into the afternoon sun. It was a bright day for September, much too bright a day to conceal such dark secrets.

"Isn't that the guy's truck there?" Ethan asked.

"Yep, he's here, although I don't see much work going on. I thought the captain cleared the scene so they could go back to work."

"He did. Can't say why no one's here, except for the manager. Probably something we should ask, hey?"

"Probably." Riley made her way toward the entrance, and once they stepped inside, she noticed virtually nothing had changed since she was here with Ward after the discovery of Chloe's body. "Hello? Mr. Bayliss, it's Officers Thompson and Pruitt." Her voice echoed inside the massive structure.

A moment later, Roy Bayliss emerged from the rear of the building wearing his hard hat and yellow vest. "Well, hello. I'm sorry, I was in the back. I wasn't expecting you folks to be here today. What can I do for you?"

"Mr. Bayliss," Riley started.

"It's Roy, remember?"

"Sorry. Roy. I had a new development in the murder investigation and I was hoping I might be able to take a look at some of your company records?"

"Well, like what? We've turned everything over to you people already."

"Yes. I know. And we appreciate the cooperation, but I'd like to take a look at your contracts with the other trades. Would that be possible?"

"Why is that, Officer Thompson?"

"Roy, Chloe Dawson was submerged in concrete, had it poured into her mouth. I have to think there would be a record somewhere regarding the concrete company you hired. There might be someone there we need to speak with. Someone who had access to this building and who made the deliveries."

Bayliss eyed the officers. "Yeah. Okay, sure. Follow me." He started into the rear of the building again and toward his office. "So you folks don't have any leads yet as I understand it, is that right?"

"That's not entirely accurate," Riley continued. "Which is why we're here now."

"Of course." He walked toward a tall metal filing cabinet and opened the second drawer. "Let me see. Capital Concrete." Bayliss turned to them. "That's who's contracted to do the work here." He continued in search of the file. "Ah, here we are. If you don't mind, I'd like for this not to leave my office. You're welcome to view it here."

Riley was suspicious but played it off. "Sure, no problem. We really appreciate your cooperation." She held out her hand and waited for him to give her the file.

"Well, have at it. I'll be in the yard if you need me." Bayliss left the officers.

"He doesn't think we're all that bright, does he?" Ethan asked.

"Nope. His mistake." She eyed him. "See any cameras in here?"

He casually scanned the office and shook his head.

"I'll look at this. Maybe have a look around and see what you can find." Riley opened the file folder and the top page was a contract issued to Capital Concrete, LLC. She scanned the agreement in search of names and found who appeared to be the president of the company. With her phone in her hand, she snapped a picture of the signature. "I need to find an addendum or bill of sale. Something that shows deliveries and who signed for those deliveries."

Ethan walked near a credenza. "Take a look in the back of the file. I worked as a file clerk during my senior year in high school. It was for a car dealership and I had to file away the parts receipts. I always filed them in the back, in date order. Worth a shot."

She flipped to the back of the stack of papers, which looked to be about twenty deep, and smiled. "Have I told you lately how glad I am we're partners?" She showed him the receipts.

"No. And don't you forget it."

Riley took pictures of the deliveries including the dates, times, and who signed for the receipt of the concrete. "Here we go."

"What'd you find?" Ethan stopped in his tracks.

"An order was placed the day before Chloe was found. It was signed by someone other than Bayliss."

"One of his guys?"

"Probably. It was supposed to be for the rear yard retaining wall on the north side of the building, according to the receipt. It was a small order, only ten yards."

"Is there any way to know if there was anything left over from the wall pour?" Ethan asked.

"I don't know, but I think we need to find this person and talk to him." Riley started toward the back. "I'll find Bayliss and ask him where we can find the man who signed it. Stay here and keep doing what you're doing. I'll keep Bayliss occupied with this." She made her way outside and held her hand at her forehead to shield the sun from her eyes. "Mr. Bayliss? Can I have a quick word?"

He started toward her. "What is it, Officer Thompson?"

"Can you tell me how to reach Virgil Howard?"

"He's one of my foremen. What do you want with him?"

"He signed for a concrete delivery the day before we found Chloe Dawson. I'd just like to clarify the use for that concrete."

"Sure. I can call him in. Might take a while to reach him. I think he's at another job somewhere in Fort Wayne. I'm not sure."

"I've got time. Thanks."

[12]

The window blinds on the second-floor office of Jacob's former employer snapped shut and he pulled back. "They're here."

"Okay, man, just chill. Follow my lead and we'll get out of this just fine, you understand?"

"Yeah, I understand." Jacob did, but he also feared he might not make it out of the building alive. And if he didn't, then Rachel probably wouldn't either.

"We'll go downstairs and meet them together. You got the money?" Blake asked.

"I got it. As long as they don't change the terms of the deal." He followed Blake to the stairs and both walked down as the kidnappers stood beyond the glass doors of the entrance. They looked exactly as Jacob pictured them, like New York mafia, only this wasn't New York. This was Indianapolis and it was a city no less dangerous or with fewer problems than New York. And there was no shortage of mafia here.

Blake continued toward the door, a smile plastered on his face as though he was greeting potential clients. "Just act naturally," he whispered to Jacob.

Upon opening the door, Jacob wore the same forced smile and he knew they'd see through it. They'd see his fear.

"We appreciate your willingness to work with us, gentlemen," Blake began. "I believe you've already spoken to Jacob Biggs."

Eddie Costa nodded to Jacob. "Mr. Biggs, glad to see you've come around. Rhodes says you two have been working hard to find our money, and that an amicable solution awaits."

"I believe one does." He returned a greeting, which was nothing more than Costa proving he was the alpha with a bone-crushing handshake.

"Why don't we go upstairs to the conference room and discuss the proposal I mentioned on the phone." Blake started back up the steps but stopped when no one followed. "Gentlemen?"

"Maybe we should just do this here. No need to make it more complicated than it needs to be," Costa replied.

"Okay." Blake returned to the others.

"Where is she?" Jacob asked. "Where's Rachel? I have the money, but I need to get her back before I can do anything else."

Blake eyed him with some measure of disdain.

"I guess there's no point in pussyfooting around, is there, Jake?" The other man, who still hadn't offered an introduction, spoke up. "So I'll get down to brass tacks. Rachel's fine. She's being looked after with care. That, I can promise you."

"Look, mister, whoever you are." Jacob stood a few inches

taller than this man but wasn't nearly as muscular. "I didn't take your damn money. My boss did. Blake will tell you the same thing, despite his previous misstatements. So I'm not sure how you got it into your head that I could come up with that kind of cash. I was just an employee here. Low man on the totem pole paying his dues."

"I thought we had an agreement in place, Rhodes?" The man turned to Blake. "What's your boy talking about, he ain't got the money?" He returned his attention to Jacob. "You want your girl back, isn't that right?"

"Yes."

"Then I suggest you stick to the plan, or you'll never see her again."

Jacob eyed Blake, whose face clearly indicated it would be in his interest not to antagonize this man. But Jacob was pissed. Somehow, he'd gotten wrapped up in this shit storm and so had his ex-girlfriend. "I'm not giving you a dime until you let her go. This has nothing to do with her. It has nothing to do with me either, but I can see that argument isn't working for you."

"What is this bullshit, Rhodes? You came to us to make arrangements. Now your boy here is reneging on that?" He pushed closer to Jacob, staring him down.

In that moment, a split-second decision would change the course of Jacob's life. He threw a powerful right hook that landed hard across the man's jaw.

He staggered back in shock.

Jacob yanked the man's gun from his waist, a gun he'd eyed from the moment these guys walked in. And now, he aimed it at both of them.

"What the fuck, dude?" Blake reeled at the bold move.

"Get back, man. I know you're in on this. For whatever reason, this shit's falling on me. I don't know why, but I'm going to find out. Now I suggest you tell me where the hell Rachel is because I bet this magazine is full and I'll make sure I use every last bullet. And tell your lap dog to drop his gun." Jacob aimed the weapon at Costa. "Drop it, man."

"Do as he says," his partner replied.

Jacob's heart pounded and it left him feeling queasy. But he couldn't show any signs of weakness or these guys would pounce and he'd be dead. "Blake, stand over there with them."

"You're making a huge mistake, dude. I'm telling you, you got it all wrong."

"Do I? Why don't you tell me about Chloe Dawson?"

"Who?"

Jacob noticed the flicker in Blake's eyes. "Your girlfriend."

"The fuck are you talking about?"

"The girl who's dead. You know, had a ton of concrete poured into her mouth. Then was encased in it? I know you're working with these guys. What did she do? Threaten to expose you?"

Blake's expression hardened.

"You didn't know." Jacob peered at the men on whom his weapon was trained. "She was found in the old Caterpillar plant that's being refurbished, using the plans we drafted for these pricks."

Blake turned his attention to the two thugs. "You killed her? She didn't do anything wrong. What the fuck? You killed her, you sons of bitches!"

"Got no idea what the hell you're talking about, Rhodes."

Costa returned his attention to Jacob. "As for you, you little shit. You'd better take your shot because if you don't, your girlfriend will be next."

"Give me your phone," Jacob said. "Both of you. Give me your phones now."

"You got a hell of a set on you, son." The larger of the two men set his phone on the floor and pushed it toward Jacob. "Give it to him, Eddie."

Costa laid the phone next to the gun. "Come on, bend down and get them. I dare you."

"Kick them over to me," Jacob replied. "Blake, pick up the phones. Don't touch the gun or I'll shoot you too."

"Okay, man. Here." He handed Jacob the phones.

Jacob stepped closer to the gun that lay on the floor and with his foot, pulled it nearer before picking it up. "Now then, I'll need you three to have a seat right over here while I make some calls."

———

Roy Bayliss shook his head and dropped his phone into his pocket. "I'm sorry, officer. I got his voicemail, but I left him a message."

"Thank you. I'll tell you what, we'll get out of your hair. I'll keep trying to reach Mr. Howard. I'm sure he'll be able to answer our questions. Appreciate your time, Mr. Bayliss." Riley started back inside and caught up with Ethan. "We're leaving."

"Okay." He appeared surprised but followed her out.

She hadn't said a word until they stepped inside the patrol car and she started the engine. "Did you find anything useful while I was outside?"

"As a matter of fact, I think I did. But why don't you tell me how your conversation went? Was he surprised, cooperative?"

"Oh, he was cooperative. At least, he made it appear that he was. I asked him to call his foreman, Virgil Howard, and he did, but there was no answer. So I said I'd keep trying and Bayliss was obviously troubled by the idea of us reaching out to his foreman. This entire situation is looking really bad."

"I came across some shady-looking corporate documents and took pictures," Ethan added.

"Like shady how?"

"Subsidiaries. No parent company listed. It's worth a look. What are we supposed to do now? Jacob still hasn't called."

"No. But he wasn't supposed to meet those guys until six o'clock. It's what, like three now?"

"Yeah."

"Okay. We'll head back to the station. I want to try to call Virgil Howard again and I think we should do a background on him."

"This is making the hairs on my neck stand on end, Riley."

"Me too. I can't fit all the pieces together yet, but I will. I need to know why Chloe was here in the first place. Was she kidnapped? Her apartment had no signs of forced entry. Her car wasn't there. I think she came here of her own will, but why? And who did she see?"

"Maybe she's just a pawn and Blake Rhodes is the reason she's dead."

"That's entirely possible, but Jacob said it seemed like Rhodes didn't know about it."

"Guess we'll have to find out," Ethan replied.

———

THEY RETURNED TO THE STATION, WHERE WARD STOOD outside with a coffee in his hand.

"Uh oh, this can't be good. Captain doesn't drink coffee this late in the day." Riley parked her car and the two stepped out.

"How'd you fare at the warehouse?" Ward asked as they approached.

"Got some interesting information. What's been happening here? You don't usually have a coffee at three in the afternoon," Riley replied.

"I got a call from the owner of the plant. You know, the dog food company?"

"The owner?" Not only were the hairs on his neck standing, but now the hair on Ethan's arms were too.

"He said that a couple of my officers showed up and started harassing one of his employees."

"What? We talked to Bayliss. He let us take a look at the contractors," Riley started. "Why did he have a problem with that? I can tell you, Captain, we were nothing but respectful. I don't know why he would say otherwise."

"Neither do I, but it sure makes me think there's something else going on," Ward added. "Don't worry about it. I apologized and said we wouldn't come by unannounced again."

"That sort of defeats the purpose, doesn't it?" Ethan said.

Riley followed as Ward started back inside with Ethan in tow. "We did find a concrete company. An LLC named Capital Concrete. A man by the name of Virgil Howard, Bayliss' foreman, signed the contract and was there to accept delivery of ten yards the day before we found Chloe."

"Interesting," Ward replied.

"What's even more interesting was that when I brought it to Bayliss' attention, he tried to contact the guy but got his voicemail. Said he was in Fort Wayne or something on another job. So I said I'd make it a priority to reach out to Mr. Howard myself."

"Must be why I got the call," Ward said.

"They don't want us looking into their people," Ethan added. "But why?"

"Maybe because we're onto something," Ward replied.

JACOB WAITED FOR A CALL ON ONE OF THE MEN'S CELL phones. There was a boss somewhere who would be asking how this little pow wow of theirs had gone. And when that call came, Jacob would demand Rachel be set free if he wanted his men to live.

"I'm getting tired of sitting on this floor. My ass hurts. I need to stand up and stretch. We've been here for two hours," Costa said.

"You can stand up when your boss calls and tells me he's letting Rachel go."

He laughed. "You are going to find yourself in a world of hurt, man. You have no idea what you've gotten yourself into."

"I haven't gotten into anything. It's you people who've dragged me into something I know nothing about. I don't know why or how, but I guarantee you, I won't fold. You all have seriously underestimated me. Even you, Blake."

"Man, I don't have anything to do with this."

"Don't lie to me. You set this up from the beginning. You and George both. Figured I'd make a pretty good scapegoat, right?

Small town kid and all? Guess that's probably what you thought about your girl, Chloe. And now she's dead."

"She didn't deserve to die," Blake said. "She was a good kid. We were just having fun. I don't know how she got pulled into any of this, but I'll damn well find out."

One of their phones rang. "Finally," Jacob said. "Let's see who this is." He answered the line. "Hello?"

"Who's this?"

"I'll tell you who I am after you tell me who you are." He didn't recognize the voice or the phone number and the ID showed "unknown caller."

"Where's Virgil?"

"Is he one of the men you sent here for me? Names didn't seem a big priority for either of them." He turned to the man who hadn't shared his name. "You must be Virgil?"

Virgil Howard eyed Jacob.

"I should've figured." He returned his attention to the call. "Yeah, Virgil's here. But before you talk to him, I need to know where Rachel is."

"Who's Rachel?"

"Dude, I've got a gun on your boys and I really don't have a problem shooting either or both of them, which is exactly what I intend to do unless you let Rachel go."

"You must be smarter than you look, son. Okay. You want to play this game? I'll give you the girl in exchange for my men, but that won't release you or your friend, Rhodes, from getting the money you owe me."

"I don't owe you shit and you know it. My boss took your money. Maybe Blake did too. I don't know and I don't care."

"That really doesn't matter to me. I just want it back. So either you find your boss or the money comes out of your ass one way or another," the man said on the other end of the line.

"Bring Rachel here and I'll give you back your men."

"You have a deal. She'll be there inside of the hour."

"We'll be waiting." Jacob ended the call. "So, Virgil, I guess your boss is willing to work out a deal. He's bringing Rachel here within the hour. And then you'll both be free to go."

Virgil Howard bared a sly grin. "I hope you have an exit strategy for you and your girlfriend. Cause I'd be real surprised if he lets you both live."

Jacob checked the time again. It was almost 6pm. He knew what would happen if Riley hadn't heard back from him. It would jeopardize everything and potentially cost his life and Rachel's. He was close to a solution, but if what Virgil Howard said was true, he needed a way out.

"Oh, I can see the wheels spinning, friend," Virgil said. "You know I'm right and now you're starting to realize you're shit out of luck."

"I think your boss wants his money too badly to end my life," Jacob said. "I think he knows I'm his only chance at getting back his sixty grand."

Virgil spit on the floor in front of him. "When the money doesn't turn up, you'd better get your affairs in order."

Blake sat on the bottom step of the staircase and eyed Costa and Howard. "Why'd you kill her?" He turned to Jacob. "Man, I'm sorry about this. I am. I didn't know what they did to her. If I had..."

"Then what, Blake? You would've put an end to all of this? I doubt that. I figure you must be getting some kind of cut or else you would've been in the wind along with George."

"He's got your number, Rhodes," Virgil replied. "Your boy's been setting you up to take the fall. Once he realized he couldn't get Georgie to give back the money, he figured he could squeeze it from you."

"Well, I guess you figured wrong, Blake, didn't you?" Jacob eyed him. "I won't be the one to pay for what you and George did."

[13]

With a pocket full of cash, a gun in his hand, and three hostages, Jacob's day had played out in a way he never expected. He'd devised a plan of escape once the handoff occurred. It was pretty simple really. Go outside, have the boss man send Rachel over, leave the cash. Both would then jump in his car and drive like there was no tomorrow. Because if they didn't, there might not be one.

These guys were clearly mafia. Construction contracts, kickbacks, payoffs. Yeah. And they'd been here before. They'd dealt with far more dangerous adversaries than Jacob Biggs. But he couldn't show weakness. These types of men responded to strength and so he had to muster as much as possible to pull this off.

As Jacob kept his sights locked on the men he held, only occasionally breaking away in anticipation of the arrival of the boss,

Virgil Howard's cell phone rang. Jacob still held both of their phones and eyed the caller ID. "Owensville PD. Oh shit." He knew immediately who was on the other end. How Riley got this man's number was beyond him. Her gift was exceptional, but she'd never met this man. It seemed to be beyond even her abilities. "Hello?"

"Virgil Howard?" she answered.

"Riley, is that you?"

"Jacob? How do you have this phone?"

"I'd tell you, but I don't think you'd believe me."

"I need to speak with Virgil Howard. Is he there?"

"Um, yeah, but I'm kind of holding him hostage at the moment. Can I take a message?"

"What? Are you being serious right now? This guy is a foreman working at the plant. I think he has something to do with Chloe Dawson's murder. You'd better explain to me what the hell is going on right now, Jacob, or I'm sending PD in there."

"No, you can't. Look, I have this under control. I'm about to get Rachel back. It's a long story, but I'm fine, for now. I just need you not to call in the dogs, you understand? It'll be a blood bath in here if you do."

"Where are you?" she asked.

"Still at my old office. I've arranged a handoff with the man who says George took his money and is making me repay him."

"Look, Jacob. This guy—I think he could be the killer. You can't let him leave."

"If I don't, I won't get her back."

"I'm calling PD now," Riley replied.

"No! Please. Don't. They'll kill her for sure. Just trust me, okay? This is the way it has to be. I'm sorry." He ended the call.

"Sounds like you got problems," Virgil said.

Jacob eyed him. "Shut up."

———

Riley stared at the phone. "Oh my God." She looked at Ethan. "Jacob's holding Virgil Howard hostage. And some other people too."

"What? Holy crap. Why? How did this happen?"

"I have no idea. He says he's making an exchange for his ex-girlfriend. They've got her."

"Who's got her?"

"These people, I guess. I have no idea what's happening. Last thing he said to me was that he was going to the office with Blake Rhodes and that he thought the guy was setting him up."

"Sounds like he was right. How does Chloe fit into all this? What did we stumble onto?" Ethan asked.

"I wish I knew." She stood from her desk. "We can be there in an hour if we hurry. He's going to need help."

"We can't go there. For one thing, it's not our jurisdiction. For another, did he say when this handoff was scheduled to happen?" Ethan asked.

"No. Just that it would happen soon."

"Then we could be too late. There has to be another solution. And I think it's going to have to involve IMPD." Ethan returned to his desk and picked up his phone.

"No. Don't. We need to talk to Ward." Riley started toward his office, when the night shift arrived.

"You two still here?" Abrams asked in his usual arrogant tone. "The A-team's just arrived. You can go home now."

They both ignored him and continued to Ward's office.

"Captain? Can we have a word?" Riley entered without waiting for a response.

The captain sat up at attention. "What's going on? What happened?"

Riley told him what had happened and about the call with Jacob. "I think we need to go there and help him."

"No. Pruitt was right to want to call IMPD. I should've done it sooner. Jacob could be dead by the time they get there. I'm making the call now. I won't have Jacob's blood on my hands or anyone else's." Ward picked up the phone. "I need to speak with Captain Pryce. It's Captain Daniel Ward, Owensville PD." He waited while the line was transferred.

"Don't do this, Captain. Please," Riley said.

"Captain Pryce. Thank you for taking my call. I'm afraid I have an urgent situation."

———

TWO CARS PULLED ALONGSIDE THE FRONT OF THE OFFICE building where Jacob had taken the hostages. It was the boss and his lackeys, and they'd blocked the entrance. That could be a problem and might contravene Jacob's plan of escape.

"Looks like our people have arrived," Virgil began. "I hope you're ready, Jakey boy."

Jacob watched as two men from one vehicle stepped out and two men from the other car emerged. "Where is she?" he whispered. Then he saw her. The men flanked her on both sides, holding her arms. She appeared terrified, but he was grateful to see her unharmed.

He was outnumbered, outgunned, and had begun to see the flaws in his plan. These guys were professionals. He was a second-rate architect from a small town. Not exactly a level playing field, but he couldn't falter now, not when she was standing right there.

Jacob pointed the gun at the men. "Stand up. You too, Blake." He waited for them to stand. "Start walking toward the door. The three of you will stand in front of me."

"Smart move, kid," Virgil replied. "Didn't think you had it in you, from what your boy here has said about you."

He eyed Blake. "Just keep moving until I say so."

The men continued toward the glass doors.

"That's far enough." Jacob stared ahead in the small gaps between the men. He watched as the others moved in toward the front doors. They were using Rachel as a shield. Guess they were smart too.

The man who Jacob assumed was the one in charge used the knuckle on his index finger to knock on the glass.

His dark eyes held a pointed contempt. "Jacob Biggs. Are you ready to do this?" His voice was slightly muffled through the thick glass doors.

"How do you want to handle the exchange?" Jacob asked.

"Like we talked about, son. Let my men go and you'll have your girl back. But I want the six-K down payment or this deal goes away and so does she."

Jacob regarded the man who stood just outside the doors. Would this guy stick to his word or would he gun them all down just for the hell of it? He'd come this far, so there wasn't much point in turning back. He and Rachel both stood a better than fair chance they'd find themselves with bullets in their backs, but better than fair was looking like decent odds right now. "Send her in."

The man laughed. "How about you send one of my men out and I'll send her in at the same time, but you'll need to give him the money."

"Fine. I assume you'll want Virgil. He seems like the smart one."

"Right you are, son. Now give him the money."

Jacob reached into the pocket of his jacket and pulled out the fat envelope that contained every last dime he had; money he didn't owe but was being forced to relinquish. And all because of Blake Rhodes. "I'm handing him the money now." He slipped the envelope inside Virgil's coat while the man remained with his hands in the air. "Go outside. Walk slowly."

Virgil Howard started toward the door, each step measured with caution. No one wanted an itchy trigger finger from anyone. He pushed open the door and placed one foot over the threshold.

"Send her over now," Jacob said.

"A deal's a deal." The boss looked at his lackey. "Let her go."

Rachel walked to the door and she met Virgil in the middle.

"You got yourself a brave boyfriend, little girl." He continued past her.

She made her way inside and toward Jacob. "Oh my God." Tears streamed down her face.

"It's okay, you're safe now. Get behind me," Jacob said.

She slipped behind him and huddled at his back.

"Okay. How do we move..." Jacob's words were cut short at the sound of sirens and racing police cars. "What the hell?"

"What did you do, son?" The man turned to his people. "Go. Now!"

Jacob could hear him shouting orders. Police cars, SWAT trucks, the entire damn force had just arrived. "God damn it, Riley!" He still held the gun at two of the men.

"We need to get the hell out of here!" Blake shouted and watched the cop cars race to the front of the building. "Shit! What the hell did you do, Jake? Are you crazy?" Blake ran toward the back of the building, nearing the rear exit.

Jacob held his gun on him but couldn't fire. In fact, he'd never fired a gun in his entire life.

"I knew you were too chicken shit to use that." Costa bolted through the doors.

"Stop! Police!" an officer yelled from a distance as he brandished his weapon, still running head-on toward the entrance.

Meanwhile, the boss and Virgil Howard managed to get inside their vehicle. The tires spun and they hauled ass out of the lot. Shots fired at the back of the car, but they had escaped. And that meant Jacob was going to have even bigger problems.

As Costa made his way outside, an officer yelled, "Stop!"

But Eddie Costa didn't stop. He pumped his legs hard and tried to make it to the end of the building. The officer fired his gun and Costa went down.

Jacob watched and was rendered speechless, but only for a moment. He grabbed Rachel. "Come on!"

"Where are we going? The cops are right there. No!"

"I can't stay. They'll take me in and keep me there. I won't get a chance to warn Riley they'll be coming for her. Blake knows about her and he'll sell her out the way he sold you out."

"Let go of me! I'm not going anywhere with you! You did this!" She yanked away her arm.

Jacob eyed her, then the scene outside. "I'm sorry. I have to go." He ran toward the rear exit and pushed through the doors. Outside, he had only one option: veer right and he'd make it to the car dealership nearby where he could hide, then he could figure this out. Now he had IMPD on his tail. He didn't know what they could charge him with, maybe nothing, maybe something. But either way, it would take hours to sort it out. He didn't have that kind of time, not anymore.

———

RILEY SHOULD HAVE HEARD FROM HIM BY NOW. IT HAD BEEN at least an hour since Ward made the call. In fact, she thought IMPD would've made contact.

"Why don't you go home, Thompson?" Decker began. "There's nothing you can do."

"I have to know what's going on."

"I know you do, but you won't get answers until Ward gets answers," he continued.

Ward opened his door. "Thompson."

"There you go," Decker said. "Maybe he's got something for you."

"Maybe." Riley entered Ward's office. "Please tell me you heard back from them. Is Jacob okay?"

"Sit down." Ward closed his door and returned to his desk. "I just got off the phone with Pryce. They took down one man. They're working on an ID now. The others got away before they pulled in. They were just minutes too late. Except Rachel Freemont was there."

"That was his ex-girlfriend. What about Jacob?"

"I don't know what happened exactly or where Jacob fled to,

or why. Kid should've stayed put. Now I've got IMPD wanting to know what's going on. I told them about our investigation. Riley, whatever went down over there, I have a feeling will spill into Owensville. We know there's a connection to the plant. You have to find Jacob. He's at the center of this and we need to keep him safe. Do you know if anyone was aware that he'd been in town?"

"Just his cousin who he'd been staying with. Maybe Blake Rhodes."

"He could be our weak link. Look, I still don't know how all this ties to Chloe Dawson, but I'm pretty damn sure it does," Ward replied.

"What are we going to do?"

"Try to reach Jacob. I know it's risky, but if he has any chance of making it through this, he's going to need us. And we're going to need him."

"What if I call and they've got him?" Riley asked.

"It's a risk, like I said. And we have no idea who made it out of there. Or who was there in the first place. But, Riley, we have to track him down. And who knows, he might still call you."

"If he's able to. We know Virgil Howard was with him, which means he's tied up somehow with Chloe. He might be the killer. It's possible Rachel has some idea who the men were as well, besides Virgil Howard."

Ward nodded. "Possibly. I'll make sure Pryce keeps me informed on that end. But why kill some twenty-year-old-girl?"

"Maybe Rhodes crossed the wrong guys and killing her was the payback. It's just..."

"What?" Ward asked.

"I didn't get the impression that she died at the hands of those people. I don't know. I felt something when I got into her laptop and when I collapsed."

"If not them, then who?"

"That's something I'll have to find out." Riley pushed up from the chair. "I'll figure out a way to get hold of Jacob and get him down here. Even if I have to go and get him myself."

"Riley, be careful."

"I will." Riley returned to the bullpen and headed straight for her desk. She shut down her computer and gathered her things.

"You're leaving? What's going on?" Ethan asked.

Riley turned to Abrams and Decker, who sat at their desks. "Hey, guys, if I give you a picture of a car, you think you can run down the plates for me? It's important."

"But you don't have plates?" Decker asked.

"No. A make and model with Indiana plates, number's illegible. You think you can pull BMV records on who owns that type of car here in Owensville?"

"What do you need it for?" Abrams asked.

"Can you do it or not?"

"We'll give it a shot, Thompson," Decker replied. "I'll touch base if we find anything."

"Thanks. Goodnight." She turned to Ethan. "Follow me out?"

Ethan jumped from his desk and reached her as she waited outside. "What's up?"

"Jacob's in trouble. Ward said the IMPD got there too late. We don't know Jacob's whereabouts. Luckily, his ex-girlfriend is safe."

"What do you want me to do?"

"Can you run by his cousin's house? Ask if he's heard from him?"

"And if not?" Ethan asked.

"I'll call his parents. Right now, I don't want to freak them out, so I'll have to come up with some excuse."

"Got it. What are you going to do right now?"

"I need to see Carl. I have to talk to him about something. I'll be home later. Call me when you're done."

[14]

When Riley knocked on Carl's door at nearly 8pm on a Wednesday night, she wondered if he might already be asleep in his chair. So when he opened the door and peered at her with expectancy, she was taken aback.

"Figured you'd show up, so I stayed awake." He stepped aside. "Come in."

"I didn't mean to keep you up. I just needed to see you." She followed him inside.

"I know you did." He groaned as he sat down in his chair. "Tell me what's happened."

The bond they shared was still strong and, in fact, never really wavered. Riley hadn't needed him this much in a long time and he'd sensed it.

"I need to find him—Jacob. He's in danger and I'm afraid if I make contact, it might jeopardize his safety."

"Have you foreseen anything that might point you in the right direction?" Carl asked.

"No. I'm completely blank and that's what scares me."

"He's been away too long," Carl added. "You don't feel the same about him as you used to. The connection you shared is damaged."

"Maybe, but that doesn't change the fact that I have to help him. I asked Ethan to talk to his cousin. If that turns up nothing, then I'll reach out to his parents."

"If he had the ability to contact anyone, why don't you think it would be you? You tried to help him today, didn't you?"

"Yes, but I failed spectacularly. I could've cost him his life and that of his girlfriend's."

"Ex-girlfriend, as I understand it."

"Right," Riley replied. "Last night, when I had the episode—that whole thing with Chloe Dawson, I knew those people were tied to it somehow, but there's more. When I first sensed her, she told me to stop him. I didn't know who 'him' was, let alone how to stop him. Still don't."

"What are you not telling me, Riley? If you want my help, I have to know everything you're feeling. And I can feel that you're holding something back."

"A few days ago, maybe longer, I don't really remember, but I kept seeing this car."

"The one you told me about. You got the cameras like I said, right?"

"Yes, except it hasn't been by the house since that night Jacob was there. He saw it passing by the next morning when he was having breakfast at the diner. Unfortunately, he didn't capture the plates, so I asked the guys at the station to run BMV to see if anyone here owns the make and model."

"So you saw it alone one night. Then again when Jacob was there, but not since?"

"That's right."

"Sounds to me like this car wasn't keeping tabs on you, but on Jacob. You ever think it could be the guys who are after him now?"

"The thought had occurred to me, and the timing..."

"Right. So Jacob brought them here."

"If he did, I truly don't believe he had any idea, which is why I think he hasn't made contact with me yet. He doesn't want to bring trouble. He remembers the last time someone brought trouble to Owensville."

Carl looked away.

"I'm sorry, I didn't mean...Carl, you know how much I cared about CJ. He tried to save my life. None of what happened was his fault."

"It was, we both know that, but that was a long time ago. And I suspect you're right in that Jacob doesn't want anything to happen to you, so he's trying to find a way out of this himself. I admire him for that."

"Admiration won't keep him alive. I need a solution," she said.

"You already have a solution. You just want me to give it my blessing. Riley, you know I'll help you in any way I can."

"I know."

"But now that I'm stuck here, an old useless man, I can't help you and it kills me. Look, I can't see what you see. I have a bad feeling about this, but it's you who needs to see the endgame and work toward it. Do you see it, Riley?"

"I think so."

"Then I will stand behind you one hundred percent. I just can't help you."

"Thank you, Carl. I needed to hear you say the words."

"There will come a time when I'll no longer be able to offer words of wisdom or offer my sardonic wit. And you need to prepare yourself for that time. You are stronger than you know. You always have been. 'Bout time you realized it."

———

RILEY KILLED THE HEADLIGHTS AS SHE PULLED INTO HER driveway. It was almost 9pm and still no word from Jacob. If he was safe, he would've called.

Inside, she flipped the switch to find CJ on the couch. "Hey, what are you doing there? Get down, boy."

He jumped off and ran toward her, offering a warm greeting.

"I know you're hungry. I'll get you some dinner." She walked into the kitchen and dished his food into his bowl, like she had every night. But tonight, Riley felt helpless. Who were these people and why had they killed Chloe Dawson? Now they were after Jacob. She just didn't have any answers. And then a knock came upon her door.

She swiftly approached and peered through the security lens. Her heart sank just a little. She opened the door. "Hey, you didn't have to come by, you could've just called. Come on in."

"Thanks." Ethan removed his coat and draped it over a chair in her living room. "How's Carl?"

"He's fine."

"And was he able to help you?"

"I think so. Can I get you a water or something?"

"I could really use a beer, if you got one. I know you don't really drink."

"I always keep some in the fridge for guests." She made her way to the kitchen and opened a bottle of Heineken for him. "Will this do?"

"You bet, thanks." Ethan gulped down half of it. "The guys didn't have any luck with the car."

"No? Well, I shouldn't be too surprised. I have a feeling it was the same guys who are after Jacob, but it was worth a shot."

"Yeah, I did make it out to see Jacob's cousin. He's going to call his aunt and uncle and leave a message to have Jacob call you."

"You told him not to make them worry, right? That cousin of his isn't the most tactful man I've ever met."

"I told him it was personal, a message from you. So I think he's cool."

"Good. Sit down, please." She made her way to the sofa and got comfortable. "I'm sure he's safe."

"I wish I had your confidence. I might not be keen on the guy, but I don't want any harm to come to him," Ethan said.

"I'm starting to think it's more about not wanting to bring trouble here, and that's why he's not reaching out."

"Is that what Carl said?" Ethan downed another swig.

"He said if it's how I felt, then it was probably the case. You know what he's like. He's always making me figure things out myself."

Ethan smiled. "Yeah. What a jerk." He tossed back another drink before locking eyes with Riley again. "How do you want to handle this? Ward won't get involved unless it comes here. You know what a stickler he is for jurisdictional lines."

"I know. But I also think he realizes there's danger coming and he doesn't want to make matters worse," she replied.

"Geez, how much worse can it get?"

———

JACOB OPENED THE DOOR TO BLAKE'S APARTMENT. THERE wasn't a chance in hell the guy would come back here tonight. In fact, he was pretty sure he'd never see Blake again. And Jacob had been smart enough to take Blake's keys from his coat pocket when he was looking the other way inside George's office. Jacob had seen betrayal written on his colleague's face and precautions had to be taken.

Jacob sat back on the sofa where he'd slept the night before and held his phone in his hand. They hadn't called him yet, but they would. So he needed to let Riley know he was safe—for now. He could almost hear her words in his head now. She would insist he come to Owensville. Maybe that had to happen. Maybe that was the point of all of this.

He pressed her number and waited for the line to answer. "It's me."

"Jacob. Where are you? Are you safe? What happened today?"

"One question at a time, Riley, please. I'm completely fried right now."

"Right. No. I'm sorry. It's just that I've been waiting to hear from you. I was so afraid something had happened."

"That's why I'm calling. I wasn't going to, but Riley, I think maybe what I had hoped wasn't going to happen, just might."

"They're coming here, aren't they?" she said.

"I think so. I think Blake probably told them about you."

"Did Virgil Howard kill Chloe Dawson?" Riley pressed on.

"I don't know. Maybe. Blake didn't. He was shocked when he heard the news."

"Where is that piece of garbage anyway?"

"I have no idea. Rachel is safe. I did what I set out to do. But after you called about Virgil Howard and how he authorized the concrete delivery, I just know that's where they'll go."

"Considering the manager, Roy Bayliss, made contact with Howard, I wouldn't be surprised," Riley began. "They're going to know we're building a case against them. And you believe these men are mafia. That pretty much confirms they'll do what they have to do to protect themselves and their investment."

Jacob sighed before continuing, "Two days ago, I didn't even know the plans had been approved to refurbish the plant. Let alone the fact that they had already started work on it. I should've told you that I'd been working on it way back when, but I guess I didn't see the relevance at the time. I do now. These men want money from me, Riley. I don't have it and I don't know how to get it either."

"Then come home. Come home so we can work through this together. Ethan's here with me. The guys at the station were trying to ID that car. You remember? The one that showed up driving by my house the other night?"

"The same one I saw at the diner," Jacob replied.

"Yeah. Only the search didn't turn up anything. But at least we know who we're looking for. We have names. We can get everyone in on this, Jacob. We don't have to do this alone."

"I couldn't bear it if something happened to you, Riley. The last thing I wanted was for you to get involved. But here we are."

"It's okay. You can't stop them. This was started by someone else. It was started by whoever killed Chloe Dawson. I don't know why they're coming after you for money. Going through this much trouble for sixty grand just doesn't sit right. There's something else at play and I need you to come home, Jacob. How soon can you be here?"

"I have to sleep. I just need a few hours. So I'll try to hit the road by dawn or shortly after."

"Then you call me as soon as you leave, you understand?"

"I understand. Geez, you're starting to sound like my girlfriend again." Jacob attempted to lighten the conversation, but it only created silence. "I'm kidding, Riley. I'll call you when I'm heading out of town."

"And you're sure you're safe where you are now?"

"I am."

"Okay. I'll talk to you tomorrow. Bye." Riley ended the call and looked to Ethan. "He'll be here in the morning. He's safe. He bought himself some time."

"He's always been a lucky bastard. You want me to stay here tonight?"

"No, that's fine. I'll be okay here."

"You don't know that, Riley. You don't know what Bayliss might've said to Virgil Howard."

"What do you want me to do, Ethan? Tell Ward we need Abrams and Decker to patrol the neighborhood?"

"Maybe. Why not? I mean, these men had a car scoping out your house. That scares the crap out of me."

"You're being paranoid," Riley said.

"Okay. So, when we went to the plant, unannounced, met with Bayliss, asked about their concrete contractor, you don't think any of that information could've been relayed to Howard or his bosses? They know who and where you are."

Riley was quiet because Ethan was right.

"So, for that reason alone, I'm staying here whether you want me to or not. I'm perfectly happy on the sofa."

"I can see nothing I say will change your mind."

"You're darn right it won't."

"I'll get you a pillow." Riley walked to the linen closet and grabbed a blanket and pillow. She was reluctant to accept Ethan's offer but knew it was probably the right thing to do. And it would give her a chance to keep him safe too. One of the benefits of her so-called gift was that she could often sense when a close friend or loved one was in trouble—or about to be. Right now, she didn't feel like Ward was in any danger. He was the captain, after all. He lived alone, no kids, and he had an arsenal in his basement. In fact, the more she thought about it, maybe they should both stay with him.

"Here you go." Riley dropped the linens on the sofa. "I can take first shift."

"I'll do it. I'm not tired. You go and get some sleep."

"Thank you, Ethan."

"You don't need to thank me. I know you're more than capable of handling yourself. So this is really more for me than you."

"Sure it is. You want CJ out here with you?" She eyed the dog, who appeared content to stay where he was, which was at her feet. "He's a good watch dog. He'll bark before he runs away."

"I'll take all the help I can get."

"Good. I'll come out in say, four hours, to relieve you."

"Yep."

She walked to her bedroom and closed the door. It was

unlikely she'd actually sleep, but maybe if she could just close her eyes for a few minutes. Maybe it would help her to see things more clearly. Like how she was going to keep Jacob safe when he returned home. How she was going to keep Ward and Ethan from getting hurt.

Riley had always worried about protecting others, whether it was her mom, her dad, or even Carl. She'd tried to protect him too. It had been a heavy burden for a ten-year-old girl. Now she was an adult. A cop. Now protecting people was her job.

———

RILEY STOOD ALONE INSIDE THE PARTIALLY RECONSTRUCTED plant. Darkness surrounded her. She wore only a t-shirt and underwear, the very same thing she'd worn just before crawling into bed only minutes ago; at least, it felt like it had been only minutes.

In her bare feet, she traversed the plant. Its concrete floor felt newly poured, her toes leaving slight indentations. Riley knew this was a dream, but whose dream was it?

She continued toward the rear of the vast manufacturing facility, right back to the place where they found Chloe. Only she wasn't there this time. There was no washout pool. There was no body. "Hello?" her voice echoed. "Anyone here?" Riley waited for a reply, but none came. "Someone has to be here." She knew this because it didn't feel like her own dream. She could usually tell the difference. This felt like another world, even though the place was the same. She continued in search of the person to whom this dream belonged. "Jacob?"

"Riley?" Daniel Ward emerged from the back office. "Riley, is that you?" He wore a white t-shirt and boxers. Why are you here?"

She was frightened. Never before, in all the years they'd known each other, had she ever crossed over into one of his dreams. "Dan? What's going on? Why are you here?"

"I asked you first."

"I don't know why I'm here. Something brought me to you. What have you seen? Did you see Chloe?"

"No. I was out back and then I appeared in the office. I was looking at the files. I don't really know why I'm here either."

"I think we should leave. I need you to wake up," Riley said.

"Why? Maybe we're supposed to find something."

"No. That's not what's happening. Dan, something's wrong. We shouldn't be here."

He offered her a confused smile. And then his eyes widened when a shot rang out.

"No!" Riley watched as blood seeped from his lips. "Dan! No!" She reached out for him. "We have to go, now!" His blood continued to spill from his mouth like some horrific creature. "No!"

Riley shot up in bed, a pool of sweat surrounding her. She jumped up and ran into the living room.

"Riley, what is it? I heard you scream. Are you okay?" Ethan appeared as panicked as she had as he braced himself on the sofa.

"It's the captain. Something's going to happen to him. I saw it, Ethan. I saw it!"

The alarm clock on Jacob's phone sounded off, brutally yanking him from his sleep. He sat up on the sofa, still yawning, having only had a couple hours' rest.

He walked into the small kitchen for a glass of water. There was no more time to waste; he had to return to Owensville to stop the men who'd almost killed him yesterday and to keep Riley out of the line of fire. Jacob returned to the sofa and pulled on his t-shirt and jeans before walking to the bathroom to splash water on his face. It had been two days since he'd had a shower or worn fresh clothes, but his small suitcase he'd taken to Owensville remained in his car. That suitcase and the few items inside were all he had left in his possession. The apartment he shared with Rachel was hers and so was pretty much everything inside it. For a man in his mid-twenties, he had virtually nothing to his name. This wasn't how things were supposed to turn out.

With his cell phone in hand, Jacob headed out the door and

made his way to his car. The morning sun was still hidden behind gray clouds and it didn't appear to have much chance of breaking through them today. Fitting.

Inside the car, he texted Riley. "I'm on my way."

———

CAPTAIN WARD EYED RILEY AS SHE SAT ACROSS FROM HIM. "I can't just sit back and let you take on these men. I won't do that. I know what happened. It was my dream, remember?"

"Dan, if what I saw had actually happened to you, I don't know what I'd do," Riley said. "You have to let me do this and you need to sit this one out. I won't risk your life."

"You and I both know that sometimes when you see things, it can take on different meanings than the literal ones. And this is likely one of those times, especially considering all that's happened in the past 24 hours."

Riley glanced at her phone. "He's coming. Jacob's on his way." She returned her attention to Ward and Ethan, who sat next to her. "We need to protect him."

"Okay, let's take a step back here," Ward continued. "We assume Virgil Howard is connected to Chloe's death. He signed for the concrete delivery and he was one of the men who threatened Jacob."

"And helped kidnap his ex-girlfriend," Riley added.

"That's who we need to find," Ethan said. "We don't know anything about these other men who were a part of the exchange yesterday with Jacob, but we know about Howard. Captain, I think it's time we get the state police involved in this. We'll have

State issue a BOLO on Virgil Howard and maybe we can stop him before he gets here."

Ward appeared to consider Ethan's proposal and continued. "Here's what we're going to do. This mysterious car that has shown up at your house, Riley, is the same one Jacob took a picture of at the diner, is that right?"

"Yes, but he couldn't get a shot of the plates."

"Okay. I'm going to assume it belongs to one of the men who's involved in the plant operation. Now, you asked Abrams and Decker to pull a report? Any luck with that?"

"No. No one in Owensville is a registered owner of that make and model."

"Let's be on the lookout for that vehicle, first of all. Secondly, Pruitt, I like your idea and I think it's the right call. Someone has to have something on Virgil Howard. A man like that has to have dirt on his hands. But what we really need to know is who's running the show? Bayliss?"

"I don't think so. He doesn't seem that high up on the food chain," Riley added. "But I can try to get closer to him today. I might be able to pick up something from him."

"That would mean you'd have to go to the plant. I'm not sure I like that idea," Ward added. "Not right now. I'd rather wait until Jacob arrives and we can get him under our protection."

"We don't have that kind of time, Captain. I think I should go there this morning," she said.

"Well, you're not going alone," Ethan replied. "We can go together."

"Neither of you are going down there right now. I can't chance it. What I need to do is get in front of this situation. I need to get with IMPD about Howard. I'm sure they'll find a connection to the man in charge."

"You met with the owners the other day. They wanted to keep a lid on the situation. Who were they?" Riley asked.

"I did meet with two men. They were the lawyers representing the company, but I'll follow up on that. I have a feeling, though, that these people, meaning mafia-types, know how to create shell companies and shuffle things around so as not to be linked back to any identifyable names. But these are questions Jacob might have some answers to. He helped draft the plans. He might have more insight into this than we know."

"What's been bothering me the most is the fact that they're after him for what seems a paltry amount of money, in the grand scheme of things. Someone was murdered in their plant and they're concerned with sixty-K?" Riley asked.

"It's possible they believe Jacob knows something about the organization. Something that could expose them. That's something you'll have to ask him when he returns, which, by my math, should be in about an hour. Until then, let's get to work with history on Virgil Howard, and I'll reach out to State Police and let them know about our situation. The coordination with them and IMPD will be critical. Let's hop to it. We've got a lot of ground to cover."

———

BLAKE RHODES HELD THE LIGHTER TO THE END OF THE JOINT hanging from his lips and inhaled. With this thumb and forefinger, he pulled it from his mouth and held on to his breath.

"Hey, asshole, you mind putting that out or go the fuck

outside?" Virgil Howard appeared from the kitchen of the apartment where they were holed up. "Jesus." He continued toward the sofa and sat down. "You screwed this up. Costa's gone because of you."

"I didn't know that chick-cop from Owensville would be onto the situation. Bayliss never should've let her look at the contracts," Blake replied.

"If he had stopped her, that would've put a spotlight on him and the big man. He didn't have a choice. But, I'm telling you, man, I didn't kill your girl. It had to be some kind of accident or some shit. Boss would've had my ass for doing something so stupid and inside our own operation."

Blake extinguished the joint. "I'll find out what happened." He eyed Howard, trying to read him and understand if he was telling the truth. Right now, he was pissed because Chloe never did nothing to nobody. She was just some kid he liked to hang out with sometimes. Hell, he didn't even know why she was in Owensville. Maybe that was a question for her friend, Rehnquist. He knew the kid was crushing on her and played it up, giving him shit whenever he saw him, which wasn't often. But Virgil Howard was a soulless son of a bitch with empty eyes, impossible to read. He would get to the truth about Chloe one way or another.

"What's the plan, Virgil?" Paul Kearns, the man who'd stood next to him yesterday and only narrowly avoided a bullet, approached from the bathroom. "We can't sit here all damn day. Boss wants to know why we haven't found Hammond and how we plan on getting our hands on the kid."

"We know where he's going. At least, Blakey boy over here feels pretty confident he knows. So we'll go to the plant, talk to Bayliss, and get a feel for how far up his ass the cops down there are. Back road hicks like that can't be too smart, right?" He laughed.

"I don't know, man. I think if Biggs knew about Hammond, he would've fessed up by now. The money he gave us yesterday, I bet he's tapped out. He's going to know it ain't about the money soon enough. Why are we going after him so hard?" Kearns asked.

"Cause according to Blake, Jacob knows where Georgie boy is, isn't that right?"

"Like I said, he knows. Them two were tight."

"And if you're wrong? What do you think the boss is going to do to you?" Virgil continued.

"I'm not wrong."

"You must have some kind of beef with Jacob Biggs." Virgil stood and reached for his coat. "Let's go. I want to stop by Starbucks on the way."

WARD EMERGED FROM HIS OFFICE AND HURRIED TOWARD Riley. "I got something back from IMPD on Virgil Howard. Pruitt." He waved him over. "Here's the deal. Howard is the chief treasury officer for Capital Concrete."

"Wait, I thought he worked for the plant owners?" Riley asked.

Ward raised his index finger. "Get this, he's a company officer for the concrete contractor and for the plant. And, he's a former employee of Sandoval Manufacturing."

"Who are they?" Ethan asked.

"Sandoval Manufacturing is a subsidiary of Golden Grains dog food. The same company who bought and is refurbishing the plant.

And that's not the only thing. There's a list of people with similar histories. All worked for other companies and almost all of them are the same trades working on the plant right now. Most of those same people are now employed, in one form or another, by Golden Grains."

"It's all a big circle. They're awarding contracts, getting kick-backs, setting up other companies," Riley said. "Jacob thought these guys were mafia."

"IMPD thinks so too," Ward replied. "They've been after them for years. Drug trafficking, racketeering, money laundering. The list goes on."

"Why are they still operating?" Ethan asked.

"According to Captain Pryce, every time his people get close, they shut down operations and open up under new names, new owners. He sent the case files to the feds but says they're too slow to act."

"So now it's up to us." Riley looked to Ward. "They're coming here. Are we going to get any help?"

"Pryce is trying to round up everyone he can who's involved with those organizations, but it hasn't been easy. He's going to try to extract information in exchange for immunity."

"What about the Feds?" Ethan asked.

"He says don't bother. They aren't interested in small potatoes apparently. He said he'd help us as much as he could, and offered to assist State police too."

"We're going to need backup, Captain," Riley added. "Are they going to help with that?"

"Once he rounds up whoever he can, he's sending a team to help. It'll take the day, most likely, but he knows we're in deep here."

Riley eyed him. "Good. Because I have a feeling a storm's coming and we're running out of time."

———

JACOB PULLED OFF THE HIGHWAY AND HEADED TOWARD THE station house where Riley would be waiting. The idea that he was the one bringing this trouble and that some girl was dead as a result almost made him keep on going straight out of Indiana altogether. But they would still come and Riley would be in their crosshairs or whoever else happened into their sights. It amazed him still how he was in this mess when only days ago he'd returned home in hopes of finding a place again in Riley's heart. That now seemed an unlikely feat. How could she forgive him for leaving her? He just wasn't cut out for small town life, or so he thought. He'd wanted more, but now that he'd seen what his ambitions produced, he'd begun to reconsider that small town life might not be so bad after all. If they could survive this, maybe she would again find a place for him.

He eyed the rear-view mirror, as he had several times en route to Owensville. So far, it didn't appear anyone followed, not that it mattered because they were coming regardless. But what he still hadn't pieced together was Blake's involvement with them. In light of the revelation his girlfriend had been murdered at the plant, why would he possibly want to remain a part of what they were doing? Was he getting a cut of the money? Did they have something on him? "If I could get my hands on you, George," he said to himself. George had been the real problem and he was going to get off free as a bird. No one had kidnapped his wife. No one had killed a member of his family. Why was there no retribution against him? Only Jacob, it seemed. Unless you counted Blake's girlfriend. Who was letting George off the hook? And could Jacob find him when the others couldn't? After all, he had Riley in his corner and she could do incredible things.

The station was just ahead and he'd made it within his stipulated time. Hopefully, that wasn't going to be the only thing to go right today. Jacob parked his car and walked toward the entrance. He spotted Riley inside and opened the door.

"Jacob, you made it." Her face masked in relief.

"I made it. Are you okay?" Jacob embraced her but felt her flinch. "Sorry. I..."

"No, I'm sorry. I'm on edge. We all are. Ward's been working with IMPD and it looks like this involves a web of intertwined companies all owned and operated by the same people."

"The mob," he replied.

"Most likely. How did you get caught up in this?"

"Guess I worked for the wrong guy." Jacob continued inside and shed his coat. "Ethan. Good to see you again. I'm sorry it has to be for something like this."

Ethan stood and offered a greeting. "It's okay, man. This isn't on you. Glad to see you're okay."

Jacob felt some relief hearing that from Pruitt. The guy had a thing for Riley and didn't care much for what he'd done to her, but he was all right in Jacob's book. "Where's Captain Ward?"

"Right here." With an outstretched hand, he approached Jacob. "Glad to see you, son. It's been a hell of a time waiting for you. But as I was telling my people here, help's coming. We're dealing with a well-oiled machine that has managed to slip under the FBI's radar, but not us locals. We'll get the sons of bitches who killed Chloe Dawson and took your girlfriend." He turned to

Riley. "Riley, I'll let you fill him in on what's been happening. I need to get back on the horn with Pryce and see how he's coming along. We don't have much time, and I expect those men will be here soon enough. Give me twenty minutes. Then, we're going to the plant to bring Bayliss in."

"Are we arresting him?" she asked.

"Yes, we are."

"Under what charge?"

"Don't know. We'll figure that out later. I just need to shut down operations over there. Get everyone out because that's where those boys will be headed, I imagine." Ward started back toward his office.

"You want a coffee or something, Jacob?" Ethan asked. "I'm grabbing one for myself."

"Yeah, sure, coffee would be great. Thanks."

"Come sit down." Riley made her way to her desk and took a seat. "I know these guys have something to do with Chloe's death, but I'm still getting a feeling there's more to it than that. I just can't pinpoint it yet. And last night..." She eyed Ward's office. "I found myself in Dan's dream. I don't want him to go to the plant, but so far, I haven't been able to change his mind."

"His dream? That must have been a surprise. You think he's going to get hurt?"

"I saw it, Jacob, and I won't let it happen. He's like a..."

"I know. Look, there's something I wanted to ask, Riley. I think if we found the man who took these guys' money, I think we could end this without anyone getting hurt."

"Even if that was possible, Ward's working with IMPD. They're licking their lips waiting to get their hands on them. Guess they've been after them for a long time. So whatever money they're looking for, at this point, I don't think it's going to matter. And frankly, I'm not so sure this is about the money. Jacob, do you know more about George Hammond than you've mentioned?"

"What is that supposed to mean?"

Riley felt his defenses rise."I'm not pointing fingers. I'm just asking if there's more to this than meets the eye. Was Hammond in on something else that might expose these men who are after you now?"

"I have no clue. I'm telling you the truth. Look, it was Blake who pointed them in my direction, claiming I had the money George stole from them. That's all I know. I swear. I came here ready to ask if you could help find him—George Hammond. He's the one who we need answers from."

Ethan returned with a coffee. "Here you go, man. Sorry, I didn't know how you took it."

"Doesn't matter. Just need the caffeine. Thanks, I appreciate it."

"So what are we planning on doing right now?" Ethan grabbed Abrams' chair and rolled it over to Riley's desk. "I know you're planning something, Riley. I can see it in your eyes."

"Jacob wants me to find George Hammond, the guy who really took the money. And who I think has more to do with this than we know."

"What's that going to matter? Isn't Priority One finding Chloe's killer?" Ethan replied.

"Of course it is, but if Jacob thinks tracking down Hammond could help, what harm can it do?"

"What harm?" He looked at Jacob. "We're already in this up to our knees. We've got mobsters running the plant that we thought was going to be this town's salvation. Turns out, they're just crooks, and once this goes down, so will the plant. So what harm it could do is to risk more lives. No. We have enough to deal with, Riley. If George Hammond stole the mob's money, he'll pay the price. Chloe Dawson deserves justice."

"Jacob?" she asked him.

"I can see I'm outnumbered and maybe you're right. But what I don't think anyone's considered here is that these guys went to great lengths to find me, but not the man who took their money? That doesn't make sense. Unless..."

"Unless he's a part of their organization too," Riley said.

"He could be the one holding the cards. He could be the boss of this entire shit show. So I'm trying to figure out why I'm the only one who cares about him."

Riley stood up, placing her hands on her hips. "I'll be right back." She left the two alone and headed into Ward's office. "Captain? Can I talk to you?"

"What's up?" He drew back in his chair.

"What can we get on George Hammond? He's the owner of the architecture firm Jacob was working for. Jacob has a theory that maybe Hammond is part of this organization behind the plant operation."

"I can ask Pryce and see if he's popped up on their radar. He made no mention of the name when we spoke earlier."

"I think if we can understand his motives, or who's paying his bills, we'll understand why he and Blake Rhodes are pointing the finger at Jacob for the sixty grand."

"I'll see what I can get. And in the meantime, I think it would be a good idea for you to find a place for Jacob. Someplace these guys won't find him."

[16]

The floral wallpaper and green carpet of the home where Carl lived held a familiar scent to Jacob. "This place reminds me of my grandparents' house. I know what he means to you, Riley, but what if you're putting him in danger?"

"I'm not. Those guys don't know about Carl; they know about me. And if the car that's been driving past my house and past the diner belongs to them, then they know where I live too. It's best if we hole up here."

"Please don't make me sit on my hands while you track down these men. Riley, I brought this on and I should be the one to finish it."

"Unless you're the one who killed Chloe Dawson, you didn't bring on this problem. There's a connection to her I can't yet see, but it's there. So we're going to talk to Carl, let him in on what's happening, and ask that he let us stay here tonight. We don't know when those men are coming, but we need to be prepared."

"Then let me at least help you to prepare."

She knocked on Carl's door. "One step at a time."

"Come in, Riley," Carl sounded through the door.

Riley opened the door and the two walked inside to find Carl on his recliner. "How you feeling, Carl?"

"First of all, let me say that these walls are pretty damn thin. I heard every last word you two said outside my door. So how I'm feeling is a little uneasy at the moment."

"Right, sorry." She eyed Jacob. "You remember Jacob, don't you?"

"Course I do."

Jacob offered his hand. "Nice to see you again, sir. It's been a long time."

"That it has, son. That it has." Carl returned the greeting. "Sit down, both of you. So I hear you need a place to hang your hat —temporarily."

"Riley insists that I keep out of sight for the time being," Jacob replied.

"She's usually right about these things and I figured you of all people would recall that."

"I do, sir, but I also don't think she should be taking this on alone."

"I'm not alone," Riley began. "I have my department and the help of the Indianapolis police." She turned to Carl. "Just until this is over. I could send him to see his parents, but I think that would create more problems."

"I agree. He should stay here. No one will think to look for you here, son. And we've got pretty tight security in place. Mostly to keep the old folks in, but it helps to keep some people out too."

"Fine, but I can still help. They aren't here yet," Jacob replied.

"That you know of." Carl turned to Riley. "What's your senses telling you? How much time do you all have?"

"I can't see anything right now, which worries me even more. So the plan is to get something on Jacob's boss, George Hammond, and find out he's involved with this group of men. The captain's working on that now. I'm hoping that will shed some light on a plan of action."

"What can I do to help?" Carl continued.

"Just knowing you'll keep Jacob hidden here is enough. I can't say which direction this is headed."

"Riley, please, let me work with you on this. I'll come back here tonight and hide out. But I can be of some use. I know these people. I spent hours holding two of them hostage yesterday, and Rhodes, well, I know him like the back of my hand. So let me help."

"Boy's right," Carl added. "He'll be nothing more than a limp noddle sitting here with me. I'll keep cover for him tonight, but you and Ward are going to need all the help you can get. And I think you can sense at least that much. I know I can. Despite his past behavior, I'm inclined to suggest you take the boy up on his offer."

It was two against one and it seemed Riley was on the losing side of this battle. And while Carl couldn't help getting in a dig about their previous relationship, he was urging her to do what was necessary. "Fine. How do you propose to help, Jacob?"

"Let me call Blake. I can convince him he's in danger too. That they'll turn on him and come after him and probably frame him for Chloe's death. If there's one thing I know about Blake, it's that he's easily swayed by money, power, and women. I can convince him all three are at stake if he chooses to side with Virgil

Howard and his boss, who may or may not be George Hammond."

"And you'll find out what their plans are?" Riley asked.

"Yes. You work on finding George, I'll get to the bottom of the rest of them and get a feel for if they're coming here."

"If?" Carl interrupted. "If isn't the problem. It's when."

———

In the car, as Riley started back toward the station, Jacob regarded her. "He's been like a father to you all these years, hasn't he?"

"Yeah, he has. If it hadn't been for him, I would've probably ended up like my grandfather. He couldn't handle the gift. It ate him alive."

"But that's not you, never has been. You feel too much responsibility to let anyone down and that's exactly what you feel it would be—letting people down. It's the one thing I saw as your biggest flaw, Riley."

"Flaw? Being responsible is a flaw?"

"No, of course not. Taking responsibility for things you have no control over, people you owe nothing to; that's your flaw."

"Is that why you left me?"

Jacob shook his head. "No. I left because I had to. I didn't feel the same way about this town that you did—that you still do."

"Then why come back?"

"And bring with me all this trouble?" Jacob asked.

"That's not what I said."

"You didn't have to say it. Riley, I didn't know. Well, maybe on some level, I knew I was working for a man of questionable scruples, and a partner who had virtually no conscience. But I swear, if I'd known this was going to happen, I never would have come back. I honestly can't tell you what drove me to it. Maybe it was my breakup or losing my job. Maybe I wanted your sympathy and I was just looking for a shoulder to cry on."

"You're not helping your cause here," she replied.

"I'm not trying to. I'm trying to be honest with you," Jacob replied.

"And what happens when this is over? When we stop these people and we're left with just each other? Will you leave again? No longer needing my shoulder?"

"If I survive this without ending up dead or in jail, well, I don't know what I'll do. I guess that depends on you." When she didn't respond, he continued. "You're coming back to Carl's tonight? With me?"

She eyed him briefly before peering through the windshield again. "That's the plan. I can't stay with Dillon, so I don't have much choice."

The patrol car radio sounded. "Riley, come in." It was the captain.

"I'm here. What is it, Captain?"

"Where the hell are you?"

She eyed Jacob for a moment as an uneasy feeling enveloped her. "Heading back to camp. What's going on?"

"I have information on George Hammond. Come see me as soon as you arrive. Ward out."

"He's got something and I hope it's good." Riley pressed on the gas pedal and picked up some speed. "We could use something going in our favor today."

"Maybe he found him. Man, I hope so." Jacob grabbed hold of

the safety handle above the door frame as she continued to pick up speed.

With a turn to the left, the station house was in sight. "Looks like he called in the night shift," Riley said. She arrived and pulled into the parking lot, nearly slamming on her brakes to stop at the front of the building. "Come on." Riley jumped out and didn't wait for Jacob, but he soon caught up and joined her as they entered.

Ward was in the bullpen with Ethan, Abrams, and Decker. "Riley, come here." He eyed Jacob. "Why are you still here?"

"I think I can help, sir."

Ward cast a chary eye to Riley. "This your idea?"

"Not exactly, but I don't disagree."

"Fine. Here's the deal. Captain Pryce found something interesting on George Hammond." He looked to Jacob. "Your instincts served you well on this one, son. Hammond used to work for an architectural firm called G3 in Indianapolis."

"I remember him mentioning that," Jacob said.

"So one of his first clients was a company called Sandoval Industries."

"Oh my God." Riley folded her arms and waited for the shoe to drop.

"Yep. And apparently, he was written up on more than one occasion for accepting what could only be described as personal gifts. The people he worked with at Sandoval took him out, wined and dined him."

"But why? If he was just an architect, why invest in growing a relationship with him?" Ethan asked.

"I suspect it was because Hammond's brother sat on the city

planning commission. They approved all construction projects submitted to the city."

"Well, that would make sense. Schmooze him to get to this brother," Riley added. "And how did he happen to give up that cushy gig?"

"I can answer that," Jacob said. "George mentioned his brother used to serve on the commission when we were working on a bid for a government building. I asked him why he wasn't still there. He said he got caught taking bribes, lost his job, and went to jail."

"So George Hammond outlived his usefulness to Sandoval Industries," Ward began. "He decided it would be best to convince them he could offer help in other ways."

"And that was when he started our firm," Jacob added.

"Oh, and there's something else." Ward turned to Decker. "Can you pull up that note?" He waited a moment and continued. "Pryce presented his case to the DA's office and the DA placed a temporary freeze on Great Grains' bank accounts last year when he was knee-deep in this deal, only they weren't called Great Grains at the time. And what he found then, but it only makes sense now, was a promissory note to Hammond and issued by the owner of what is now Great Grains and Sandoval industries."

"They lent him the money to start the architecture firm," Jacob said.

Ward placed his index finger on his nose. "Bingo."

"So he's not the head honcho, but he's been wrapped up with them for years," Jacob said. "He had to have taken the money and fled. And it was after the girl, Chloe Dawson, was killed."

"There's a connection." Riley looked at Ward. "He has to be involved in her death or else why steal money from your own people? The operation was going smoothly. None of us ever questioned what was happening at the plant except that it was going to bring jobs again."

"You think George killed her?" Ward asked.

"All signs seem to point in that direction." Riley eyed Jacob. "You were let go. He was closing down the office. He had to have planned it, but who was Chloe to him?" She recalled her vision at the girl's previous home. *"You have to stop him."* That was what she said, but why? Stop Hammond? What had he done to her?

"Riley? Are you okay?" Ethan asked as he steadied her.

"What?"

"You went quiet and started zoning out. Are you okay?"

"Yeah. Sorry. Captain, how are we going to find the connection to Chloe? I know those men are coming. I just don't know exactly when, but they're coming for Jacob. And they're coming to cover up any connection to the death of Chloe Dawson."

"George must've somehow convinced them Jacob was the real culprit. The one who stole the money and killed Chloe at their plant." Ward looked at Jacob. "What did you do to piss this guy off?"

"Nothing, I swear. I came in every day and did my job. It's Blake. The two had to be working together on how to set me up. Blake probably got a split of the cash too. That way, he keeps Virgil Howard and his boss off his back and I take the fall."

Riley peered at the team. "I have to find the correlation between Chloe and George. What am I not seeing?"

Chris Decker chimed in as he and Abrams sat in virtual silence, since this was the first they were hearing about any of this. "Did he know her?" He asked Jacob. "You say she was Blake Rhodes' girlfriend. Did Blake Rhodes hang out with George Hammond socially? And if so, might he have met Chloe then?"

"It's possible. We were a small office. We did hang out as a group on occasion. If George met Chloe, I wasn't there," Jacob replied.

"Captain, is Pryce monitoring Hammond's financial activity?" Riley asked.

"He is."

"Good. If Hammond thinks he's in the clear, he's probably been using his bank account or credit cards or whatever else because why wouldn't he? And that's how we're going to find him."

"That doesn't solve our present and chief problem," Abrams continued. "We've got a bunch of mobsters headed into town and I don't know if you all realized this, but there are only four of us." He peered at Jacob. "You're a civilian."

"I'll get on the horn with Pryce and let him know what we've discussed. He's going to have to move up his timeline." Ward returned to his office.

"Something still doesn't sit right with me." Riley turned to Ethan. "I think we should talk to Justin Rehnquist again."

"Why?" Ethan asked.

"I need to know more about their relationship. And he knows Blake Rhodes too. Let's ask him about that."

"If you say so."

She turned her sights to Jacob. "I need for you to stay put. You'll be safe here. I don't know how much time we have until this storm hits, but I need to know more while Ward is working the other angle."

Jacob's face masked in disappointment.

"You know I'm right."

"Fine. I'll stay here. Not that I have much choice. Just keep me posted, please?"

"I will." She turned to Ethan. "You ready? We should get on the road."

———

RILEY TURNED SHARPLY TO THE RIGHT.

"Wait, the Auto Zone is left," Ethan said.

"I know. I need to stop by the school and talk to Dillon. You don't mind, do you?"

"Does it involve our current situation?"

"I think so."

"Then do whatever you have to do," Ethan replied.

She continued into the parking lot and noted the kids leaving. "What time is it?"

"Two thirty. Looks like school's letting out," Ethan said.

"Damn. Okay." She unbuckled her seat belt. "If we hurry, we can catch him probably still in his classroom."

"You want to rush through the school in uniform? You think that's a good idea?"

"Right. Okay, we'd better check in up front and we'll casually stroll through." She reached for her phone. "I'll just text him to stay put and that we're heading his way."

"That might be more prudent." Ethan stepped out of the car.

With her phone in her hand, she viewed the returned message. "He's waiting for us in his classroom." Riley started toward the front office and both entered.

"Wow, third time this week?" the woman behind the desk said.

"I know. I don't mean to cause a disruption. Just working on something with Mr. Thompson for his class. You know, career day type of stuff. That's why I brought Officer Pruitt with me."

"Oh sure. You both go right on back. I'm sure he's still in his classroom."

"Thank you." Riley took the lead and started through the school again. And among the stares and slacked-jaws, finally turned to Pruitt. "I never got this much attention when I attended."

"Neither did I." He smiled.

She peeked through the door of Dillon's classroom. "He's there; come on." And upon opening it, she was greeted by her haggard brother. "Hey. Wow, rough day?"

"Standardized testing today. I really wish there was a better way. My kids are always so panicked about it."

"I'm sorry to hear that. I know it puts them under a lot of stress. Not to be rude and change the subject, but I need another favor."

"Okay." Dillon turned to her partner. "Hey, Ethan."

"Hey, Dillon. Good to see you." He offered his hand.

"What's going on now? Must have to do with the girl," Dillon said.

"It does."

"Like I said before, I don't have access to a lot, and what I gave you..."

"I know, Dillon. What you've done so far has been really helpful, but I was hoping you could do something else for me." She revealed a sheepish grin.

"And that would be?"

"Justin Rehnquist, Chloe's friend, and who I believe might have been the last person to see her alive. Can you look into him for me? They graduated the same year. I just need to see his records. I want to know if he was ever written up or suspended for any sort of violence. Any disruptions, really."

Dillon regarded her with caution. "Don't tell me you suspect he's the killer?"

"Can't rule it out. I've got a few ideas and I need to sort through them before I take anything to Ward. We've got a storm coming, Dillon. And I think it could be worse than before."

"If it's that important, I'll look into him." He eyed the both of them. "Are you two in danger?"

"I think a lot of people might be in danger," she replied. "But I don't know when or how to stop it."

[17]

The delivery of the feed belts for the manufacturing plant had arrived and Kilroy "Roy" Bayliss ensured their installation. There had been plenty of setbacks in the past week and it was his job to get everything back on track. Now there were even bigger problems coming out of Indianapolis, problems that would take the project offline were certain conclusions drawn.

Bayliss knew what needed to be done now in order to keep those conclusions from forming in the first place. He turned on his heel and marched back to his office. He yanked open the filing cabinet drawer and began pulling the files and dropped them onto his desk. From the corner of his eye, he noticed several workers eyeing his actions. But with one swift glance back, they'd hastily returned to their tasks, forgetting what they'd seen.

With several files in his hands, Bayliss approached the large shredder that sat in the corner of his office. By the end of this afternoon, there would be nothing left that would connect Great Grains manufacturing with any of its so-called "subcontractors," which had really been nothing more than shell companies that funneled back into the parent organization. Neither would there be left any trace of the use of the trucking companies that hauled the goods across the border, which would expose them to the real money-making operation. He was no stranger to the drill and had been through this plenty of times before. Bayliss was to take care of not only the paper trail, but the electronic trail as well.

———

THE SCHOOL GROUNDS WERE CLEAR. THE KIDS AND STAFF HAD all gone home, with the exception of Dillon Thompson, the brother of a cop who had been embroiled in a murder investigation. He would have to be stealthy because if anyone caught wind of what he was doing, getting fired would be the least of his problems. What he was doing was illegal. No warrant. No probable cause. He was a civilian, which made this a theft, but he wouldn't refuse Riley. Not ever. And if he could dig up something that might help solve the murder of a former student, then he should. Rule of law be damned.

Once again, he found himself inside the Records Department. The door was unlocked, the lights were on. The cleaning staff usually locked up after they were finished, but they usually didn't clean the administration office until the very last. So Dillon had at least forty-five minutes before they would appear. He didn't know why Riley had the sudden interest in this kid, but it wasn't wise to discount her intuition.

He searched through the files, most of which contained

current students, but there was a whole section of files in which the administration maintained older student records, only sending them to archives after three years. And Rehnquist graduated two years ago, along with Chloe Dawson.

"Mr. Thompson?"

Dillon spun around. "Oh. Hi."

"What are you doing in here?"

"I was—um—looking for an old student file. I thought it might still be here, but I can't seem to find it."

"Well, who are you looking for? Did you fill out the proper request forms?" The woman who'd appeared from nowhere now stood with her hands on her hips, gazing at him with suspicion.

"You know what? I didn't send in the form, but I was just about to. You see, I was grading some essays and I came across one that sounded awfully familiar and so I came back here to search the name of the student who I believe might have written the original essay."

"Oh my. That is a problem. But you mustn't forget that those records can only be accessed after the forms are approved."

"Yes. You're right. Who knows how long that might take, though, right?" He tried to appear casual, resting his arm atop the cabinet.

She walked inside. "I can show you where the forms are and we can get your request in tonight."

"You're too kind, Monica. I appreciate it, but I'll come by in the morning and fill it out. No point in keeping either of us here any longer than necessary."

"Okay. If you're sure. I don't mind. I only came back because I forgot my sweater and it's getting chilly out."

"Sure. Sure, but thanks. I'll plan on stopping in tomorrow."
Dillon started toward the door. "Thanks for letting me know."

"Anytime."

He tried to keep measured steps, but his pace quickened as he returned to his classroom. Once inside, he collapsed onto his chair. "For crying out loud." Not only did he not get anything on the Rehnquist kid, but he was also nearly caught red-handed. Although, he had to admit, his reasoning was sound. Perhaps that was what would have saved him too if he had been caught with the file. Still, he had nothing to give to Riley because making another attempt was out of the question. He didn't have the strong stomach she did. Maybe there was another way he could help.

Dillon stood up and recaptured his composure. What Riley was looking for was a history on the kid. Had he been punished for any display of violence against another student or teacher? Had he been suspended, expelled, or anything of that nature? And if he had, why? Dillion assumed this pertained to Chloe Dawson and that Riley must have suspected Rehnquist could be involved in her death. So where else could Dillon look for this information?

Maybe the time had come for him to step up for Riley as she had for him on many occasions. It was she who kept him on the straight and narrow after their parents split. He'd already been prone to hanging out with the wrong crowd, smoking pot on the steps of abandoned homes, coming home after curfew because he and his friends were drinking beers behind the Casey's. In fact, the more he considered it, the more he realized if it hadn't been for Riley, he wouldn't have become a teacher. No one ever believed he would, except for her.

So he would go back to that building, talk to Monica—hell, flirt with her if he had to—but get that file because if this kid did have something to do with Chloe's death, he didn't want to be the one who let him slip through the cracks.

Dillon started back toward the office, more determined than before. If Monica was gone, the door could already be locked, assuming janitorial staff hadn't yet been there. And she was only there to pick up her sweater. But he needed to focus on the fact that he could still obtain access because Riley was short on time. She said a storm was coming and that meant bad things were coming.

The building was just ahead and Dillon spotted the light on inside. It was either Monica or the cleaners. Either way, it wasn't too late to get in. He reached the door and turned the handle. "Hey, Monica, I was hoping you'd still be here." Dillon closed the door behind him.

"You're back," she said. "I thought I'd just check on a few things before leaving. You know how it goes. Tough to leave the job behind sometimes. So did you want me to go ahead and help you with that form?"

"Actually, I was hoping you could help me expedite things a little."

"Okay. I'm not sure how I can do that, but I'll try." Monica appeared pleased by his request.

"Look, I'm working on something with my sister."

"Officer Thompson?"

"That's right. She asked me to check on the file of a kid who used to attend here. Justin Rehnquist. Now she didn't want anyone to know and that was the reason I said what I said. It's imperative to the investigation that this remain hush-hush."

"Oh, I don't know, Mr. Thompson."

"You can call me Dillon. We are colleagues."

"Of course, Dillon. Student records are privileged information. I can't just hand something over to you without a form. You know that. And if it's your sister, well, that adds another dimension to the situation, doesn't it? But she can make the request."

Dillon walked closer to her. "Monica, this is really important. You know Riley wouldn't ask if it wasn't. She's working on a case. It's on the q-t for right now. But if you could do me this favor, I know it would mean a lot not only to me, but to Riley too. I just want to see if the kid was ever written up for anything. That's it. I don't care about his transcripts, absences, standardized tests grades. Just disciplinary action."

"Well, I guess if that's all it is. That should be okay."

"I sure would appreciate it and I know my sister would too."

Monica stood from her desk. "You say Rehnquist?"

"That's right. He graduated two years ago."

She opened the files and began to search for the name. "Hang on. Okay, here he is." With the file in her hand, she laid it on the desk. "The discipline records are kept on the right-hand side." She began to flip through the manila folder until the section appeared. "Here we go."

Dillon moved closer, standing squarely inside her personal space. He was a handsome man, which many of the female teachers had decreed. He was, of course, happily married, but in this instance, it was okay to use what he had to get what he needed. "This is perfect. Can I take a look?" He held her gaze.

"Of course."

Dillon scanned the reports, noting minor infractions, just like any other high-schooler. Nothing major. "Wait a minute. This one says he was given a week's detention for striking a boy in the lunchroom." He continued reading with Monica peering at the same file.

"Yes. According to the report, he did it in defense of a girl."

"Chloe Dawson." He eyed her. "Thank you. I don't see anything else in here that might help Riley, but this might." He placed his hand on her shoulder. "Monica, I can't thank you enough for helping me, for helping my sister with her investigation. Now, can I trust you to keep this between us?"

"Yes, of course, Dillon. Anything I can do to help local law enforcement. Are you sure there's nothing else?"

"This is absolutely perfect. You have a good evening, Monica. And I'm sure I'll see you tomorrow." With a flirtatious smile, Dillon left.

———

THE AFTERNOON WAS GIVING WAY TO EVENING AS THE SUN fell behind the police station. Riley returned with Ethan in tow.

Ethan pushed through the door and eyed Jacob. "What's he still doing here? I thought you set him up for the night?"

"I brought this problem here. I'm responsible for fixing it," Jacob replied.

Ethan laughed. "Really? Wow. I knew you were arrogant, but assuming this all revolves around you is something else."

"Ethan, what's wrong with you?" Riley eyed him. "He knows more about these people than we do. And while I'll agree he's not the sole person responsible for this, I won't reject his help and neither should you."

"Sorry, Riley. It's just..."

"Forget it, man," Jacob said to him. "It's fine. I understand. Everyone knows how you feel about Riley, so don't worry about it."

"For God's sake, can we stop now?" Riley's irritation turned to anger. "The last thing we need is you two pissing on each other. Where's the captain?"

Ethan kept his sights on Dillon but replied, "Looks like he's in his office."

Without another word, Riley continued to the captain's office and leaned inside the doorway. "Hey, Cap. What's the word on our reinforcements?"

He raised his index finger and continued the call. "Great. Thank you. We'll see you soon." He ended the call. "That was Pryce. He's got a team that'll be heading our way inside the hour. Should put them here by dark. We can figure out a plan of action on their arrival. I heard something going on out there. Everything okay?"

"It's nothing. So there's nothing we can do in the interim?"

"There's not a chance in hell our small team is going to go down to the plant, guns blazing, and take on these fellas. We don't know if they're here yet. And we don't know how many of them there will be. So, yeah, we're going to sit tight until IMPD gets here. If that's okay with you?"

"Yes, sir. I'm sorry. I'm just anxious."

"We all are, Riley, but we need to be methodical about this. We have to cover all our bases to be sure no one gets hurt. My gut tells me they'll put out feelers for Jacob first, maybe split up their team. Some heading to the plant and then others into town. So there's a decent shot we'll spot them out and about. They have no idea we're getting help from the big boys. We need to keep it that way."

"Jacob's still here."

"You need to consider getting him in place for the night."

"I'll take him later, before IMPD gets here. There was something else I wanted to run by you." She moved in to sit down. "I asked Dillon to check into Justin Rehnquist for me. Ethan and I were going to head down to speak to him again, but I wanted to get more information about him first."

"You can't keep running to your brother. You'll either put him in danger or you'll cost him his job."

"I know, and after this, it won't happen again. I just need to know more about this kid."

"Look, Riley, we've got about a dozen theories about what happened to Chloe and half a dozen possible suspects. This kid—you'd better be sure about because I don't see it. Find me something more and I'll let you run on it. In the meantime, I've got Abrams and Decker staking out the roads leading to the plant. If they spot something suspicious, they'll let me know."

Riley's cell phone rang. "It's Dillon."

"Better take it, then."

"Dillon, hi. What'd you find?" She listened to him relay the story along with bringing to her attention that he could have been fired were it not for his quick thinking. "I was hoping for more than that, but it does lend credence to the idea that he tried to protect her. I have to assume he loved her too, but she probably didn't know it." She nodded. "Thanks, Dillon. I'm sorry you had to go through this, but it helps. And I won't ask again. I'll talk to you later." She ended the call and looked at Ward. "Dillon says Justin was given a week's detention for hitting a guy in defense of Chloe."

"That's it?" Ward replied.

"I know you think I'm off base here, but she spoke to me. She told me I had to stop him. I just need a little more time. I'll get you something."

"Fine. Run on it, but remember, we've got a much more pressing problem," Ward said.

"Bringing down the mob?"

"You got it, kid."

———

JUSTIN REHNQUIST LIVED IN A ONE-BEDROOM APARTMENT alone. He had always been sort of a loner, even back in school, which was why it was so hard to believe that Chloe Dawson had wanted to be his friend. She wasn't the most popular girl in school, but she was pretty, smart, and had a small group of friends, to which he had also belonged. Now he waited for a man who had entrapped him. He thought he was helping Chloe when all he was really doing was letting this guy get close to her.

He had no place to go. There was no running from people like them. If only he'd known, he never would have agreed to get her there. It was all so messed up now. The girl he loved was gone and it had been his fault.

[18]

On the once tranquil road that led to the station house, several patrol cars appeared. Ethan Pruitt caught sight of the vehicles as he stood at Riley's desk. "Hey, they're here."

"It's about time reinforcements arrived." Riley peered through the window and noted the cars pulling into the lot. "It would've been nice if they could've made less of a spectacle of themselves. The entire town will be talking by now."

Ward appeared from his office. "I see the cavalry's arrived."

"Yes, sir," Riley added.

"These boys are the big league. I hope they have a plan of attack ready." Ward stood at the entrance and opened the door. "We sure are glad to see you fellas."

"You must be Captain Daniel Ward? I'm Lieutenant Moody. Captain Pryce sent us your way to help end this situation that seems to have spilled over into your peaceful community."

"You are most welcome." He held the door for the officers. "Come in, find a place to park it, and we'll get started."

Half a dozen officers arrived in full tactical gear and Riley was picking up a troubling feeling, like maybe this had just gone from bad to worse. These guys were here to help, and while that was all well and good, they also looked like their orders were shoot to kill. She wasn't opposed to taking drastic measures when necessary, but this felt like overkill. The storm was building.

"I'll start off by introducing my staff." Ward returned to the bullpen. "This is Officer Riley Thompson, Officer Ethan Pruitt, and Jacob Biggs. He was personally involved with the men we're after. I have two officers in the field staking out the area leading to the plant in search of our out-of-town guests."

"If you don't mind, Captain, it might be best to call your people back to base. We've been monitoring this group for over a year and they are dangerous. They won't hesitate to take out your officers if the mood strikes them," Moody said.

"Fair enough. I'll call them back now." Ward stepped away to make the call.

Riley looked to Moody. "Do you have any idea where George Hammond is? I believe he's going to be key to containing further escalations."

"He's the one who pulled me into this situation," Jacob said. "Right now, I'm wearing a big fat target on my back."

"And you led them here," Ethan replied.

The lieutenant seemed to pick up on the friction between the men and brushed it aside. "Hammond hasn't yet been located. We're tracking down his financial activity. Credit card use, ATM use, anything that might point us to a location. So far, he seems to be keeping a low profile. More so than I would've expected for a man who has no idea we're here."

"But you said you all have been after these men for at least a year. Seems to me he's flying under the radar for that reason. And if that's the case, we might not track him down after all," Riley said.

Jacob approached Riley. "Can I talk to you for a moment?"

She eyed the lieutenant before replying, "Please excuse us for just a moment."

Moody continued to discuss the situation with Pruitt, though Pruitt's gaze followed the two of them until they disappeared beyond the corridor.

"What is it?" Riley began. "You can't just pull me away like that, Jacob. This is my job and we're doing everything we can to make sure you're safe."

"I didn't mean any disrespect; I needed to talk to you about Blake Rhodes. We discussed a way I might reach out to him and get a feel for what his people were doing. I think the time to act on that is now."

"Okay. I'm listening."

"I'm going to use Chloe. I want to tell him that the cops think it was George who killed her."

"We have no idea..."

"I know, but hear me out. Blake is a good architect, but he's driven by jealousy. I've seen it first-hand. And if he thinks George had anything at all to do with his girlfriend's death, he might give him up, or at the very least, help us avoid an all-out war with these people. I don't know if it was George or not, but neither does Blake and neither do any of the men he's with now. Who's to say I'm not right? Virgil Howard is protecting his boss. Even the captain at IMPD doesn't seem to know who he is. What if Blake does? What if I can get that from him?"

"You're pinning a lot on 'what ifs'."

"Look, I didn't want to say any of this in front of all those cops. I'm telling you because you know that if I can get a sense for what Blake is up to, then you can too. And that might give us the advantage we need."

Riley considered his suggestion. If he was right, then they could put a plan into place that might preempt what she had already seen in her mind as a storm to end all storms. A gun battle that could cost Ward his life. And that was a risk she was unwilling to take. "If you're right and he talks, then we might just get ahead of this situation. Maybe even stop them before they get here. But if not, then Blake will inform his boss and that could make matter worse. They could bring reinforcements."

"I'm not wrong. In all the years we've known each other, I've put my trust in you. Now I'm asking that you do the same for me."

"Okay. Make the call, but do it here, not in front of those guys. If this goes wrong, I don't want them to know. I'll pull the captain aside and tell him. At which time, I fully expect to be fired, but I'll deal with that if it comes to pass."

"It won't, Riley, I promise you." Jacob reached for his cell phone and pressed Blake's contact information. "Blake, it's me, Jacob."

Riley was only privy to one side of the conversation, so she tried to read Jacob's expressions as he spoke. What she really needed was to be in front of Blake so she could see him for who and what he was. Then she would know if he was being truthful.

"Look, man, forget what happened back there, okay? I'm telling you, the men you're with now—they have no idea who killed Chloe. So who does that leave? Who would take that poor girl's life at the very plant that tied George to these men. And who took the money? I'm just saying, it's entirely possible it was George who did both." Jacob looked at Riley and revealed a smile as though he might get what he needed. "Dude, if it wasn't him, then who was it? Cause I'm not seeing any other possible reason for her to be dead in a pool of concrete. Do you?"

Riley believed he might have been making progress. The fact that he was still talking was a good sign.

"They're running down George's banking trail right now, Blake. They will find him. And I can be the one to tell you when they do. But you have to help me too. Regardless of what's happened, we were friends, man. I need your help and you need mine."

Riley peered at Jacob and tapped on her wrist, indicating his time was up.

"I'm running out of time, Blake. Please, we can work through this and both come out of it on the other side. You can take down the person responsible for this entire raw deal." Jacob held Riley's gaze as he continued to listen to Blake. "Thank you. Contact me when you can via text." He returned his phone to his pocket.

"Well?" she asked.

"He said they're tying up loose ends now and plan on heading here tomorrow morning. Riley, he says Bayliss was instructed to destroy computer files and documents."

"They're trying to cover their asses. Meaning Bayliss and Howard had talked. They know we're close to proving Chloe's death was at their hands. So we have until morning. Better let the captain know."

The two returned to the stares of everyone in the room, including Abrams and Decker, who'd just arrived.

"You two ready to join in on the discussion now?" Ward asked.

"Actually," Riley looked at the team. "Jacob reached out to his former colleague, Blake Rhodes, who we all know has been instrumental in attempting to frame him for the supposed money he stole. And who also happens to have been Chloe Dawson's boyfriend."

"You made contact without informing us?" Moody appeared hot under the collar. "That's something we really need to coordinate on. I'm sorry, but we didn't come down here to have you folks go off half-cocked."

"He didn't," Riley said. "He thought he could make progress with this guy. He knows him and his personality. And frankly, he accomplished just that. Jacob, you want to let them know what you found out?"

"They're coming tomorrow morning. Someone instructed the plant manager to destroy files and documents."

"That won't do them any good," Moody added.

"They might not realize that at the moment and that will work for us because it means they aren't in a hurry to get here. We've just been handed the gift of time, but in exchange for the information, I agreed to provide him with the whereabouts of George Hammond when he's located. I made sure Blake believed that he was the man who killed Chloe."

"We don't know that," Ward said.

"It was the only leverage I had, so I used it," Jacob replied.

"Do we need to stop these guys from destroying evidence at the plant?" Abrams chimed in.

"No. I want the rest of them here first," Moody said. "We wait until morning. In the meantime, the captain and I will work to find Hammond. In fact, I should be getting an update from my captain at any time."

"What do we do until then?" one of his team asked.

"If we locate Hammond, we'll get on him. If not, then we'll sit tight until morning. We'll have them on extortion, kidnapping, and possibly murder. And I won't even go into the trafficking operation I'm sure the plant was set up for. It'll take days for their lawyers to sort through the red tape I'll be piling on. That'll give us enough time to build a solid case."

———

BLAKE RETURNED TO THE LIVING ROOM OF THE APARTMENT, where the others were discussing the plans. What had started off as an effort to extort Jacob Biggs and recruit the unwitting man to help them find Hammond had now become an attempt to discover who killed his girlfriend. Blake was going to play both sides and needed to find the confidence to make it believable because if any one of these men got a whiff of what was really happening, Blake would find himself wearing concrete shoes to match Chloe's.

"Was that your boy, Jacob?" Virgil asked.

"Yeah. He still thinks we're after the money, but I told him that if he knew where Hammond was, it was in his best interest to give him up. Hold Hammond accountable and he would be let off the hook."

"Good, but you see the problem now is that Jakey caused the

death of one of our own. Eddie's gone because of that prick. That isn't going to fly, you feel me?"

"I understand. He doesn't know we're coming, just that we're still after the money. You gotta do what you gotta do. Eddie's gone, and yeah, he'll have to pay for that," Blake replied.

"That boy should've left the cops out of it. They'll be after us too, if they aren't already. Won't take long for them to put two and two together once they ID Eddie, which means they'll be watching us. If they see we're headed to the plant, they'll be right behind us," Virgil added.

"How are we going to handle that, boss?" Kearns asked.

"Once I get confirmation from Bayliss all the evidence has been destroyed, I'll let the big man know and he'll tell me what to do next. But he's not happy we lost Eddie. He wants revenge. And he wants to know who killed that girl and how the fuck she ended up inside our operation." Virgil's phone rang. "I gotta take this." He walked outside and answered the call. Standing on the balcony that looked out over the city, he started, "Yeah, boss?"

"I'm going to need you to get our sacrificial lamb ready, you understand?"

"Yes, sir. He's still here with us and has been in touch with Biggs. He has no idea we've been watching him."

"Let's keep it that way for now. Keep monitoring his phone. I want to know what he's telling Biggs because that's what IMPD will get. Biggs will pass along everything to them, I guaran-damn-tee you that."

"What about Bayliss?" Virgil leaned against the balcony railing.

"Let me take care of him. He's been a good soldier so far. I'll do what I can to repay his loyalty. In the meantime, keep Rhodes on ice."

"How are you going to get out?"

"I have an idea. You just make sure to keep Rhodes and Biggs on a short leash. They're both going to become very important to us."

"Understood." Virgil checked his phone at the sound of the click, as though he'd accidentally ended the call, but it wasn't him. He returned inside.

"Was that the boss man?" Blake appeared overly eager for an answer.

"Our orders haven't changed. Head to the plant in the morning to take care of any loose ends and then find Jacob Biggs. And kill him."

———

RILEY STRAPPED HER HOLSTER AROUND HER WAIST WHILE SHE stood at her desk. She looked through the window as the street-lamps in the parking lot flickered on. "I think we have one last shot at Justin Rehnquist. If we can't get anything out of him, I have a feeling he'll pack up and leave town."

"You really believe he killed her?" Ethan approached her desk. "With the connection to Rhodes and what we think is the mafia?"

"I can't say for sure if he killed her, but I do believe he played a part in her death. There was no reason for her to be at the plant. None. Ward asked me to build a better case, so I did. I searched through more of Justin's Instagram posts. There was a lot more there than we initially looked at."

"Well, he wasn't really a suspect at the time."

"No, but maybe he should've been. We were focused on identifying her, so when we initially met up with him, we didn't know if our victim was Chloe or not."

"Now that we do, you want to revisit this? Just like you said when we left him that day," Ethan continued. "If you're right, then where does that leave our investigation? This money Jacob says he's being blamed for. The plant and its connections to the mob."

"It's all connected, but this is the first step in finding out how." She started toward Jacob. "I want you to stay here. Depending on what happens, on our return, I'll take you to Carl's place. We'll stay there tonight."

"We?" Ethan asked. "You and him? At Carl's?"

"Can you think of a better place? I can't go home. I'm sure the car that I've seen belongs to those guys, maybe Bayliss himself. Jacob can't go back to his cousin's. But no one knows about Carl. And he lives in a secured facility. I think we'll both be safe there tonight."

"You can stay with me," Ethan continued. "I've got no connections to any of these people. They aren't going to just start showing up at cops' houses and start shooting. I mean, Carl doesn't have much room."

"I appreciate your offer, Ethan, but I need to see Carl for other reasons too. And it's best if I stay there."

"Fine. Whatever. Are we leaving, or are we going to stand around here all night?" His frustration became obvious.

"Let me just check in with Ward." Riley continued to Ward's office, where he sat with the lieutenant. "Pruitt and I are headed out to have another chat with Justin Rehnquist. I don't know what will happen, but whatever it is will probably happen quickly. So, I don't expect us to be gone for long."

"Okay. Take your shot at him, just be careful," Ward replied.

"You want one of my guys to go with you?" Moody asked. "They're getting anxious. I can see it. I don't think any of us planned on sticking it out for the night."

"No. I don't want to spook him into taking off the moment he sees us. Besides, I thought you all had your hands full tracking down Hammond?"

"Doesn't take all of us, but we're talking with the bank and reviewing surveillance footage from an ATM it looked like he stopped by earlier today."

"Oh yeah? Where was he?"

"By the looks of it, on his way here," the lieutenant replied.

"Then that makes this mission all the more important."

"If you say so." Moody snickered. "No offense, Thompson, but how long have you been in uniform? And here in this town where nothing much happens?"

"That's not necessary Lieutenant Moody," Ward started.

"Look, I get this is your town. I do. And again, I'm not trying to belittle any of your officers. Please know that."

"Sure sounds like you are," Riley said.

"I don't mean to. What I mean to say is that I've run these types of operations many times. And until I know for sure Hammond is heading this way, my guys are going to continue tracking him down. That's what we should be focusing on. Look, I can't stop you from doing whatever it is you're about to do, but I think it's a waste of time."

"That's not up to you to decide," Ward added.

"No, it's not. Just giving you my two cents," Moody added.

Riley brushed over his remarks and looked at Ward. "I'm going to talk to Rehnquist and Pruitt's coming with me." She started toward the door. "Captain, let me know if anything pops up and we'll get back here as soon as possible."

Ward watched as she left and turned his sights again on the lieutenant. "I understand where you're coming from, but when Thompson gets something in her head, nine times out of ten, she's right. So I put a lot of faith in her. And by the end of this, you will too."

Despite the fact Owensville had changed very little since Riley was a kid, it now seemed to her to be different. She viewed it through different eyes—older, wiser perhaps. Of course, as a child, she had been preoccupied with a chilling gift she couldn't control, an alcoholic father, and gun-running militia men. Now that she thought about it, perhaps things hadn't changed at all.

Except that there were a few more apartment buildings, a couple of new stores, mostly retail chain stores, and it was nice having a Wal-Mart nearby. And the apartment building they were driving to now had been built only two years ago, around the time Justin Rehnquist graduated high school, along with his friend, Chloe Dawson.

"I wanted to thank you for sticking up for me back there at the station." Ethan kept his eyes on the road ahead as he spoke.

"What do you mean, sticking up for you? I was sticking up for all of us. I know IMPD is a hundred times bigger than we are, but that doesn't give Moody the right to tell us we don't know what the hell we're doing."

"Well..."

"Well what? You agree with him?"

"Not entirely, but when was the last time we handled a homicide, let alone a vast mafia conspiracy?"

She pursed her lips. "I'll give you that one. Still, he should respect our work regardless."

"Yes, he should, and from what you said, Ward put him in his place anyway."

"He did." She eyed the road ahead. "That's the building up there."

"What's going to be our approach to this?" Ethan asked.

"I'll know more when I see him." She parked in the lot and cut the engine. "And if Chloe's ever been in his apartment, I might be able to pick up something there too. We'll just have to take this one step at a time." Riley stepped out of the patrol car and waited for Ethan to join her. "There's one other thing." She regarded him. "You and I are partners—and friends, right?"

"Of course."

"Then I'm going to need you to step back where Jacob is concerned, I mean, from a personal perspective. Whatever happens after all of this is over is my business."

"Okay, fine." He followed as she started toward the building. "You want him to break your heart again, I guess that's on you."

She shot him a glance but continued on until they reached the unit. "105. This is his place. Ready?"

"As I'll ever be." Ethan palmed his weapon and she knocked on the door.

"Justin, it's Officer Thompson. We spoke the other day. Can I come in?" She waited, anticipating an answer or a door opening, but neither occurred. "Justin? We want to ask you a few more questions about Chloe." Riley looked at Ethan with concern before drawing her weapon. "Justin?" With her gun aimed at the door, she tried the handle. It was locked.

"Should we try his cell phone?" Ethan asked. "I've got his number here."

"Go around back, check behind his patio fence for lights inside."

Ethan nodded, and with his own weapon drawn, started around to the rear of the building. Riley peered through the windows, but the curtains were drawn and heavily lined, making it impossible to see anything inside. "Damn." That familiar feeling grew inside her. It was a gnawing, gut-clenching sensation that told her something bad was going to happen or had already happened.

She quickly turned her sights to the parking lot, looking for Rehnquist's car, and in the spot marked "105," there it was. Riley was going to have to find a way in because his car was there and yet there was no answer at the door. This was not a good sign. She raised Ethan on the radio strapped to her shoulder. "Ethan, I'm heading your way."

Before he had a chance to reply, she started around the side of the building and his voice sounded. "I'm here. No lights on."

"Stay put." Riley continued to the back where an alley abutted the small fenced-in patios of the ground-floor units. She spotted Ethan and caught up to him.

"I don't think he's here, Riley. I was able to peek over the fence. No lights and I don't hear anything either."

"His car is here. Ethan, we're going to have to find a way in. I'm getting a really bad feeling about this." She grabbed the top of the wood fence and positioned herself to be hoisted over. "Help me up."

"Wait, you can't just go inside. We don't have a warrant."

"I believe Justin's life is in danger. That's enough probable cause to get inside. Ward will see it that way too."

"For crying out loud, Riley." He clasped his hands together and leaned over for her to place her boot inside his laced fingers. "Just don't break your leg or anything."

"Then don't throw me over. Go easy, got it?" She raised up with his help and straddled the fence. With careful maneuvering, Riley lowered herself onto the concrete patio. "There's a latch down here, but it's padlocked. You're going to have to jump over too."

"What?"

"You got a good six inches on me, you can do it, Ethan. Come on, we're wasting time." She eyed the top of the fence and spotted his hands. "Just pull up."

The top of his head surfaced and soon he was halfway there.

"Damn it." Ethan tumbled onto the patio. "Shit!"

"What happened?" she asked, staring down at him on the ground.

He showed her the cut on his hand. "I'm fine. Let's just get in there before someone calls the cops on us."

"Funny." She inspected his injury. "You'll live. Now how are we going to get in?"

"Thanks for the sympathy." Ethan approached the sliding glass door. "You sure you want to do this?"

"Have I steered you wrong before?"

Without another word, he returned his sights to the door and pulled up on the handle. "I saw this on TV once. Apparently, there's a track and the door can just lift off..."

The slider lifted from its track and the lock disengaged.

"There you go." He turned to her with a smile.

"See, I knew you could do it." Riley aimed her weapon and crossed over the threshold and into the dark apartment. "Justin, it's me, Officer Thompson. Are you okay? Are you hurt?"

They both continued inside with guns ready, and side by side, they moved cautiously through the darkened room.

"I can't see a thing." Riley found a light switch and turned on what was the breakfast nook light, but Ethan struck the fixture before she'd flipped the switch.

"That's going to leave a mark." He rubbed his head.

It took a moment for the scene to register. The place had been ransacked and Riley turned an anxious gaze to Ethan. "This is bad." She immediately dashed through the apartment and toward the back, where a bedroom and bath were tucked away inside the short corridor. She reemerged from the bedroom. "He's not in there."

"Well, someone's been here," Ethan said. "He could've been kidnapped, like Jacob's girlfriend." He started down the hall where she had just been and stopped at the bathroom. "Riley, you check in here?" He moved inside.

She joined him. "You see anything?" Without warning, she doubled over in pain.

"Riley! What's wrong? What's happening?" Ethan grabbed hold of her.

"The bathtub." Her words were a mix of syllables and groans.

Ethan turned slowly toward the tub with dread in his eyes and reached for the curtain that was pulled closed. He yanked it open. "Oh my God."

Justin Rehnquist lay in the tub, naked in a pool of blood-stained water.

Riley gasped for breath before she was able to stand upright again. She walked toward the tub and stared at the body.

"It looks like suicide," Ethan said.

By the look of him, he hadn't been dead long and Riley knew what she had to do, so she reached for his shoulder and lay her hand on him. The images exploded in her mind, powerful and seething with pain. She gripped the edge of the tub with her other hand.

"Are you okay?" Ethan touched her, but she shrugged him off. All he could do was sit back and wait.

In her mind's eye, she was transported to where Justin stood, ready to enter his apartment. Someone he expected was waiting inside. And in a flash, another image burst in her head. Inside the living room, Justin was fending off his attacker while she stood only feet from him.

"It has to be this way. You should've kept your mouth shut," the man said.

The attacker's back was to her. "Show me," she whispered. And Justin looked at her as though she'd been physically there as it was happening.

The man who came at him with relentless vigor saw the shift in his gaze and turned with curiosity.

"Stop! You're hurting him!" Riley screamed at him, but he looked right through her. She wasn't really there. She had been too late and all this had already happened.

The man choked Justin until he fell unconscious before dragging him toward the bathroom and placing him in the tub. He then grabbed a knife from his pocket and slashed Justin's wrist. Blood spurted from his veins, landing on Riley's face. She flinched and outstretched her hands to somehow attempt to save him, but there was no use.

The attacker went for the other wrist, slicing it again. The tub and walls were now coated in Justin's blood while the man turned on the faucet and the water ran, creating a marbled, swirling piece of bloody art.

She yanked her hand away. "It wasn't suicide, Ethan. Someone killed him." With wild eyes, sweat on her brow, and out of breath, Riley turned to her partner. "I saw him. I don't know who he is, but I know he's with the rest of them."

"I'll call this in. Why don't you go sit down a minute?" Ethan reached for his radio as Riiley stepped back. "We'll need to see what these men look like too. All of them, including George Hammond. Maybe you'll be able to ID this perp."

Riley stared at the lifeless body of the young man with whom she had talked only days before. And this did nothing to solve the mystery of Chloe's killer, and in fact, it only muddied the waters.

"Dispatch, this is Pruitt, we're going to need an ambo at 1839 Mineral Way, unit 105."

"Ten-four, ambo will be dispatched."

The radio cut out and Ethan turned to Riley as she stood in the hall, still pale. "They're sending an ambulance. We'd better get Ward out here too." He studied her for a moment. "How are you going to explain who you saw here tonight?"

"To Ward? He'll know, but as for the lieutenant, I'll have to figure out something."

"He won't believe any of this," Ethan said.

"I wouldn't either, if I was him."

―――――

By the time Riley and Ethan returned to the station, it was approaching 11pm. Justin's apartment was secured, Moody's team swooped in for forensics. And now the time had come to explain what she saw and who. The "who" she hoped someone else could provide the answer.

"Oh, thank God you're back." Jacob rushed to her side. "Are you okay? You look pale. Do you need something to drink?"

"I'm fine, really." Jacob always worried when she had an episode. Of course, one like that hadn't come in some time, but it was clear he was afraid for her. Even now, she sensed fear in him. And there was reason to be afraid. Dangerous people were out there waiting for him, maybe waiting for all of them.

"Why don't you give her some space, man." Ethan helped her inside.

"I'm okay. I don't need any help." She eyed Ethan's hand that held on to her arm. "You can let go of me now."

He pulled away. "Where's the captain? He's not back yet?"

"He and the lieutenant are setting up a team to surveil the plant," an IMPD officer spoke up. "You uncovered something pretty damn important. Moody's pulling out all the stops now."

"Good. It's about time." Riley started toward the breakroom, motioning for Jacob and Ethan to follow. Once inside, she began, "Look, I don't know who it was I saw, but, Jacob, we need to get our hands on a picture of Hammond, for starters. And if it wasn't him, then I need to get in front of a sketch artist. Whoever killed Justin might've also killed Chloe."

"What about Blake Rhodes?" Ethan asked. "Is it possible it was him?"

"I know what he looks like from the legwork we've already done. It wasn't him," Riley replied.

"Right. So let's get a picture of Hammond." Ethan started toward his desk.

"Riley, wait." Jacob held her back for a moment. "You don't look well. I think this one took a heavy toll on you. Are you sure I can't get you anything? How's your stomach?"

"You remember."

"I remember. Nausea, loss of color, clammy hands, and oh wait, let me check." He placed the palm of his hand on her forehead. "Yep. Brow's still sweaty too. All the symptoms are checked off."

She tried to smile, but her chin quivered.

"Hey. Hey, it's okay." Jacob pulled her close. "Just relax. It's just his emotions leaving you, remember? There's always some residual feelings. Just take a breath."

Ethan reappeared in the doorway and caught sight of their embrace. He stopped for a moment, then cast his gaze away and returned to the bullpen.

"Are you okay now?" Jacob regarded her closely. "Yeah, you look okay now." With his thumb, he wiped away a stray tear. "We'd better take a look at those pictures."

She'd forgotten how comforting it felt to have him around. These episodes didn't happen a lot, but when they did, she was drained, just like she was right now. And Jacob always knew what to do.

He started ahead without her but stopped and turned back. "Are you coming?"

"Right behind you." Riley followed him out into the bullpen.

"Riley, come take a look at this." Ethan pushed away from his computer and waited for her approach. "Look familiar?"

She stood behind him with folded arms and peered at the screen.

Jacob made his way next to her. "That's Hammond. Was he the one?"

"The one what?" Lieutenant Moody entered with Ward behind him. He walked toward them. "What are you looking at?" He eyed the image on the screen before looking at Riley. "Hammond. You think he's responsible for killing that kid you found?"

Before she could answer, Captain Ward interrupted, "Officer Thompson, can I have a quick word. I'll have her back in a flash, Lieutenant." He headed into his office and waited for her.

Riley already knew what this conversation would entail. She'd been prepared for it since they made the call about Justin.

"I wanted to stop you before you said anything to Moody," Ward began.

"He's going to want answers. I can't keep this from him."

"Riley, you're going to have to. There has to be another way. If word gets out about your abilities..."

"Yeah, I know. They'll kick me off the force. Any case I've been involved with, they'll think I'm just some crazed lunatic who sees things."

"Something like that, but I know you. I've seen you in action more times than I care to recall. But this has to stay here, in this station house."

"How do you propose I go about explaining that I saw who killed Justin?"

"First of all, that picture you were looking at was George Hammond. Did he do it? Did he kill Justin Rehnquist?"

"No, it wasn't him."

"Then who did you see, Riley?"

"I don't know who he is. But if I can just see what the other guys look like, the ones who are coming here. I'm sure he's among them."

"Then you'll have to do it someplace else. Go to Carl's, take Jacob. That was your original plan anyway, and take your laptop. You can log into the system from there and track down the names we already know. If he's one of them, call me. I don't care what time it is. I have a feeling me and the lieutenant have a long night ahead of us."

"I can't leave you guys here."

"That's an order, Riley. We just put a surveillance team in place. Moody's got his guys here and back in Indianapolis tracking Hammond. There's nothing more for you to do tonight. Besides, after what happened, you need some rest. I know how draining it can be for you."

"I wish people would stop treating me like I have a disease. 'Go, get some rest. You look pale. Can I get you anything?' I can look after myself. I always have." Riley turned on her heel and approached Jacob. "Come on. We're leaving."

[20]

When the door opened, Riley expected to see Carl half-asleep and wrapped in a robe, irritated because it was so late. But as he stood before her, alert, almost energetic, she knew he'd been waiting for them and was invigorated to be included in something again.

"I'm sorry it's so late," Riley said.

"Don't be. Come in." Carl stepped aside and let in the two kids with whom he had been so close over the years, one in particular. The other, well, he was still a little pissed by what he'd done. But that was going to have to be tabled for the moment. "You want something to drink? Water? Pop? I wish I could offer you something stronger, but they don't let me keep booze here."

"You go and sit down. I'll get us some water." Riley walked toward the small kitchenette. The bar-sized refrigerator still had bottles of water inside from when she stocked it up the other day. She grabbed a few and returned to the living room. "Here."

"Thanks," Jacob replied.

"Looks like you've had an interesting day," Carl began. "Care to share what happened?"

"Is it that obvious?" Riley asked. "We found Chloe Dawson's friend—dead—made to look like a suicide."

"And you must've seen who did it?" Carl asked.

"I did, but I don't know who he is. We started looking into it at the station and that was when Ward essentially ordered us out."

"Ah, he didn't want the big city cops getting wise to your gift, because that could jeopardize everything."

"That's right. So here we are." She opened her laptop. "Jacob knows what most of these men look like and while not all of them will be in the system, some of them will most certainly be. And, if he isn't here, Ward will have to get access to Lieutenant Moody's files of the men they've been following for the past year."

"I hope you recognize one of them." Jacob tossed back the rest of his water.

"And if this killer isn't one of these men you're looking for?" Carl asked.

"Then I guess we sit here until morning. According to Jacob's friend, that's when our guests will arrive," Riley said.

"He's not my friend anymore," Jacob replied.

"Well, isn't this some kind of shit storm? This is the gnawing feeling I can't shake," Carl said.

"You've picked up on it too, huh?" Riley logged into the department's servers and checked her email. "Jacob, I need a name."

He walked toward Riley's chair and crouched down next to her, peering at her computer screen. "Virgil Howard, that one you already know."

"Right." She pulled up his information and looked at a picture. "That's not him. Pretty much what we expected. Who else?"

Jacob cast his eyes upward. "Oh yeah, check out Paul Kearns. It seemed to me he was Virgil's right-hand man. At least after Eddie Costa was gunned down by the cops."

She pulled up the name. "No, definitely not him either."

"I don't who else." Jacob sighed. "Those were the only guys there the other day."

"Unless it isn't one of these men at all," Carl said.

"It has to be. Who else had reason to kill Justin? He was Chloe's friend and she's dead," Riley added.

Carl studied her. "Look deeper. Remember who you saw, remember what she said to you."

"She warned me," Riley began. "And when we initially talked with Justin, I felt he might've been holding something back. I couldn't see it at the time, but I felt it." With immediate recollection, she looked at Jacob. "We have to go back to his apartment."

"Why?"

"Because there's something there. We've overlooked something obvious. I can feel it and I can almost see it. And I have to find out what it is."

"Riley, it's not safe out there. They could already be here, regardless of what Blake said. The captain sent us here to keep a low profile," Jacob said.

"He sent us here so I could figure out who it was I saw choking the life from Justin Rehnquist." She looked to Carl. "I'm right, aren't I? You can feel it too."

"I do believe you're onto something. Whoever this was, his face is seared in your mind's eye. And while I can't see who you saw, I can see that you aren't sure he's with the rest of them coming here to town."

"Jacob, you should stay here. I'll go," Riley said.

"Not a chance am I letting you go back there alone. Someone found Justin. That someone might find you too."

"Oh, so now you want to stick it out with me?" She closed her eyes. "I'm sorry. I don't know why I said that. I didn't mean it."

"Somehow, I think you did. Look, I'm not letting you go out there by yourself. Think whatever you want, but it's not going to happen. This is all because of me."

"This isn't about you anymore. Not this part," Carl said. "Go, take my car. I don't drive it anymore, but I keep it in the storage unit at the back. Last thing we need is for someone to spot your patrol car. And, Riley, this has to be resolved tonight. It could change the course of what's about to happen."

"I can't believe this car still runs." Jacob eyed the massive green dash, metal door handles, and analog clock in the 1979 Lincoln Continental.

"Carl would never get rid of it. It's the only thing he has left that reminds him he isn't in a grave yet," Riley replied.

"That's dark."

"He's a dark guy who's seen a lot." Riley pulled into the parking lot of Justin's apartment building.

They stepped out and continued along the walkway until reaching the unit that now had police tape stretched across the front door.

"How are we supposed to get in?" Jacob said.

"Justin dropped his keys when he was caught by surprise by his attacker. When Ethan and I were here, I found them on the floor. Figured they might come in handy, so I swiped them." Riley removed the police tape and unlocked the door. "Voila." She entered the apartment and immediately felt her chest tighten.

Jacob noticed the grimace on her face. "Are you okay?"

"I just have to push through it," she replied.

"I hope you and Carl are right about this because I don't think you need to go through this again," Jacob added.

"The man I saw doesn't seem to be one of Virgil Howard's guys. So if he isn't, then who sent him? I was in a state that I couldn't see anything past what Justin was feeling at the time of his death. So we didn't keep looking for clues. My mistake, which I'm here to rectify now."

"I know what happened between you and Carl way back, but how did it end up that he is somehow connected to you? I mean, does he see things like you do?"

"No. He senses feelings in me, same as I do him. Only not quite the same. I don't know how it happened exactly. When I crossed over into his dreams, something was left behind. I've never had that connection with anyone else. Not even my own family. I can't really explain it."

"That's why you visit him so often, isn't it? You share that bond."

"Yes, but it's also because I love him. He's always been there for me, no matter what."

"And I haven't."

"I didn't say that." She turned away and continued to survey the apartment. "Without Justin here, I don't know what I'll find."

"You said whoever it was tried to make it look like a suicide.

That does seem strange if it was these same guys who are after me. What would be the point?"

"There wouldn't be one. I should've picked up on that sooner."

"It takes a while for you to recover. Don't be too hard on yourself."

Riley continued in search of something that would help her connect to Justin once again. She started toward his bedroom. "If I'm going to find something to latch on to, it'll be in here."

Jacob followed closely behind until they reached the bedroom.

"If I can find something personal," she began.

Jacob veered off toward the closet. A moment later, he returned to Riley's side. "How about this?" He wore a broad smile. "Right coat pocket. Jacket was still hanging in the closet. Guess Moody's men didn't search the place as well as I would've thought."

"A cell phone?" Riley was stunned.

"I don't know if you'll pick up anything from this, but I bet you'll find some interesting phone calls or text messages." He handed her the phone.

"I can't believe you found this."

"Maybe I have a touch of the gift too."

"Careful what you wish for." She turned on the phone. "I'm sure it's password protected." As the phone loaded, she found she was right. "Damn it."

"This is a cake walk for you. Come on, Riley, focus. You know what it is. I know you do."

She exhaled and studied the phone. "He had it recently. I don't know, I'm not seeing." She stopped dead, and after another moment, keyed in a code. The phone unlocked. "I saw him entering the code."

"It is stronger now, isn't it? Stronger than when you were younger?" Jacob asked.

"Yeah. Sometimes it's a little frightening, even for me."

"I don't doubt that at all."

She swiped the phone and immediately checked the email. "Looks like a burner. I wonder why he needed this? How deep was he in this?"

"I don't know, Riley. I guess I was hoping you could figure that out."

She began checking the text messages. "Jacob, there's some here from Chloe. This doesn't make sense. Why wouldn't they text on his regular phone?" She opened one of the conversations. "This was last week, three days before we found her. It's the last one on here. I don't recognize the phone number." As she read the messages, it became clear what had been happening. "Jacob, are you reading this? Am I reading this right?"

"This is bad, Riley. I mean, really bad."

"He was using her," she began. "I thought he loved her, but if that was true, how could he do this?"

"Did you know she was pregnant?" Jacob asked.

"No. She kept that from me. Who was she trying to protect? I don't even know if the coroner is aware. I doubt he's gotten any of the labs back yet. Do you know what this means?"

"According to these texts, he brought her there; to the plant."

"Yeah." She peered at Jacob. "He signed her death warrant. He took her there, knowing she was pregnant and knowing what would happen to her."

"But who did he take her to see? He doesn't mention a name at all. All we have is a phone number and I'll bet it's a burner too. Probably in a river somewhere by now. How are we supposed to find out who this number belongs to? These phones aren't traceable."

"I have to get this to the captain. Maybe there's something Moody can do with it. They have resources we don't."

"Are you sure you want to bring this to his attention? You could find yourself in a lot of hot water for coming here tonight. Moody will want to know why. What are you going to tell him? That you had a feeling something else was going on?"

"You know, there was one thing that has been bugging me since we found Chloe. And that was why in the world her ID was still there. I mean, would you go and kill someone, then make sure to leave behind identification for someone to find?"

"It was that manager at the plant who found it too, wasn't it?"

"Yes, and he called us."

"Like it was planned," Jacob added. "Riley, are you sure you can't pick up anything else here? A little more information sure would be helpful. We need to know who this number belongs to that Justin was texting. You saw a face, you have to find more."

"I know that!" She paused. "I'm sorry, I didn't mean to raise my voice. I'm freaking out over here, and I know it's on me to find more. Sometimes I just can't see everything." She scanned the bedroom again before walking to his closet. Upon opening the doors, she reached for his clothes, touching every last article that still hung on the rod. "Where's the coat, Jacob? The one you found the phone in. I might get something if he'd worn it that day."

Jacob retrieved the coat he'd found from the closet. "Here."

She grabbed hold of it. Riley closed her eyes, but nothing came. She slipped it on and waited. "Come on. Show me something, Justin. Whatever you did, you can make it right."

237

Jacob kept his sights glued on her, waiting, ready to catch her if she succumbed to a vision.

Riley saw an image appear before her. It was a woman. She was standing inside the plant with Justin. "Who are you?" Riley's brow began to bead with sweat. Her breath grew shallow. In her mind's eye, she stood not more than ten feet away and watched them talk.

"And you promise not to hurt her?" Justin had said to the woman.

"I'm only going to make a point. She won't be harmed, I promise you."

"I don't know."

"Justin, I know you need the money. Chloe will never ever know it was you. I promise you, this will just be a warning."

"Okay," he replied.

"You're making the right call. Here's half the money. You'll get the other half after you bring her here tomorrow night. Someone will be waiting."

Justin appeared confused. "Wait, you aren't the one who's going to talk to her?"

"No. I'll send someone to deliver the message. Don't worry. He knows what to do. This is the last thing I'll ask of you. After that, we'll never have to see each other again. It's for her own good. She has no idea who she's involved with. You're doing her a huge favor."

Riley's eyes flew open, revealing a terrifying glare.

"Are you okay? Is it over?" Jacob grabbed on to her shoulders to steady her. "What did you see?"

"A woman. She was trying to convince Justin to get Chloe to the plant. He was being paid to bring her."

"Was this woman the one who killed her?"

"No. She said someone was going to meet Chloe there. Get her to understand that Chloe didn't know how much trouble she was in."

"She was going to be warned to back off?"

"I think so, and he agreed. Justin agreed to do it because he needed the money." Riley looked at him.

"But if he did what he promised to do, why was he killed?"

"The man who killed him has to be the same one who killed Chloe. A hired hitman? I don't know why they would've come after him."

"Unless it was to take back the money?"

"They could've easily just not paid him in the first place. No, I think Justin was talking to us and that spooked whoever paid him off. He was scared. I saw it. It felt like more than just losing his friend. Unfortunately, I didn't see everything clearly."

"This is so much bigger than I thought. Where does it stop and with who?"

Riley pulled off Justin's coat and stared at it. "I have no idea."

———

CAPTAIN DAVE PRYCE SAT IN HIS CAR, ELBOW HANGING OUT of the driver's side window and peering into the darkness. The skies were laden with clouds as thunder rolled above him. He waited for the woman to show up. And she was late.

The parking lot of the shuttered Best Buy in the suburbs of Indianapolis was a good place to lie in wait. It had been all but forgotten by everyone, including law enforcement, making it an ideal location to set up this little rendezvous.

He spotted headlights approach and leaned over the door until the car pulled alongside him and the driver rolled down her window. "I was getting worried you weren't going to show."

"He wasn't supposed to die."

"He was talking. It couldn't be helped. Collateral damage," Pryce said.

"It was almost over. Why? You only had to wait another day."

"Like I said, it couldn't be helped. Is that the only reason you wanted to meet? To scold me for doing what I had to do to protect you?"

"You weren't protecting me. You were protecting yourself," the woman replied.

"Just stick with the plan. Stay out of sight. My people are already in place. You just have to ride this out and it'll all go away. So long as you keep to your end of the deal. Your hands are just as dirty as mine. I need you to remember that."

She eyed him. "Don't you worry about that. I remember. But after tomorrow, I'm gone, you understand? No one will have need to find me. No one cares at all about me."

"Well, that's where you're wrong. I care."

She laughed and shifted the gear. "Goodbye, Dave."

"Goodbye, Kelly. You take care of yourself."

[21]

The assisted living facility where Carl lived was just ahead. Riley pulled around to the storage units at the back and parked Carl's car inside his unit. She pulled the keys from the ignition and turned to Jacob. "I need you stay here with Carl, okay? I'm going back to the station to talk to the captain. I have to tell him what we know."

"I want to come with you."

"No. Please just stay here. It's the only way I can be sure you're safe. I have no idea what I'm going to run up against. This isn't what we thought it was. In fact, I'm not sure I have a clue at all about what we're up against. Carl will be awake. He won't sleep until he knows we're okay."

Jacob held her gaze, and in a moment of desire, his hand slipped behind her neck and his lips pressed firmly against hers.

She surrendered to him, but only for a moment. "Stop. You can't do that. Not now when everything is so messed up."

"I'm sorry. I just—I couldn't help it. It won't happen again." He opened the car door and stepped out.

Riley waited as he walked inside the building. "Damn it, Jacob." She missed the way his lips felt on hers. The way he touched her. Despite the fact that he left, she never stopped loving him, even when he moved on with another woman. But she couldn't give in to him now. She couldn't divert her attention, not when she was so close. He only kissed her because he was afraid. "It was nothing more than that," she reminded herself.

Riley returned to her patrol car. Carl would be annoyed she wasn't staying, but there was too much happening and Ward had to be briefed. There was still the dream of his and she believed he was in danger. Maybe there was something she could do to stop whatever was about to happen.

———

At the approach of midnight, Riley drove back to the station, sure that the captain would still be there, and her only concern was explaining to Moody why she'd returned. And Riley being who she was, was desperate to know if they'd tracked down Hammond. Now there were two faces she'd seen, the woman in the plant and Justin's killer, neither offering an identity and knowing both were important.

The station house was ahead and she was not wrong in her assumption. Ward was still there. In fact, it appeared Moody and a few of his men were still there as well. She wondered about Ethan and her other colleagues.

Her patrol car pulled up next to one of Moody's team and Riley stepped out. She made her way inside to find only Abrams and Decker. "Hey. Anything new happening?" she asked Decker because Abrams generally got on her nerves.

"They're still monitoring Hammond, but he's been MIA for the past few hours. I think they lost track of him."

"Yeah. With all their modern technology, you'd think those IMPD pricks could do better than that." Abrams was displaying his usual machismo.

"What about the captain?" she added.

Decker thumbed in the direction of Ward's office. "Been in there with Moody for a while. Hey, I thought you were done for the night. Wasn't that Captain's orders?"

"Since when do I obey orders?" She smiled. "What about Pruitt? He get sent home too?"

"Yep. It's just us chickens now," Abrams said.

Riley started in the direction of Ward's office, but his door opened before she reached it.

"What are you doing here?" Ward said. "I saw you pull in. Where's Jacob?"

"He's safe. I needed to see you." She peered around him in attempt to spot Moody, but he didn't emerge from the office.

Ward continued into the bullpen. "Let's go into the breakroom."

"Where's Moody?" she asked, following him closely.

"On the phone in my office. He has a lead on Hammond," Ward continued.

"About time. Maybe we can find out if he's coming here or not."

Ward stepped into the breakroom and stood with his arms folded. "Okay. What's so important you came back here, directly disobeying an order. Which, by the way, you seem to be making a habit of lately." He leaned against the countertop of the kitchenette.

"I went back to Rehnquist's apartment."

"Why would you do that? You went alone?"

"No, I didn't go alone. I brought Jacob with me, but that's beside the point," Riley said.

"Then you'd better get to the point quick."

"I was trying to figure who it was I saw who murdered Justin. We were at Carl's place and I did as you asked, logged into the system. But none of the men, at least the ones we had on file, were the killer. So I thought I could pick up something if I went back and Jacob refused to let me go alone."

"For your sake, I hope you found something worthwhile," Ward replied.

"I did. A woman. I saw a woman with Justin at the plant. She was asking Justin to bring Chloe there and that he would be paid well for doing it. But she promised him nothing would happen to her; that it was just going to be a talk, a warning. And that's all I saw. So now I have two faces—no idea who the hell they are."

"What am I supposed to do with this?" Ward appeared to mull a solution.

"I think we should try to track the numbers on this." She held out the burner phone that belonged to Rehnquist. "If we can figure out who he's been in contact with, that will bring us closer to figuring out who killed Chloe."

Ward reached for the phone. "You should've led with this. This is something we can work with. Let's get it to Moody. He'll have the resources to trace these numbers." He started back into the corridor and toward the bullpen, where he found Abrams and Decker at their desks. "You two, come with us." He continued to his office. "Moody, we've got something." Ward held out the phone. "This belonged to Justin Rehnquist, the kid who just died."

"We already have his cell phone."

"This one's a burner. If the kid was hiding something, it'll be on here," Ward replied.

"How did you get this?" Moody eyed Ward but glanced to Riley too.

"It's still my crime scene," Ward said. "Suffice it to say, we got it. Now do you want to look at this or not?"

———

CARL TAPPED HIS FINGERS ON THE ARM OF HIS RECLINER AS he eyed Jacob. "And you just let her go?"

"You do know Riley, don't you? Do you really think I could've stopped her?"

Carl groaned. "I suppose not, but you could've insisted you go along."

"I tried, Carl, I did. She's at the station with Ward."

"Something's not right. I know it and she knows it. The problem being is what the hell are we going to do about it? I feel so damn useless here in this old folks' home, which is really just a holding place for those about to die, including me."

"Carl, that's not..."

"Oh, hush, I know. I'm just frustrated as hell because I don't know what to do."

"I'm not sure there's anything we can do. Ward will take care of her, not that she needs taking care of. She's made that pretty clear."

"I'll bet she has, and then some," Carl said. "But that don't change the fact that I can't see us sitting here while she and Ward take all the risks."

"That's their job," Jacob replied.

"Well." Carl pushed slowly off the chair. "I, for one, can't sit back and wait. I won't do it, not where Riley's concerned. We're going down to the station."

"What good will that do? You know Ward will send us back here, or have his boys escort us back. Either way, we won't be there long enough to make a difference."

"Boy, I never guessed you'd be the one to give up so quickly. Of course, you were the one who left her, not the other way around."

Jacob turned thin-lipped. "Absolution is not my friend in this town. That's okay, I don't suppose I deserve it, after everything I did."

"Yeah, well, maybe you can do something about it now, show your worth," Carl said.

"How do you propose I do that?"

Carl made his way to the kitchenette for a bottled water. He tossed back half of it, then continued. "The way I see it, going to the station probably isn't the best idea I've ever had. Ward will do as you say and send us packing. So what if we tried to track down your friend, what did you say his name was? Drake or Blair or some shit?"

"Blake. His name is Blake Rhodes. You want me to call him and find out what's going on?"

"Why not?"

"I don't know how much more he'll be willing to share. Honestly, I still can't figure out whose side he's on."

"I bet he'll be choosing sides when you tell him that Rehnquist boy was killed and that you know it was on orders of the man he's with now."

"But I don't know that for sure."

Carl eyed him. "Boy, you're going to have to play like you do. You understand me? Get him talking. He learns that kid is dead and so is his girl, what do you think he'll do?" He paused while Jacob appeared to consider the question. "He'll spill the beans on their plans, won't he? He'll want retribution, believe you me. That's all anyone wants who thinks they could be next."

"Right." Jacob retrieved his cell phone. "I'll do it now."

———

RILEY PROPPED HERSELF AGAINST THE LATERAL FILING cabinet behind Ward's desk. They listened while Moody made the call to Captain Pryce.

"If we get this to IT forensics, they might be able to trace the cell towers where the calls originated. If it turns out they came from someplace near Howard or his cronies, we can start putting two and two together," Moody said into the phone.

Riley sensed this was not going well. She could see it in Moody's eyes, and he seemed to be avoiding contact with hers. Another bad sign. She looked at Ward, who returned an equally disappointed glance. This was all they had right now. When morning came, and it was speeding down the highway, they were going to have to face Virgil Howard, Roy Bayliss, and whoever was running the show at the plant, and whether that was George Hammond was still a big question mark.

"Yes, sir. I understand, Captain. I'll let them know." Moody ended the call and peered at the small town cops. "He says it'll take too long to pull the information. And it would only waste valuable manpower. Best thing to do is ride it out till morning, like we planned."

"But if we do that," Riley began, "we'll be putting lives at risk. Yours, mine, and all these guys here. Including your people staking out the plant now."

"I understand, but he says these burners take a lot of time, and more often than not amount to zilch, as he put it."

Riley eyed Ward. "Are you going to do something about this? This is still our case."

"What do you want me to do? We don't have an IT department, let alone IT forensics. Unless that burner has pictures of a potential suspect, or names, or any identifying factors at all, sounds like we got ziltch at this point. Now, I appreciate what it took for you to get this. I really do, but we're going to have to put it aside and keep to our initial plan."

"No one seems to want to put a stop to the impending blood bath." Riley pushed off the cabinet.

"What makes you think this is going to end in some sort of shootout at the O.K. Corral?" Moody asked. "I have no intentions of going in there with guns blazing looking to take people down."

"You might not, but they do," Riley began. "They're coming here looking for Jacob Biggs. They're coming to hide any trace of a connection to Chloe Dawson. Virgil Howard made sure the concrete was there and gave the order to take Chloe's life with it. I'm sure of it. What I don't know is why you can't find George Hammond. He's the key to this and you know it as well as I do."

THE RAIN FELL IN HEAVY DROPS AS HAMMOND DROVE A CAR that was not his own. He fumbled for a moment to figure out how to turn on the wiper blades and finally, they began to clear the windshield. His meeting was going to be a wet one, but in light of the present situation, what the hell did that matter? Hammond was being hunted by those on both sides of the fence and the outcome wasn't looking to break in his favor.

The prearranged location was just ahead and he noticed he was the last to arrive, meaning he hadn't been left to hang out to dry—just yet.

"I wasn't entirely sure you were going to show. We haven't heard from you in two days." The man placed a piece of gum in his mouth. "Figured you might just drive on through."

"Thought about it for a second." Hammond figured the gum was one of those nicotine gums designed to help quit smoking. "Don't suppose you got a cig on you? I could really use one right about now."

"No sir. Trying to quit." The man walked toward the sidewalk with a covered awning. "Let's get out of the rain, shall we?"

Hammond followed him. "Where the hell am I supposed to go? They got the entire force looking for me."

"I wouldn't worry as much about the cops as I would your colleagues. The cops won't shoot you. Can't say the same about your own people. You really screwed the pooch, didn't you?"

"Doesn't help when they're one in the same. Look, I need to know my family is safe before I agree to anything else." Hammond glossed over the truth that had been so eloquently stated.

"I'm working on making that happen, but as you know, we have to keep a low profile until this blows over."

"Blows over? With these guys, things don't just 'blow over.' I'd think you of all people would know that." Hammond cast his sights toward the street, watching the rain bounce off the asphalt. "You people were supposed to protect me."

"We did, until you decided you couldn't keep your pants on. This isn't on us."

"I see. So whatever I can offer doesn't matter to you at all? Is that what you're saying? After I've been cooperative for the past few months? Guess I should've figured as much."

"Just keep your panties on. I'm working on getting you someplace to hunker down. And your family. But right now, we're trying to make sure IMPD doesn't get wind of the fact that we're pulling the strings. That happens and your family is toast. Now we know you don't want that."

"Fine. So get me the fuck out of here and do what you need to do to end this." Hammond was losing his patience with this man who did nothing but make promises.

"As I said, we're working on that. In the meantime, stay off the grid. I'll reach out to you soon." The man spit out his gum. "This stuff doesn't work for shit." He began to walk away, but stopped short. "Regardless of what you might think, your intel will lead us to the man we're after."

"And what about the dead girl?"

"We'll get to the bottom of that too." He started away again.

———

JACOB STOOD OUTSIDE ON THE SMALL BALCONY OF CARL'S apartment. He wanted a drink and a smoke, though he wasn't a smoker, but neither were available to him at the moment. Instead, he'd have to make the call sober, with all cylinders at full speed.

With the exception of the other day when he'd held those men at gunpoint, never in his life had he been the type to be good in a situation like this. But he surprised even himself at the way he handled the so-called meeting with those men. So perhaps now he could summon that same mettle and push through the phone call that would force Blake to, once and for all, take a side. And if it wasn't Jacob's, then so be it.

Jacob held his phone and typed in the message. "Can you talk? Urgent." He pressed send and waited. For a moment, he considered the idea that Ward could track down Blake's location using his cell number, then have IMPD storm the place, if that was possible. That would bring all this to an end. But there was still the question of George Hammond. And he still believed Blake might know how to find him, that they were working together somehow. With Hammond still out there, Jacob would always look over his shoulder. And that wasn't something he wanted to consider for the rest of his life. No. This was the way it needed to play out. He had to convince Blake to turn on these men and give up Hammond. With Rehnquist dead, he might accomplish just that.

Jacob was pleased Carl saw his initial plan to go to the station as a mistake. The last thing he wanted to do was drag the old man around town, risking his safety, because if he let something happen to Carl, Riley would never forgive him. Hell, she hadn't forgiven him for leaving in the first place.

Blake replied to his message. "I'm walking outside now. I'll call you."

"Okay." Jacob steadied himself. "Let's do this." He waited for a moment when his phone rang. He answered the call. "Blake?"

"Dude, this wasn't the plan. I said I'd call you with news. I don't have news, brother. Plan's the same as it was a few hours ago."

"That's not what I need to talk to you about. Look, man, you know Chloe's friend, Justin Rehnquist? You mentioned him before?"

"What about him?"

"They found his body earlier tonight in his apartment. Someone tried to make it look like a suicide, but the cops here don't think it was."

"What the fuck? Are you sure?"

"Yeah, man, I'm sure. Dude, this is messed up. Who would've killed that guy? Why?" Jacob waited while the line went silent for a moment.

Blake began to reply, "Shit, I don't know. I mean—fuck, I don't know."

He heard the panic rise in Blake's tone and now the time had come to put the nail in the coffin. "That's not the worst of it. Blake, Chloe was pregnant. I saw a text message from her myself to Rehnquist. I have to assume it was yours."

"Do not screw around with me, Jake."

"I'm not, bro. You gotta do something about this. It had to be one of your people up there."

"No way. No one even knew her or Justin."

"Wait, I thought Hammond knew her? Didn't she come into the office a few times to see you?" Jacob said.

"Well, yeah, but she probably said two words to him the whole time."

"You sure about that, man? You know what George is like. He takes what he wants. Just like he took the sixty grand."

"No fucking way. I don't believe you," Blake replied.

"You don't have to believe me. I'll show you the messages. Look, man, the only other conclusion would be that the kid wasn't yours—and she's dead. So is her friend. You can put that puzzle together, can't you?"

"I gotta get down there. I have to see what the hell you're talking about."

"Can you get away or are you being watched?" Jacob waited while it seemed Blake was pondering the question. Maybe he'd planted the seed well enough to take root. "You need to find Hammond and find out what the hell is going on. And you got an opportunity to turn the tables on Howard. Someone knows what the real story is and I think someone is protecting Hammond and Virgil Howard. Maybe they don't want you to know the truth. They want to keep you on a short leash until they get their money. And who knows, maybe Kelly lied to me. Maybe she does know where George is."

"If what you're saying is true, she wouldn't have known about Chloe. I can't believe it myself. Look. I'll figure this shit out. I'll call you back."

The line went dead and Jacob smiled. "Guess I could do it." He walked back inside.

Carl eyed him as he closed the sliding door. "You look like the cat that ate the canary."

"I got him on the hook. I got him thinking it could've been Hammond and everyone's about to hang him out to dry. And I told him Chloe was pregnant."

"She was? Damn, that poor girl. You best get on the horn with Riley. She'll want to know about this."

Moody's expression over the question of his department's ability to locate Hammond appeared as though she'd struck a chord of doubt in him. And as Riley awaited his reply, she noticed a text appear on her phone. It was from Jacob, and as she read it, she realized that he had just jeopardized his own safety. He'd told Blake about Chloe's pregnancy. This was something she had yet to reveal to Ward, primarily because it wasn't officially determined by the coroner's office yet. But also, because not only had Chloe not shown this major life event to Riley at their previous encounter, Riley hadn't picked up on it either. And this too gave her pause. Was Chloe telling the truth to Justin?

"Thompson? You okay?" Ward appeared concerned by her silence as she stared intently at her phone.

She glanced at him before turning to Moody. A way out of this might have just presented itself. "Lieutenant Moody, do you have any contacts, outside the usual ones, who could help you track down a name or location if I give you a number that had called Justin's burner phone?"

"Given that Pryce has already made clear he doesn't care about the burner, you want me to disobey orders from him?"

"It's not a matter of want. It's a matter of need. And I think you know that. I think you've known that for a while now." Riley felt that seed of doubt in Moody growing. He was a man conflicted and she only needed to nudge him.

"There might be someone I can call," he checked the time, "who might still be awake at this hour."

"Then we should get on it now, before we're out of time," Ward said.

Moody headed outside to make the call where his men couldn't overhear. Ward and Riley returned to the bullpen and waited.

"You saw something, didn't you?" Ward asked.

"Picked up on it, more like. I don't think Moody trusts Pryce, not entirely. But there's something else you should know too." Riley showed him Jacob's message. "He's trying to turn Blake against the people he's with. And he might have accomplished his goal. Captain, Chloe Dawson was pregnant."

"Are you sure?"

"Well, on that burner phone, we saw messages from her to Justin. She told him she was. Whether that was true, I don't know."

"Oh my Lord. That poor girl. What on earth did she get wrapped up in?"

"We need to find out because I'm getting the feeling that Pryce is willing to put everyone at risk to get his man—whoever that might be."

Moody returned inside. He eyed Abrams and Decker, who seemed to be watching his every move.

Riley noticed his return and waited for his approach. "What's the verdict?"

"I've got a guy. I'll send him the information now."

———

CAPTAIN WARD STOOD OUTSIDE THE DOORS OF THE coroner's office at an hour when he should have been sleeping. But what Riley said rattled him because if this girl had been pregnant, that would change everything. Her case would become a multiple homicide.

A car approached, and it could only have been the doctor Ward called upon leaving the station. He'd asked Riley to stay put and assist Moody in any way she could. But what he really wanted from her was for her to watch Moody's every move. She would know whose side he was on pretty quickly, depending upon how he chose to handle this situation with his own captain.

The doctor stepped out of his car and pulled his coat around him, thrusting his hands in his pockets.

"Thanks for coming down, Doc. I know it's late."

"I figure it must be important." The doctor unlocked the door and walked inside the dark office, switching on the lights. "If what you're thinking turns out to be true, that sure will change things for your investigation."

Ward followed him inside. "Yes, it will. That's why this couldn't wait. I have to know for sure."

"Then we'd best go find out." The doctor continued into the corridor, flipping on the lights as they walked through. Eventually, he approached the room where Chloe was still being kept on ice. "The autopsy hasn't been performed yet, but I can draw additional blood and test for the presence of the pregnancy hormone until such time as I can complete the autopsy and take a look."

"How long do you think it will take to get the results back?" Ward asked.

"On a pregnancy test? Minutes. We're going to find out right now." The doctor pulled Chloe from her steel cabinet and folded down the sheet to her chest. With a careful touch, he exposed her right arm and drew the blood.

"So, even after her death, you'd still be able to detect the hormone?"

"Absolutely. I could also perform an ultrasound, but if this girl was pregnant, God forbid, she wasn't far along and probably not far enough along to see anything inside. So we'll go this route first." He began to draw the blood and turned back to Ward. "How did you discover this news?"

"We found a cell phone and she told someone she was pregnant. That someone is now dead."

"Justin Rehnquist. The young man you brought in earlier?"

"That's right. They're linked."

"So, would he be the father?" the doctor asked.

"I don't know, but I doubt it. Unfortunately, I think it may be a little more insidious than that. I think this girl was caught up with what we think could be the mafia."

"Well, that's not something we see every day here in Owensville."

"No, sir. It is not," Ward replied.

The doctor withdrew the vial and started toward the back room, where it would be tested. "Let's see what she'll show us."

Ward followed him inside the small lab. "I really should consider spending more time with you. These are things I should probably learn."

"It's not like we have a daily or even monthly need for such things. But that appears to be changing." He began to test the sample. "This shouldn't take long. I wouldn't mind a coffee from the machine if you'd like to grab some for us?"

"After dragging you down here at one in the morning, it's the least I can do." Ward stepped into the hall toward the coffee machine. It was usually horrible stuff that came out of these machines, but it would help keep him awake.

Upon his return, he held two paper cups in his hands. "Here you go."

"Just set it over there if you would." The doctor observed the results. "I'm sorry to say, Captain, but Chloe Dawson was indeed pregnant. And given these increased levels of the HCG hormone, I'd say she was roughly four weeks at time of death. Not enough to see on autopsy, but enough to pick up in the bloodwork."

"Damn. This wasn't the conclusion I was looking for, Doc. Now we're dealing with three murders. And I don't have a clue who's responsible."

———

SMOKE FROM HIS CIGARETTE DRIFTED INTO THE NIGHT SKY AS Blake stood on the balcony of the apartment where they were holed up until morning. He considered what Jacob had said, wondered if he'd been lied to; not by Jacob, but by the man running the show, which, for him, was Virgil Howard. It was he who convinced Blake that Jacob could draw Hammond out of the woodwork, or had it been a ruse? To what end, he didn't know. But his girlfriend was dead and now he believed she was pregnant, a troubling revelation that made Blake feel queasy at the mere thought of it.

But the question remained, who killed her? Why? Now that these ideas swirled in his head, he couldn't think clearly. All he could see was Chloe with a swollen belly, not the girl who now lay in a morgue, concrete still stuck to her body and inside her mouth. So how could he get to the truth? Morning was only a few hours away, when they would head to the plant to destroy any remaining evidence and to find Jacob—and kill him. But not before doing what it took to get him to talk about Hammond. Blake didn't know what was more important to Virgil: getting revenge for Costa's death or finding George Hammond. Right now, he didn't care. Right now, he was feeling more certain that Hammond had played a role in Chloe's death. Jacob was onto something. The two had met. And Howard didn't know about Chloe. Yeah, it was starting to look like Hammond did the deed. Now Blake had to take matters into his own hands and find him and it had to be before Virgil did. Because once that happened, there might not be anything left of him to answer the questions Blake had. And there was only one person he could turn to.

He pressed the end of his cigarette onto the wrought-iron bars of the balcony. He turned and peered inside, where a couple of the men were still awake and playing video games. But not Virgil; he'd gone to bed. The time for him to break away was now.

He walked inside and looked at the men who hadn't noticed his return. "I'm going to get some food. I'm starving. You guys want anything?" When they didn't reply, Blake grabbed his car keys and walked out the door.

Getting to Kelly Hammond, George's wife, was the first step. Jacob had tried but was unsuccessful. But that was because he didn't know what George was involved with; Blake knew all too well. This would work to his advantage when it came to Kelly. She wouldn't want to pay for her husband's mistakes. It was unclear if she'd been approached by Virgil Howard. In fact, it seemed strange to Blake that she wouldn't have been at the top of the list when it came to tracking down her husband. Perhaps she had been confronted before Blake was dragged into this when George disappeared. And then of course, he turned tail and pointed directly at Jacob. Something he now regretted. This entire thing was so screwed up. Chloe was gone. That stupid friend of hers was gone. Blake no longer knew where he stood or with whom.

It was a thirty-minute drive that would put Blake at Kelly Hammond's house at roughly 2am. The children would be asleep and so would she. And Blake wasn't a monster. He would do everything in his power not to disturb or frighten those kids. All he wanted was to know where George was and if he had anything to do with Chloe's death. And if she didn't offer information, then he would revise his technique. He had options—she didn't.

He contemplated his plan of action and carefully considered the words he would use to get his point across. And, he had a gun, if necessary, to reinforce his point.

———

On arrival to the gated home, Blake pressed the intercom button. No answer. He tried again, this time, pressing the button longer. She was there. She had no place else to go. Finally, a groggy tone sounded through the speakers. "Blake? What are you doing here? It's two in the morning."

Blake eyed the security camera mounted on the gate's column. "We need to talk, Kelly. Please. It's important."

"I already told Jacob I don't know where George is. You need to leave, Blake."

"Not until we talk. Kelly, I know about Chloe Dawson. And I bet you do too." He waited to see if she would take the bait.

The gates started to swing open and Blake returned to his car, pulling inside the circular driveway until he reached the front of the home. As he stepped out, Kelly opened the door, wrapped in a long bathrobe with her arms folded and an expression that suggested she knew exactly who Chloe was.

"I'm sorry it's so late, but I had to see you." Blake approached her.

Without a word, Kelly stepped aside to let him in, closing the door behind him. "Let's go into the study to talk. I don't want to wake the kids."

Blake followed her into a grand room lined with cherry bookcases and a large, ornate desk. A small seating area fronted the fireplace and he followed her to one of the chairs.

"Can I get you a coffee or water?"

"No, thank you. I need to ask you something important and I need you to be honest with me." At this, he pulled open his jacket just enough to reveal his sidearm.

She eyed it but didn't seem distressed by the reveal. "Like I said, I don't know where he is. Jake came by looking for him and I told him the same thing—after he hopped my fence, of course. I don't know where that son of a bitch went. He cleaned out our accounts and he's gone. No note. No text. Nothing. I haven't told the kids yet. I don't know how to."

Blake sat down on the chair. "Kelly, I have to know, were you aware if George was seeing a girl named Chloe Dawson?"

"No, I wasn't aware, but it sounds like you are. Care to let me in on the secret?"

He hadn't expected that response. He regarded her with concern and believed she could be lying. "It would be helpful for you to be honest with me. You know the people George worked with. The people George has pissed off by deserting."

"Oh, I have a feeling it's all part of the game. I knew what he was up to. He's been working with those people for too long not to be noticed." She looked around. "I mean, do you really think the owner of a small architecture firm could acquire a place like this? You're not stupid, Blake."

"Where is he, Kelly? You have to know because I don't believe he would've left you and the kids without warning. Especially to deal with the likes of Virgil Howard. He loved you."

She laughed. "Really? He had a funny way of showing it. I don't know where he is, Blake. I'm not sure how many different ways I can say the same thing. And as far as this woman you're asking about, I wouldn't put it past him to have an affair. But if he was, I was in the dark about it. Just as you are about his where-abouts. Just as we all are."

Blake reached into his jacket and pulled his weapon. "Please don't make me do this, Kelly. It's not what I want."

She eyed the gun and a hint of fear flashed in her eyes. "I'm sorry, Blake. I don't know. You have to believe me."

He shook his head. "You know what, Kelly? I don't. I think you know a lot. And it's time you fessed up. I'm pretty sure your kids would be lost without their father—and mother."

———————

The captain returned to the station and tracked down Riley, who was still with Moody.

"You're back." Riley pushed from the desk where she sat with the lieutenant. "Well?"

"It was positive. Chloe Dawson was pregnant, about four weeks, according to the blood test."

"Christ." Moody appeared as disheartened by the news as Riley had been. "So now we've got a multiple homicide on our hands and that doesn't include the Rehnquist boy."

"Appears so," Ward replied. "Please tell me you two got somewhere with Rehnquist's phone."

"I sent my guy the numbers. We're still waiting on a response. He said it would take a couple of hours," Moody replied.

"We don't have a couple of hours."

"Captain, this isn't something we have control over, not this time." Riley turned to Moody. "But once we get the intel, it should open this up for us, right?"

"It'll tell us who this kid was talking to and what part he played in the death of that girl, and her unborn child, if any."

Riley, of course, had some idea. She'd seen it, but explaining that to Moody wasn't something she could do. It would have to be proven and that was what they were waiting for now.

"Riley, can I have a quick word?" Ward asked.

"Sure. You'll excuse us, Lieutenant?" Riley followed Ward back to his office. "What's wrong?"

Ward closed his door. "Any word from Jacob about this Blake Rhodes situation?"

"No, he's still waiting. He's getting antsy, though."

"We all are. What we know now changes things. We have no real leads on this girl's death, except for what you saw, and we can't use that."

"Especially since I don't recognize the woman or the man who killed Justin. I feel completely useless right now."

"Don't. If it weren't for what you've discovered so far, we wouldn't know about Chloe's baby. But I need you to remember that Moody can't get suspicious. You have to watch what you say around him."

"I know..." Riley swung around as Moody rushed inside.

"We've got a name. Come quick." Moody led the way to the workstation and turned the monitor so they could see it.

Riley stood behind him and peered at the screen. "Wait. What the hell is this?"

"What'd you all find?" Abrams moseyed over.

"And your guy is certain this is who was in contact with Rehnquist?" Ward asked.

"Pretty damn certain." Moody eyed the two of them. "So do we go after Hammond's wife now or wait until morning?"

[23]

The clock on the satellite TV box in Carl's apartment flashed 12:00. The red glare hadn't prevented Carl from drifting off to sleep in his recliner, however, it forced Jacob to continually check his phone for the actual time. His anticipation was palpable while he waited for news from Riley.

It was past two in the morning and no word from Blake. Jacob wondered if he'd planted the idea well enough to lure his colleague into turning against Howard and spilling the beans on their entire operation.

Jacob pushed off the side chair quietly in an effort not to disturb Carl. The time had come for him to take action. He was going to have to steal the old man's car. Perhaps "steal" wasn't the right word in this instance. "Borrow" might be better suited and sounded far less devious.

He walked to the kitchenette and grabbed the car keys from a bowl on the counter before slipping out the door and locking it behind him. The old car was inside the storage unit where Riley left it and that was where Jacob was headed.

In the alleyway, he raised the storage unit's door. The old beast waited, ready to be put back into action. Jacob slipped into the driver's seat and keyed the ignition. Adjusting the rear-view, he peered into the alleyway, knowing the narrow garage left little room for error. He reversed the green monster out, getting clear of the storage unit and closing the door behind him.

The town was asleep as Jacob rolled along the streets with no clue as to a destination. Perhaps he should have laid out a better plan. "Blake," Jacob said. He was going to have to make contact and determine if in fact he'd swayed his former partner enough to take action. With his cell phone in hand, he texted Blake and waited for a reply.

A brief reply came and read, *"at Hammond's home."*

It turned out, Jacob had been able to plant enough doubt to force Blake's hand. Only this hadn't been the desired outcome. Jacob eyed the road ahead, illuminated by the yellow lights of the old Lincoln, feeling just as impotent as he had sitting in Carl's home for the elderly. And then she called. "Riley," he answered the line. "I was wondering when you were going to call. What's happening?"

"Looks like Moody's an ally after all," Riley said.

"What's that?"

"I'll explain later. Suffice it to say that Moody's decided to put his resources to better use. He found a name associated with a cell number that appeared on Justin's burner multiple times. Jacob, the number belongs to Kelly Hammond."

"George's wife knew Rehnquist?"

"She knew him, very well, in fact. Moody retrieved her social media information and found a picture of her. She's the woman I saw at the plant with Justin. She's the one who convinced him to bring Chloe there."

Jacob slowed to a crawl on the road, stunned by the revelation. "Oh my God."

"He made the call to Captain Pryce to relay the news, figuring he was going to be reprimanded for going against orders, so he was surprised instead when Pryce said he was going to bring in Mrs. Hammond for questioning," Riley continued.

Jacob immediately thought of Blake. "Um, Riley, there's something you should know."

"Yeah?"

"Blake Rhodes is with Kelly Hammond right now. You remember what we talked about earlier? Well, turns out I was able to convince Blake that he should consider the idea George was behind Chloe's death and that was the real reason he fled with the money. And if he had any way of knowing how to draw George out of hiding, then he needed to do so."

"He's there? Right now?"

"Yes."

"And Pryce's team will be there within minutes, I imagine," Riley added.

"What does this mean for Blake?"

"Jacob, he's going to be arrested. He's part of the group. Pryce is after these guys, like, hard after them. I don't know how far he'll go. My guess is, pretty damn far."

"Should I warn Blake?"

"That depends. He's involved in this. He was the one who

helped to frame you. Do you want to see him free or pay for leading Virgil Howard to your girlfriend, and to you?"

Jacob considered her question. Blake had deceived him already and had almost cost his life and Rachel's. Regardless of what George had done, did Blake deserve a get-out-of-jail-free card?

"Well?" Riley asked.

"If he gets arrested along with Hammond's wife, we might never find George. He'll always be out there and I'll always be looking over my shoulder."

"The good news is, if Blake or Kelly Hammond know where George is, they'll use that information as a bargaining chip. Pryce will get George Hammond one way or another. Blake doesn't deserve to get out of this, no matter that he suddenly found a conscience because his girlfriend and possibly his child were found murdered. We'll get justice for Chloe. Blake can go to hell, for all I care."

Jacob was silent while he pondered her reasoning.

"Where are you right now, Jacob? Please tell me you're still with Carl?"

He broke his silence. "I can't do that."

"Jacob."

He heard the disappointment in her voice. It was the same disappointment he'd heard years ago when he decided to leave Owensville. "I couldn't stay there. I thought if I could just figure out what Blake had planned, maybe meet up with him if he'd been able to get a line on Hammond, then I could track him down."

"You can't trust him, Jacob. You know that. He's been playing you since the start of this. Please, go back to Carl's. Let Pryce handle Kelly Hammond, and if Blake is there, then so be it. If you're there too, you could end up in as much trouble as Blake. He dragged you into this and there's no telling what he'll say just to save his own ass."

"Riley. I'm sorry. These men won't stop until they get from me the money or my life. They'll come after me so long as they think I stole from them. And they might use you to get to me if that fails. I won't let that happen." He ended the call and pulled back onto the road.

"Jacob? Jacob? This isn't about the money anymore!" Riley shouted into her phone as she stood outside the station house, freezing in the cold night air. "Shit!" She marched back inside.

"Whoa. What's wrong with you?" Decker asked.

"I need to leave." She ripped the jacket off the back of her chair before brushing past him and back toward the door.

"Um, okay. Where are you going in case Captain asks?"

She stopped in her tracks and spun around. "Tell him I have to stop Jacob." Riley continued outside and stepped into her patrol car.

————

WITHIN MINUTES, SHE'D ARRIVED AT HER DESTINATION AND headed to the front door. She knocked, and a moment later, the porch light flickered on and the door opened.

"Hey, I need you. Can you come with me?" Riley asked.

"Where are you going?" Ethan rubbed his eyes. "What time is it anyway?"

"It's late. Ethan, I need your help." She held his gaze with a deadly stare.

"Okay. I need to put some pants on. I'll be right back."

She waited at the door, peering inside until Ethan returned, fully dressed. "Grab your weapon."

He turned back and retrieved his holster before buckling it to his waist. Ethan began to follow her out. "Riley, you need to tell me what the hell is going on."

"I'll fill you in on the drive," Riley said.

"The drive to where?"

"Get in." Riley stepped inside the car, and after Ethan joined her, turned the ignition and sped down the quiet road.

Ethan appeared to be waiting for her to reveal their destination and why she was doing this alone at 2:30 in the morning. "You know those guys are supposed to be coming in the morning. Are we going to the plant? Did you get something on a location?"

"No. We're going to the city."

"Why are we going there?" he asked.

"Because that's where Jacob is going."

———

"WHAT?" WARD SLAMMED HIS FIST ON HIS DESK.

"She said she was going to stop Jacob Biggs. I thought he was with Carl Boyd. I have no idea what changed," Decker replied.

"You try Pruitt yet? She would go to him for backup."

"No, sir. I came straight to you."

"I have a feeling I know where she's going." Ward picked up his phone. "I'll call her now. Go on. I'll take care of this. See what you can do to help the lieutenant."

"Yes, sir." Decker left.

The captain waited while the line rang, but it went to voicemail. "Damn it!" When the message finished, he spoke. "Riley, you'd better call me back and I mean like pronto, you understand? There are things in motion that I can't stop. I can only guess where you and Pruitt are headed and you both could be stepping into something I'll have no control over. Call me back!" He ended the call.

Lieutenant Moody knocked on the opened door. "Captain Ward, is everything all right?"

Ward considered telling him, but these were his people. He would get them back. "Yes, it's fine. Any news on your end?"

"Pryce has organized a team and they'll be heading to Kelly Hammond's home inside the hour. I hope I did the right thing."

"What? Of course you did."

"I just have a bad feeling about this."

"What are you not telling me, Moody?"

"Look, your officer—Thompson. She's smart. And I think she might've figured out that I don't entirely trust Pryce."

"Okay. Care to tell me why?"

"I don't have anything concrete, but maybe after tonight I will."

———

KELLY HAMMOND STARED AT THE GUN NOW AIMED AT HER and the man who held it, a mediocre structural engineer who was easily led by her husband, the now disappeared George Hammond. "You seem to be a lot of things, Blake, but a killer doesn't appear to be one of them. George talked about you—the work you did. The way you always kissed his ass. He had zero respect for you. Just thought you might like to know that."

Blake chuckled. "I might be a kiss-ass, but I'm not an idiot. You really think your words are going to change my mind? That I'll just put away the gun and walk out of here? I don't think you know me at all, Kelly. I know who George is, though. I know he was sleeping with my girlfriend and got her pregnant." He noticed the glare in her eyes. "Yep. He was cheating on you and then killed the girl because she was carrying his child. My girlfriend."

"Doesn't sound like she was much of a girlfriend if she was cheating on you too. And what gives you the idea George did this? Do you have proof of a relationship? Do you have proof he was the father of this baby?"

Blake didn't, and the only evidence he had was hearsay from a man he tried to frame. "I'll tell you what, you let me know where George is and I'll ask him."

"I told you, I don't have a goddam clue where my husband is. You want to check my phone? He hasn't called me in two days. You want me to show you my bank account? Because it's empty. So you tell me, Blake, do you really think after what George just did that I'd hesitate one iota to tell you where you could find that asshole? And on top of that, you're calling him a cheater. All the more reason to have you take care of him for me, which is what I assume you want to do. Am I correct?"

"Mommy?" A girl appeared at the top of the stairs.

Blake eyed Kelly and noticed panic sweep through her.

"Go back to bed, sweetheart. Everything's fine."

"You sure about that, Kelly?" Blake eyed the girl. "Hi, sweetheart. I'm a friend of your daddy. Why don't you come here for a minute?"

Kelly smiled at her daughter. "Oh, he's only joking, baby. Go on back to bed now. He'll be leaving soon."

"No, really, I think I'd like to talk to her." Blake aimed the weapon at Kelly while keeping it from the girl's sight. "Come here for a second. What's your name?"

"Zoe."

"Well, hello, Zoe. I'm Blake. I worked for your dad. How old are you?"

"Six."

"It's very nice to meet you, Zoe. I was just talking to your mom. Do you happen to know where your dad is? I need to give him back something very important. I'm sure he'll need it."

"I know where Daddy's at. He calls me every day. He had to go away on business, but he's coming home soon."

"Is he? Well, I'm sure you'll be glad about that. But where is he now?" Blake continued.

The girl looked at her mother.

"Your mommy doesn't seem to know," Blake said. "So why don't you tell me?"

"Blake, she's six. George hasn't called her. She's making that up. I swear to you."

"He said he was in Columbus."

"Ohio? I see. That sounds exciting. And you say you've talked to him?"

"Sure. He gave me a special phone just so he could call me."

"Really? Could I see that phone?" Blake asked.

"She's just a child, Blake. This is a game to her. You have to believe me. She doesn't know where George is." Kelly looked again to her daughter, trying to convey calm.

"It's in my room. I'll go get it." The girl turned and ran back up the staircase.

"Please leave her alone. I'll tell you what you want to know. I'll tell you where George is. Just don't hurt my children."

Just as the girl disappeared up the staircase, a loud crack sounded. The door burst open and men in uniform spilled inside, yelling and shouting orders.

"Get down!" One of them held an assault rifle and made his way to Blake and Kelly Hammond.

"Jesus!" Blake dropped his gun.

"On your knees! On your knees! Both of you. Now!" Another officer rushed inside.

Two others entered the home.

"My children!" Kelly yelled. "Don't hurt them!"

"Mommy!" Zoe ran back down the stairs, dropping the play phone in her hands.

One of the officers spun in her direction. The girl screamed and lost her balance. She tumbled down the steps and collapsed on the landing.

"Zoe!" Kelly stood. "She's hurt! Help her!"

"Get down now!" The officer aimed his rifle at her head and approached. "Kelly Hammond, you're under arrest."

"What for?"

"For the murder of Chloe Dawson."

Blake, who was already on his knees with his hands behind his head, looked to her. "What the fuck?"

"Sir? Sir? Over here!" An officer was attending to the young girl. "We need an ambulance. She's not breathing, sir!"

Captain Dave Pryce entered the home and holstered his weapon. "Jesus. Get that girl to a hospital." He approached the other officers, who were keeping Blake and Kelly at gunpoint.

"What did you do?" Kelly screamed at him. "My baby! What did you do to her?"

"You take this one." Pryce eyed Blake. "I'll get her out of here."

"Yes, sir, Captain."

Kelly spilled tears, her face heated as she shouted. "I swear to God, I'll tell them what you did! You'd better pray my baby is okay."

Blake witnessed the exchange as he was being yanked up by the officer. His face masked in confusion. "What the...?"

[24]

The Indianapolis Metropolitan Police Department headquarters exhibited an orderly mien for a station that was the busiest in the whole of the city. And now Blake Rhodes was part of that outward calm. He was placed in a holding cell for a charge that hadn't yet been disclosed. What was more troubling was that he didn't know what had happened to the woman, Kelly Hammond, or her little girl, Zoe.

The situation had grown out of control. Blake had no way of reaching Jacob to warn him. He was about to find himself in the middle of what appeared to be some sort of setup that could involve George's wife and Captain Pryce, a theory that seemed beyond anything Blake could have considered. And now he wished he'd never gotten caught up in any of this. But it was much too late for that now.

There were other, more pressing concerns he pondered at the moment. The idea a captain at the IMPD was behind any of this was beyond troubling. And if Pryce needed to shield himself from exposure, he would do so at any cost, meaning Blake might be here for a while.

"Rhodes." An officer stood at the bars of the holding cell.

Blake approached him. "I'm Blake Rhodes."

The officer opened the door. "Come with me."

He started toward another area of the vast station house, leaving Blake to wonder where he was being taken. No charges had been set. He knew enough and had been inside enough police stations to know the drill. Though it had been some time, and in his younger years, this seemed out of place. "Am I being charged with something, Officer?"

The cop peered over his shoulder, eyeing Blake only briefly before returning his attention to his destined path.

This wasn't a good sign. The cop wasn't talking. Hindsight being what it was, Blake considered perhaps he'd given his loyalty to the wrong people. And with Jacob out there on his own, Blake had little doubt he would find himself in a similar situation, perhaps worse.

———

ETHAN PEERED AT RILEY FROM THE CORNER OF HIS EYE. SHE was weary but imbued with a determination he hadn't seen in her before. With the late hour, he was concerned for her mental state, and his own, if he was being honest. "Do you want me to drive? You look like you could use a break to close your eyes for a minute."

"No, I'm fine. We're almost there. Do me a favor, though. Try

Jacob again for me? I think he's headed to the Hammond home, but I need to know for sure."

"Why would he go there?"

"Because he's working with Blake Rhodes. They think they can track down Hammond themselves and my guess is they'll be after his wife for information."

"You mean the wife who's responsible for Chloe's death?" Ethan retrieved his cell.

"Use mine. He'll be more likely to answer if he thinks it's me."

"Okay." His tone was laced with exasperation. With the phone to his ear, he waited as the line rang. "Three rings."

"Give him a chance. Just wait," Riley replied.

"Riley?" Jacob answered.

"Where are you?" Ethan didn't correct him but laid into the important question at the heart of the matter.

"Who's this?"

"Ethan. I'm with Riley and we're headed into the city. Where are you?"

"Let me talk to Riley."

"He's insisting he speak to you," Ethan said to her.

"Put him on speaker."

Ethan pressed the speaker button. "You're on speaker. We need to know where you are, Jacob."

"Riley, what are you doing? I told you I would take care of this. You two need to go back to Owensville. I can't guarantee your safety here."

"We're the trained officers, Jacob," Riley said. "Tell me you're not headed to Kelly Hammond's house."

He was silent.

"That's that I thought. We're twenty minutes away. Have you heard from Blake?"

"No. I tried him but didn't get an answer."

"That's a bad omen, Jacob. How far away are you? We need to meet up ahead of this and figure out a plan."

"Just let me handle this, Riley, okay? I don't want you here, either of you. Go back home. You have enough to deal with there."

She shook her head. "Then we'll head to her house directly. I won't let you go there alone. IMPD is sending a team. They may already be there. If you get caught in the crossfire, I don't know what will happen." It seemed as though she might have gotten through to him. She eyed Ethan and he appeared to agree.

"I'm going to the house and you'd be better off if you didn't follow me." The line clicked and he was gone.

"Damn it!" Riley said. "We'll have to go straight there."

"Can we touch base with Ward to find out what's happening with Pryce's raid?" Ethan began. "If we get caught up in that, the captain will have our heads. This isn't our jurisdiction. This isn't even our case. We're supposed to be solving the murders of Chloe Dawson and now Justin Rehnquist."

"Seems like Kelly Hammond is a big part of solving that. I realize the captain won't be happy."

"That's the understatement of the year," Ethan added.

"We'll call him now. It's possible this is already over if Pryce's team made it ahead of us—and Jacob."

Ethan called Ward's cell phone and placed the call on speaker. The captain answered immediately but spoke before Ethan could get a word out.

"Riley, you and Pruitt better get back here and I mean now!"

"Captain, we made contact with Jacob. He's heading to the

Hammond house, where he's supposed to meet up with Blake Rhodes. They think the wife knows where George Hammond is."

"Well, you two are a day late and a dollar short. Pryce's team already raided the home and placed Rhodes and Mrs. Hammond under arrest. Both are being transported back to the IMPD head-quarters. So there's no need for either of you to be there. Just get your asses back here!" He ended the call.

Ethan's mouth hung open. "Yeah, he's pissed. Riley, it sounds like we're too late anyway. Maybe we should go back. You said yourself that your biggest concern was Ward. That you felt he was going to be in danger at the plant."

"I know. And I still believe that. But what if this is what I have to do to stop it? What do you think Virgil Howard's men are going to do when word reaches them about Pryce's raid on the Hammond home? George Hammond might have left something behind that could implicate Howard and the operation. Pryce has been watching these people for a year. You don't think he'll do everything in his power to find proof, real or otherwise? From what I've derived from Moody, I don't think Pryce is beyond doing what he has to do to get what he wants."

"That doesn't solve the current problem. We need to get back."

"I can't, not until we find Jacob. When we bring him back with us, then fine. Job done."

"Look, I've always stood behind you. If this is what you truly believe needs to happen, then I'll stand behind you again. Ward can't fire us both, right?" He spotted her look. "Okay, maybe he can, but I don't think he will. So we'll do what you say, go to the house and bring Jacob back with us. I don't know if any of this will stop Howard and his men from returning to town. Maybe it will if they know we have Jacob under our protection. Or if they know Hammond's wife is in custody. Time will tell."

———

JACOB PULLED UP TO THE HAMMOND HOUSE IN CARL'S GREEN monster. He had expected to see the gates closed, but they weren't. They'd been pushed open and appeared broken, a sign the IMPD had beaten him to the punch. But what remained unclear was Blake's whereabouts. Had he been taking into custody along with Kelly Hammond?

He continued inside the grounds and drove along the circular driveway. There was only one car and it didn't appear to be a cop car. Or if it was, it was unmarked. Had the raid ended already?

Jacob stepped out of the car and suddenly felt ill-prepared, naked even. No weapon at his disposal. Perhaps he should have waited for Riley and Ethan; at least they were armed officers. He was just a civilian, but one who desperately needed his life back. He might be too late for that now. If Blake was gone and Kelly, where would that leave him?

It appeared the home was still occupied. Maybe someone was still searching for evidence against Hammond. Now that they figured his wife had something to do with Chloe's death, they'd search every nook and cranny for ties to George.

Jacob moved closer to the home but remained stealthy to fully ascertain the situation before he barged inside and might well find himself staring down the barrel of a gun. On the left of the front door was a window. He knew this to be a living room window because he'd been in the home only days before, and had, in fact, been in the home many times prior, when things seemed normal.

He moved closer to the window to peer inside for signs of life. The window was partially enclosed by shutters. A small opening allowed for viewing inside the living room where a few lamps were on, but he saw no one.

Jacob heard the sound of voices inside as he caught sight of two people walking toward the home's foyer. "Oh shit." He immediately recognized Kelly Hammond. But the man with her, he didn't know. He wore a suit. Could have been a cop, it was impossible to know for sure. He listened as they spoke, though it was difficult to understand them from where he stood.

"I need to see my daughter. I have to know she's okay." Kelly Hammond's arms were being held behind her back as the man in the suit escorted her near the foyer.

"She's been taken to the hospital. She's fine. You'd better be worrying about what you're going to say when we get to the station."

So he was a cop. And what happened to the daughter? Jacob continued to listen.

"I'm not going to say anything. I swear it. I just want to see my girl," she pleaded.

"I'm going to need you to tell me where your husband is, Kelly. We both know he's been talking. Someone's had to reach out to you to offer protection. Look, I did my part. Now I don't know how the hell someone ID'd you, but when I got the call from my people, I came here so we could sort this out together. We're in on this together. Remember that."

"No one was at the plant besides me and that kid. And I didn't kill the homewrecking bitch. And I sure as hell didn't kill the kid."

"No, you sure didn't. But you knew damn well what the plan was."

"I don't know where he is, Dave. I wish to God I did because I'd kill him myself."

Jacob pulled back. In his shock, he stumbled over a large stone near the shrub over which he was hunched. "Shit." He peered through the window again. The man in the suit seemed to stare directly at him.

Jacob turned and ran back toward his car as the front door flew open.

"Stop! Police!"

Kelly stood next to Pryce and appeared to recognize Jacob. "Run, Jacob!"

He reached Carl's car when the cop opened fire and bullets rang out. One struck the car's front bumper. "Shit!" Jacob pulled open the driver's side door when another bullet struck it. If it weren't for the fact that this car was made of good old-fashioned American steel, he might be lying on the ground with a bullet in his chest.

It was then his sights were drawn to an approaching car. "Riley." He knew right away, and it couldn't have been worse timing on her part. "Go back! Go back!" Jacob waved his arm at her, shaking his head wildly.

Ethan peered through the windshield. "What the hell? Is that Jacob? What's he doing?"

Another shot rang out.

"Holy shit!" Riley slammed on the brakes of her patrol car as she entered the driveway. "Jacob!" She jumped out and drew her weapon, firing a warning shot near the front of the home.

"Riley! What the hell are you doing?" Ethan pushed open his door and crouched down, brandishing his gun. "We need backup!"

"That has to be Pryce up there. I think we're on our own. We have to get Jacob to safety."

"Who's the woman?" Ethan asked.

"It's Kelly Hammond. I recognize her. I have no idea what the hell is happening right now, but we need to get Jacob out of there. You're going to have to cover me." Riley started to move, heading around the relative safety of her patrol car door and into the open, toward Carl's car.

"Riley! No! Get back here!" Ethan said.

Jacob eyed her. "No! No!" He tried to wave her away.

"I'm a cop! Hold your fire!" Pryce yelled with one hand in the air, the other still clinging on to Kelly Hammond as though for a potential shield, should the need arise.

Riley had to believe this man, who she thought was Captain Pryce, wouldn't attempt to take out all three of them. He was looking for a way out. Her instincts kicked in and she saw something dark behind his eyes. She figured Pryce was on the wrong side of this. But what did that mean? What exactly had he done to get here?"

"Jacob, come on. I got you covered." She continued a low crawl toward him and Carl's car.

"No, it's not safe. It's Pryce. He's crooked, Riley. I heard him. I think he killed that girl, Chloe."

And that was when she saw it. Images flashed before her eyes of Captain Pryce. Only he wasn't the man who killed Justin. In fact, he didn't kill Chloe either, but he ordered it. "Drop your weapon, Captain." Riley slowly stood.

"What? Who the hell are you? You drop your weapon."

"I'm working with your Lieutenant Moody in Owensville. I'm going to take this man with me, but I need you to drop your gun."

"Then you're on our side, Officer. We're working on the same team."

"Somehow, I don't think that's true, Captain." She began to see more clearly his role. He had been working with this woman, Kelly Hammond, in some capacity. But the pieces hadn't quite fit together.

"Call Moody. He'll tell you. Don't be stupid, Officer. The last thing I want is for someone to get hurt," Pryce said.

Riley had never been faced with a situation like this. She needed to get Jacob to safety. She also worried about putting Ethan in danger. Riley made the call to move on him and now she was stuck. It wasn't until she peered at the woman, Kelly Hammond, that Riley began to understand what it was she would have to do. The woman conveyed pain and fear, and it wasn't for herself. No. It was for a loved one, perhaps a child. She didn't know for sure, but that was how it felt. And if that was the case, this woman would do whatever it took to ensure her child's safety. Riley would have to use her to get to Pryce. "Where is your child? Is there anyone inside?"

Kelly furrowed her brow. "They took her to the hospital. She fell down the stairs when they raided my home, looking for my husband. I swear I don't know where he is. You have to believe me. Please, I have to see my baby!"

"I believe you. Captain, I'm going to need you to let this woman go now."

"Are you giving me an order, Officer? You have no jurisdiction here. I'm the one in charge and I need you to see that, or this will end badly for you and your partners."

She was going to have to do something more. He wasn't going to just lay down his arms and surrender to her. Whatever he'd done, he was in deep and he wasn't going to go down without a fight.

Riley focused on the large wooden door behind them. The time had come to unleash what she'd worked so hard to contain. There were things she was capable of doing now that she was older. Carl knew. Ward knew. Even Jacob had been given a taste of it—once. Something had changed in her the night of the storm. While she didn't have the power to bend Mother Nature to her will, she could, if she tried hard enough, bend objects to her will. And right now, she needed a distraction. Something that would force the captain to look away long enough for her to get a shot at him. Riley was going to have to take him down.

"Officer, I'm not going to warn you again. You and your partner need to stand down. Now!" Pryce said.

Riley trained her sights on the door with all her energy focused on pulling at it. "Come on," she whispered. Her breaths grew labored, her brow line forming beads of sweat.

"Riley, what are you going to do?" Ethan looked at her in a panic.

"I've got this." She continued to stare at it. The object consumed every ounce of her energy now. Lives were at stake. It was time to use what she had to put an end to this. The two men she cared for deeply were counting on her. She would not see harm come to them.

Riley released a deep-throated roar as she threw her head back and clenched her weapon until her hands hurt.

The heavy wooden door slammed shut behind them. Pryce jumped and twisted his body to see it close.

Riley took the split-second diversion, aimed her gun at him, and fired.

Pryce released his grip on Kelly and she darted away. He looked down at his gut as the blood spilled. And as he returned a stunned gaze to Riley, Pryce fell to his knees. His gun tumbled down the steps of the entryway.

Riley tried to pull back her strength, but she couldn't. Glass shattered from the windows adjacent to the door. The house rumbled. "No. Stop!"

Ethan rushed toward her. "Riley!"

Jacob soon followed. "You have to stop it, Riley! I know you can. Let it go. You have to let it go now. It's over. We're safe."

She eyed them both, but Kelly pulled away her attention as she tried to escape. "Stop!" The gate at the end of the drive slammed shut, almost catching the woman in between it, but she slipped out.

"Come on." Jacob took hold of her. "Baby, you have to let it go."

Riley blinked hard as she looked at Ethan, and again at Jacob. She nodded. "Okay. Okay. It's over." She was out of breath and struggled to draw more air into her lungs.

"You got this, Riley. You can do it," Ethan said.

"Yeah. I got this." Riley closed her eyes, but they flew open when another shot rang out.

Jacob was down.

[25]

It was Officer Lowell Abrams, a man who wore his conceit like a badge, who made the approach to his captain. Abrams used that badge to fend off any real feelings he might have about a situation, and right now, he was hard pressed not to be worried about his brother and sister in blue. "Captain, I'm sure they're fine. You know Thompson; she's tough as nails and no one would ever get the drop on her."

Ward pulled away from the window he had been peering through for the better part of ten minutes in search of his team. "Yeah. I know you're right. Thanks." He headed in the direction of the breakroom for another coffee. It was almost four in the morning and daylight would be upon them soon. Still no word from Riley or Ethan. No word from Pryce either. Even Lieutenant Moody was growing concerned.

"Hey, I wouldn't mind one of those." Moody joined him.

"Look, I know how hard it is to sit back and wait, but without confirmation from Pryce, I think that's all we can do."

Ward poured a cup of coffee for Moody and then for himself. "Why didn't he keep backup with him? Why didn't he take that woman to the station, same as he took Rhodes?" He turned to Moody. "You said you didn't have concrete proof. What about now? Do I need to be even more worried for my officers than I already am?"

"Okay. I'll be honest with you. Like I said, it's just a hunch right now, but something smells bad about the relationship between Pryce and these mafia thugs he's supposedly after."

"Supposedly?" Ward replied.

"Yeah."

"For Christ's sake, you think he's being paid off?"

Moody sipped on his coffee. "Oh, I think it could be much worse than that."

"Captain!" Abrams rushed inside the breakroom. "Thompson's trying to reach you!"

"Shit." He tossed his half-full cup into the sink, shattering the mug on impact, and rushed back into the bullpen with Moody close behind.

"Channel 4," Abrams said.

Ward picked up the radio. "Riley? I'm here. What the hell is going on?"

"Jacob's been shot. We're waiting on the ambulance now."

"For God's sake. Are you okay? Is Pruitt okay?"

"We're fine. Captain, it was Pryce. I had to..."

"You had to what?" Ward asked.

"I shot him, but I didn't take him down. He threatened us. I thought we were safe, but he fired at Jacob and fled on foot. We're in trouble, Captain. His people will be coming."

"His people?" Ward shot a fearful glance to Moody.

"She needs to get the hell out of there. Forget the ambulance. Get that man to a hospital. Someplace where Pryce can't get to him. He has people. I'm sure he does," Moody replied.

"Riley, load up Jacob, and you and Ethan get him to a hospital. Where's Kelly Hammond?"

"She took off. She was afraid. I don't know where she's at."

"Okay. We'll figure that out later. Just get out of there and get Jacob some help. We're on our way." Ward dropped the radio receiver and eyed Moody. "How quickly can you get us to the city?"

———

Blake remained in the room alone for too long. He'd been brought here over an hour ago and still no one had come. He'd begun to get a bad feeling about this. He had no idea if they'd talked to Kelly Hammond yet. And on checking the time on an old wall clock, he realized the sun would be up soon and Virgil Howard would wonder where he was. But maybe more importantly, where was Jacob?

This situation had turned into a steaming pile of crap. He couldn't get word to anyone and he still hadn't been charged. "Hey!" he shouted. "You need to let me out of here!" He stood up, hands shackled behind his back, and walked to the heavy steel door and began kicking it. "Hey! Let me out of here! You can't keep me in here like this. I have rights!"

Perhaps if he made enough noise, they would move him. And if that happened, maybe he could glean some information as to what the hell was going on. He heard footsteps approach. "Jesus. Finally!"

The door opened and Virgil Howard walked inside. "I thought I might find you in here."

"What the fuck? How did you get in here? You should be on your way to Owensville."

"I have a few friends and pulled a few strings after I got a call from a mutual friend. Guess you thought you'd find George on your own, did you?"

"No, sir. I was just wanting to talk to Kelly."

"And why is that? You have no reason to speak with her, do you? Do you know her personally?"

"No, but I..."

"No, but I..." Virgil turned down his lips into a deep frown, poking fun at Blake. "You sound like a pussy, you know that? All you had to do was stay put. Now look at this shit."

"I didn't know about Pryce."

"And what is it that you think you know about him, son?" Virgil continued.

"I just wanted to find George and I thought Kelly would know. She probably already told Pryce where to find him."

"Hammond and Pryce got their own thing to work out. It ain't my concern right now. But see, the problem now is you sold us out to your boy, Jacob. Now we got major problems to deal with in that hick town. That's on you, Blakey."

"Did George kill her? Did he kill my girlfriend?" Blake's expression hardened.

"You think he's that ignorant? You must've been fed some kind of horseshit and now look at you. Handcuffed. Sitting in here completely defenseless."

"She was pregnant too," Blake replied.

Virgil leaned back and roared with laughter. "Of course she was."

Blake had begun to understand now why Virgil was here. "So you're not interested in finding Hammond, are you? It was all bullshit, right?"

"Winner, winner, chicken dinner! Oh, don't get me wrong, he was our A number one priority until someone figured out his wife was in on this shit. Now I'm just here to tie up loose ends, brother. Clean up the mess you made before it touches the bossman. I warned him not to bring you into the fold. Oh well." Virgil drew a knife and pulled Blake close. "Now you're a great big loose end just flapping in the wind." He plunged the knife into Blake's chest.

———

"LET'S GET HIM INSIDE, RILEY. I'M GOING AFTER PRYCE. HE'S hurt. He can't have gone far." Ethan started in the direction of the gunfire, and with his weapon ready, he searched for the injured Pryce.

"I'm okay, Riley." Jacob pushed himself forward with his arm and tried to sit up.

"You're not okay; you've been shot. I have to get you to a hospital. Can you try to stand?" Jacob was pushing six feet and weighed in at around a buck-eighty. Getting him in the car on her own would prove a challenge. Of course, she'd just managed to wield the massive entry door, but she didn't trust her gift enough to consider finessing it, nor did she really have the ability to. "Come on." She helped to lift him and slide him into the back seat. "You okay like this?"

"I'll manage. I'm so sorry I got you into this."

"You didn't. I did. I should've kept my eye on Pryce. I thought if I could just get him to the ground, I'd be able to take him in. And then I lost control and..."

"This isn't your fault, and Ethan's right. He's hurt, badly, and he won't get far."

Riley spotted Ethan in the distance. She stood up, looking around for signs he'd seen Pryce, but when he shook his head, Riley knew he hadn't found him. "Just get in. We'll worry about him later."

Ethan slipped into the passenger seat and looked back over his shoulder. "You okay, man?"

"Yeah," Jacob replied.

Riley got in and turned the engine. "Anyone know where the nearest hospital is?"

"First and Roosevelt. There's a hospital there," Jacob said.

"I'll put it in my phone. I don't know this city at all." Ethan entered the address. "Okay, pull out of here and head right."

"Sirens." Riley looked at Ethan. "Do you hear them?"

"Just keep going. Pryce must've made the call for backup. Just go, Riley. Get out of here before they spot us. We're standing out like a sore thumb in this patrol car."

"Should've taken Carl's." Jacob winced as Riley made a sharp right. "He's gonna be pissed at me."

Riley couldn't help but smirk. "I'll take the blame, don't you worry about that." She looked at Ethan again. "Call Ward, tell him where we're going. If Moody has anyone loyal to him, he might be able to get us some protection because I have a feeling we're going to need it."

———

"It's been taken care of, boss." Virgil stood outside the police station. "What about Biggs?" He listened and nodded. "Got it. But it might take some time to track down Kelly. I won't screw this up, boss." He ended the call and walked into the parking lot as a car approached him. "Bout time. I've been freezing my balls off out here."

"Get in."

Virgil stepped inside the car. "Still no word on ol' Georgie boy?"

"No."

"I bet he'll show up at the hospital when he finds out what happened to his daughter. Hammond will come out of hiding for this. We know his handlers got eyeballs on us. Word will reach him and this will be over very soon."

"I'm counting on it," Roy Bayliss pulled away from the curb and headed out.

"There's one thing I got from Rhodes before he met his untimely demise. Something we can also use to stoke the embers. Once Hammond finds out his side piece was pregnant, he'll want revenge."

"Pregnant, huh?" Bayliss looked to him for a moment. "Serves the prick right for turning tail on us."

"Must be why Kelly flipped out. Can't say I blame her," Virgil said. "I never would've stepped out on a woman like Kelly Hammond."

Bayliss eyed him before returning his attention to the road.

———

Riley pulled into the emergency area of the hospital and ran inside. "We need some help out here! Gunshot wound to the back." She returned to her patrol car where Ethan was already tending to Jacob. "There coming out now to help."

Two nurses and a doctor rolled a gurney outside and to her car.

"He's in the back seat." Riley moved so they could get to Jacob.

"Sir, we're going to get you onto the gurney, okay? I'm going to need you to stay calm."

Jacob nodded.

The nurses and doctor pulled him out of the backseat as carefully as they could, but he moaned in pain, nonetheless.

"I'm sorry, sir. We're almost there. Where are you hurt?" the doctor asked.

"Back. I was shot in the back."

"The good news is that you're moving. That means it missed your spinal cord, so let's get you inside and take a look, okay?"

"Yeah." He winced again in pain as they made the final hoist. Now he was on the gurney and appeared relieved.

Riley reached for his hand. "I'm not going anywhere. I'll be right here."

"Excuse me, Officer. I see you're not with Metro, so are you related to this man?" a nurse asked.

"He's my boyfriend," Riley replied.

"I'm going to need you to come inside and fill out some paperwork then."

"Yeah, okay." She moved next to Ethan and both watched as they rolled Jacob inside.

"He'll be okay, Riley." Ethan reached for her hand.

———

Nearly an hour had passed while Riley and Ethan sat in the waiting room and Jacob had been taken into surgery. She stood up at the arrival of Captain Ward and Lieutenant Moody.

"Riley! Do you have any idea how worried I've been?"

"It was the right thing to do, Captain." Ethan joined them. "She probably saved Jacob's life."

Riley displayed gratitude to Ethan and turned back to Ward. "He's still in surgery, but the doctors think he'll be okay."

"Thank God for that. But look, we've got a situation on our hands," Ward said.

Moody interrupted, "I got a call from some people on my team. They said a stabbing occurred at the station about an hour or so ago. It was Blake Rhodes. He's dead."

"They got to him," Riley said. "Jacob filled me in on what he overheard from Pryce and Kelly Hammond. Captain, he's a crooked cop."

"It sure as hell is starting to look that way."

"They're in CYA mode now," Moody replied.

"Has anyone seen Pryce?" Ethan asked. "I couldn't find him. I have no idea if he's alive or dead."

"We're looking," Moody continued. "Same goes for Kelly Hammond. She disappeared too. But right now, my concern is for your friend Jacob. He's the one in danger, as I see it. Especially if he overheard Pryce. We're going to have to put a guard at his door once he gets out of surgery."

"What I want you two to do is get back to our station. Moody can take it from here," Ward said.

"I'm not leaving him, Captain. I'm sorry, but I won't leave Jacob."

"That's an order, Officer Thompson. Moody's been pretty forthcoming with what he believes could be a dangerous situation concerning Captain Pryce. His attempt to gun down Jacob proves what he suspected all along. And with Hammond and Pryce still out there, there's no telling what we'll be up against. And I need you both to not be here."

"You should listen to your captain. My team can take it from here. I promise you, we will look after Jacob," Moody said.

Riley looked at Ward. "Please. I can't leave him."

"I'm sorry, Riley. You don't have a choice. If you don't return to Owensville, I'll have to ask for your gun and badge. Is that what you want?"

"Captain..." Ethan said.

"Same goes for you, Pruitt." Ward shot him a glance. "I know what you've both been through tonight, and especially you." He eyed Riley. "Go back to the station. The sun's starting to rise. This isn't over yet and we need to be ready."

"Yes, sir." Riley headed out the door.

"Pruitt?" Ward added.

"Yes, sir." He followed her outside.

———

VIRGIL HOWARD PEERED THROUGH THE WINDSHIELD OF THE

car as they pulled into the parking lot of the hospital. "Hey, lookey there."

"They're getting into a patrol car," Bayliss said. "Owensville's finest, Officer Riley Thompson and her sidekick, Pruitt. That means Biggs is here too. Imagine that. Same hospital as Hammond's girl. Looks like we'll be able to kill two birds with one stone, Virgil."

"We'll cross our fingers for the hat-trick. Kelly Hammond just might show up too."

Bayliss picked up his phone. "I'll get someone on those two cops. Who's in the area?"

[26]

The sun crept over the horizon as Bayliss and Howard stood watch from their car, waiting for IMPD to leave, waiting for the Hammonds to come for word on the daughter who lay in a bed in this very hospital. The same one in which Jacob Biggs had been recovering. It had been the perfect place to tie up all remaining loose ends. But it was almost six in the morning and still no sign of George or Kelly Hammond and no sign the cops intended to leave.

Virgil peered through the windshield. "Do you think we should gather the troops and hash out another plan? I figured Hammond would've shown by now, and his wife."

"The Feds must've caught wind is all I can figure. They'll keep George in the dark just to get what they want, and they might have already gotten to Kelly," Bayliss replied. "Sons of bitches will do anything to get to the boss."

"So what are you saying?" Virgil asked.

"I ain't leaving until we get George and Jacob Biggs. We risk too much exposure otherwise," Bayliss replied. "Bad enough we got them backwoods cops sniffing around the plant. But we got that covered. Now the time's come to protect our own right here." Bayliss opened his car door. "I'm going in."

"Wait, you can't do that. We need the okay from the top," Virgil said. "They'll get someone inside who can help."

"This needs to end and we need to join the others before shit blows up." Bayliss stepped out into the early morning light. "Stay here. If I'm not out in twenty minutes—leave without me."

Virgil watched as Roy Bayliss cautiously made his way to the hospital entrance, except he bolted right and appeared to search for a less conspicuous way inside. "Crazy son of a bitch. He's going to get us all taken down."

———

RILEY PUSHED UP FROM HER DESK IN A HUFF. "HOW LONG are we supposed to sit here?" She eyed her colleagues, all of whom had been ordered to stay on alert.

A handful of Moody's team were also still in place, waiting for instruction. "Officer Thompson, I understand your frustration. I've been there," one of the officers replied. "But until we hear from Lieutenant Moody or Captain Ward, we have to obey orders."

Abrams walked over to Riley. "Look, I know we aren't the closest of friends. I know you think I'm an asshole most of the time. But we're in this together, and no matter what happens, I'll have your back. Just like I would every last one of these guys here now."

"Thank you. And I don't think you're an asshole," Riley said reluctantly.

"Sure you do, and that's okay because I know I am."

Riley's cell phone rang and she felt a surge of anticipation, believing it was news about Jacob. But on retrieving the phone, she noticed it was Carl and figured she was going to have to do some explaining. "Carl, you're awake."

"I am. And funny thing, not only am I alone here, but I found a note from Jacob. That kid took my car."

"I know he did. Carl, things have happened, bad things, and I'll make this up to you, I promise, but right now, my hands are tied. Ward ordered us to stay here. Jacob's in the hospital in the city."

"Oh Lord. What happened to the boy?"

"He was shot. Look, I can't explain everything right now. Just, please don't be mad. I'll come see you when this is all over, okay?"

"Well, now you got me worried. What the hell's going on, Riley? Is there anything I can do to help?"

"No. I'm afraid we're on our own right now."

"Then answer me this. The storm's here, isn't it?" Carl's tone turned sober.

"The storm's here."

Carl stood in his small living room and peered through the window of his second-floor room. "That's what I thought. I'll be in touch."

"Carl? Carl, wait." Riley stared at the phone. "He hung up."

Ethan approached her. "You didn't think he'd sit idly by and let you find yourself in hot water, did you? I figured you knew him better than that. I certainly did."

"I'm going to make sure he stays put." Riley swiped at her keys.

"Not alone you're not," Ethan replied.

"You two want to find yourselves without a job?" Chris Decker quickly approached. "You leave now and Ward will have your heads. You know that."

"He's not here. And I won't allow Carl to put himself in any danger," Riley replied. "Whether those men are here now or not, I won't see harm come him—ever."

———

JACOB ROUSED FROM THE POWERFUL ANESTHESIA, CONFUSED and unsure of where he was, except that he was in a hospital. "Riley?" His hoarse voice barely sounded above a whisper. When he realized he was alone, Jacob spotted the button and called for a nurse. It was only moments before one arrived.

"Hello, Jacob, glad to see you're awake." She approached him and began checking his vital signs. "How are you feeling?"

"What happened to me?"

"You don't remember?"

He shook his head.

"It's just the anesthesia. I'm afraid you sustained a gunshot wound in your back. But fortunately, it didn't do major damage. You're a very lucky man."

"Where's Riley? I need to see her."

"I'm afraid I don't know who that is. There are, however, some police officers who I think would like to speak to you. Do you think you could answer a few questions? I'll be sure they keep it brief, but I believe it is important."

"Yeah."

"I'll go into the lobby and let them know you're awake." She left his room.

Jacob looked toward the window, and as he began to recall the events of the previous evening, he realized daylight had broken. He hoped someone could tell him where Riley was and if she was okay.

"Jacob." Ward entered the room with a broad smile. "I'm so glad you're awake and alert."

"Where's Riley?"

"I sent her back home along with Pruitt. I've been waiting here with Lieutenant Moody in hopes of talking to you about what happened. Riley filled me in on most of the details, but I wanted to talk to you about something else too."

"Well, I can tell you it was Pryce who shot me. Have you found him? Riley fired a shot and hit him in the stomach, but he managed to get his gun and fire on me."

"Moody's got some trusted folks looking for him and Kelly Hammond. She fled during the melee," Ward said.

"What about her kid?"

"The girl is fine. Took a knock to the head, mild concussion, but she'll be fine." Ward stepped closer. "Jacob, I know you were being framed. We all know that. And I also know that your friend Blake Rhodes was part of the attempt to frame you."

"I got him to come around. He was trying to help me, but I haven't been able to get hold of him."

Ward gripped the bars on the side of the bed. "I'm sorry, Jacob. He was murdered."

"What? When?"

"He was remanded into custody, but this group has long tentacles. Someone got to him inside. We don't know who did the deed but we have a pretty good guess who ordered it. Right now, the best thing is to get you back to Owensville. I'll have to get the okay from the doctors, but we need to move you." Ward looked over his shoulder toward the door. "In fact, I'm going to get the ball rolling on that now. I have an officer standing watch at your door. You're safe here until we can get transport arranged."

"Okay. Thank you." Jacob watched as Ward started to leave. "Captain, it's daylight. Do you think they're in Owensville?"

"I don't know, son. They might still be here cleaning up their mess. But just know that Riley's safe. She's at the station. Moody's guys are there too. I'll know the moment anything happens. Now just sit back and relax. We'll get you out of here soon."

———

Bayliss made his way to the emergency stairwell of the hospital building. This was one of the largest hospitals in the city with lots of hiding places. He figured someone would be protecting Biggs, but that should be an easy fix. They had men on the inside. A quick call and he could arrange for the officer on guard to be called away. And then he would slip in and take care of this nuisance once and for all. A nuisance that had well outlived his usefulness when he couldn't come up with Hammond's whereabouts, same as Blake Rhodes.

Bayliss sent a text message to Paul Kearns. Through him, a message would reach the officer inside. It would take a few minutes, so he needed to hole up in the stairwell and let the process work. If there was one thing Bayliss was capable of doing, it was waiting. He'd waited this long to rise up in the organization. He could wait this out too.

RILEY PULLED INTO THE PARKING LOT OF CARL'S BUILDING. "He's going to be ticked off about his car." She opened her door.

"I think that'll be the least of his concerns right now." Ethan followed her out. "What's the plan here?"

"I don't know yet. I'll know when I see him." She headed into the building. It was early and the doors were still locked. She peered inside and spotted one of the staff.

The woman seemed confused but approached to open the door. "Riley? What are you doing here? Is everything okay?"

"Hi, Maggie, I need to see Carl. I know you're not open to visitors yet, but it's important."

"Okay. Come on in, but don't tell the manager I let you in. It'll be my hide."

"I won't, thank you." She waved Ethan inside and they both stepped onto the elevator. "If Jacob had just stayed put, he wouldn't be lying in a hospital bed right now. And Carl wouldn't be trying to go rogue on me."

"Seems like Jacob's just as stubborn as you. I can see why your relationship tanked," Ethan said.

She eyed him. "That's not why we broke up."

"Uh huh." Ethan stared at the numbers until the doors parted. "I just hope we aren't wasting our time putting people in their places when the bad guys could already be here."

"We aren't, and we won't stay long in any case. I need to make clear to him he's to stay put until this is over."

"Whatever you say."

Riley knocked on Carl's door and he immediately opened it. "Hi."

"As you can see, I'm still here. I shouldn't have said nothing at all to you. I figure you'd show up. Come in." Carl stepped aside to let them in. "I can see by the look on your face this hasn't turned out the way you planned. So since you're here, why don't you both have a seat. Where is Jacob? You said he'd been hurt." Carl returned to his chair.

"He's still in the hospital. The captain called to let me know that he'd awakened and appeared to be doing well. But they haven't given Jacob back his cell phone, so I can't call him. I think that's Ward's doing. I think he wants me to stay focused on what's happening here."

"And what is happening here, Riley? I see that the day we feared has arrived."

"It has, Carl. I'm sorry I dragged you into this, but I do need to stress to you that there's nothing you can do. I know how much you want to help. And I know you're probably upset about Jacob taking your car. Maybe I'm really here for another reason."

"I suspected that might be the case. They're here, right? You can see it?"

"I think so. I can sense something, but I don't know who or how many."

"Okay, so tell me what you do see."

Riley closed her eyes and thought hard on the matter. Her head was clouded with thoughts of Jacob and all that happened in the night. It was hard to see anything, but she had to try. "I see three men. Their faces aren't clear to me yet, and I don't see their location. It's not the plant. They're in a car, driving." She shook her head and opened her eyes. "I can't see anything beyond that."

"Okay. That's a start," Carl said.

"There's something else you should know," Ethan began. "Riley, tell him what you did last night. The door and the house."

"I—I couldn't control it. I couldn't pull it back, not immediately anyway."

"I see," Carl began. "You did what you had to do, and that won't be the last time. I can see that too. Riley, you're going to have to find these men. You're the only one who can stop them. Ward won't be able to, not without severe consequences."

"I won't let anything happen to him. I tried to protect Jacob, but the captain—no. I'll do what I have to do to stop that vision from coming true."

"I know you will, but I think we both know this isn't going to end well," Carl added.

Ethan shot a fearful glance to her.

Riley returned a guarded gaze. "No. I don't think it will."

———

BAYLISS RECEIVED THE CONFIRMATION THAT HE HAD BUT A few minutes to do what needed to be done. He pushed through the door to the floor where Jacob was being kept. In the hallway, a nurse turned a corner and a doctor entered a room. Now all was clear.

The door to Jacob's room was just ahead. Bayliss pushed it open. It wasn't until Jacob's eyes widened with fear that he knew now was the time. "Don't yell. You'll only make it worse." Bayliss pulled a gun from his waist and aimed it at Jacob.

Jacob raised his hands to shield himself. "No! Stop!"

The door to the room flew open and Ward rushed inside, his

weapon trained on the intruder. And without so much as a word of warning, he fired, striking Bayliss in the head.

Blood splattered on Jacob's face and arms. "Jesus!"

Bayliss crumpled to the ground, his lifeless eyes staring at the ceiling.

"It's okay. You're okay. Calm down, Jacob."

"How did you...?" He was still out of breath. "I thought he was going to kill me."

"This was what we were waiting for. I'm sorry I couldn't tell you. Your reaction had to be authentic or Bayliss would've realized something was up. We were told he was here. He thought he had a man on the inside, but he didn't. He didn't have the reach he thought he did. I saw him enter the hall and followed him."

"He almost shot me."

"I know, but you're okay."

Moody rushed inside and took in the scene. "Roy Bayliss."

Ward peered at him. "Yeah, the plant manager in Owensville. Guess he was on the payroll too." He looked to Jacob. "We're getting you out of here, kid."

[27]

The time had come for Riley to call on her colleagues for help. She was not so arrogant to believe she alone wielded the power to take down these ruthless criminals. Even with her ability, and in fact, despite it, she would not rely on it solely to solve her problems. Because the more she relied on it, the stronger it became. And she feared one day it might engulf her completely and she would no longer recognize herself.

"They're on their way." Riley looked to Ethan as they sat in her patrol car keeping watch near the plant. "Time to call the captain." She made the call on her cell and waited for an answer. "Moody's guys said they got the okay to get Jacob out of there and bring him here to our hospital, meaning Ward should be on his way back."

Ward answered the line. "Riley, what's happening? We're headed back to town with Jacob."

"Thank God. He's okay?"

"He's shaken up. We all are. Roy Bayliss is dead."

"Bayliss? I suppose that shouldn't come as a surprise. Now we just need to find Virgil Howard."

"He's not the only one. Pryce is the problem now and the Hammonds are still MIA. Your intuition served us well once again. Moody opened up about his concerns regarding Pryce. He thinks he could be in the mafia's pocket."

"It's possible Pryce succumbed to his wounds. Maybe he's already dead," Riley replied.

"I don't think so. Someone's still out there calling the shots. In the meantime, Moody's men there will do as you need them to do, until we can get there."

"The team's coming now. I just spoke with Moody's sergeant," Riley said.

"Good. I'll be there after we get Jacob to the hospital. Don't do anything unless you have to, you understand? Do your best to wait for me. That's an order, Riley."

"Yes, sir."

"I'll be in touch. Be safe, both of you."

Riley returned her cell phone to the console. "Once Moody's team gets here, we'll put into place a plan of action."

"Copy that," Ethan replied.

Riley looked through the windshield, staring at the plant. "I think I've come to hate this place now. I hope it burns to the ground."

"You don't mean that. It could bring a lot of jobs. Just not from these crooked guys running it now."

"No. This place holds way too many bad memories for me. And yet here I am again, facing the very thing that frightened me as a kid."

"Maybe that's the way it was supposed to be, Riley. Maybe that's the reason we're here right now."

"You might be right." Riley looked to her friend and colleague. "Thank you, Ethan."

"For what?"

"For putting up with me, for getting me through some tough times. You're always there for me, even when I ask you to go against your better judgment."

"Yeah, well." He shrugged and looked away awkwardly.

"I know how you feel about Jacob," she continued.

"The guy's been shot. He gets a pass from me from now on."

Riley smiled. "I also know how you feel about me."

He peered at her. "I figured as much. Sucks working with a mind reader."

"I can't read your mind, only sense your feelings."

"Yeah, well, same thing," Ethan replied.

"I just want you to know that no matter what happens today, I do care for you. Very much. That will never change."

Ethan faced her, holding her gaze. "I was hoping for a little more than that, Riley. But I'll take what I can get."

Two patrol cars appeared in the distance.

"That's IMPD." Riley sat at attention, watching the cars approach.

"Good timing, and guess who else is coming to dinner?" Ethan pointed to the right. "Honey, the mafia's here..."

Riley picked up her radio. "This is car 1-8-9, our target has arrived." She started the engine. "Meet me at the rendezvous point. 1-8-9, over."

The radio buzzed. "Car 1-8-9, be advised, IMPD headed to the rendezvous point."

"Time to get this party started." Riley pulled around to the far south end of the property where trees would obscure their vehicles.

"I don't think I've ever been this scared." Ethan turned to her. "Did I say that out loud?"

"You did. And you're not alone, but we have help. There they are now." Riley watched the two IMPD patrol cars roll to a stop next to her.

The officer rolled down his window. "Officer Thompson, are we ready to lay this out?"

"Yes, sir."

———

After the sound of gunshots from the hospital reached him, Virgil figured either Biggs had been taken out or Bayliss had. "Holy shit." He was about to take off when his phone rang and he recognized the number. "Yeah Boss?"

"Hammond made contact."

"He did? Shit, I just heard gunshots, Boss. Bayliss went inside to take care of Biggs, like a dumbass. I don't know who fired, but I need to get the hell out of here."

"Bayliss is gone. They knew he was coming and took him down before he had the chance to get to Biggs. Things are going tits up and everyone's turning against us. So here's the plan. Go to the plant. Hammond will be there. I made clear it was the only way we'd let his kid live. He's going to confess to the murder of that girl and he's going to leave sufficient evidence that he was at the plant."

"But Boss, how are we going to make sure none of this tracks back to you?"

Sirens sounded and an onslaught of patrol cars screamed up to the entrance. "Ah hell, I gotta get out of Dodge, Boss. Cops are swarming the place."

"Go. I'll be in touch."

Virgil ended the call and pulled away. He was going to Owensville. "I sure as shit hope you're right about Hammond, Boss," he said to himself.

———

Virgil stopped the car near the plant entrance and began to step out. He approached

the massive doors. Inside, most of the equipment had been set and the walls enclosed, but it wasn't completed yet. "Too bad. Money down the damn drain now. Boys?" he called out.

Paul Kearns appeared from the back office along with a few other men Virgil hadn't known all that well.

"Virgil." Kearns approached. "Where's Bayliss?"

"Dead. What's going on?"

"Shit, man, we're losing too many people."

"Look, Boss said Hammond was coming here. They struck a deal and Georgie boy is going to surrender. Our instructions are the same until then. Any trace of our association with the affiliate groups needs to disappear." Virgil surveyed the area. "I expect our friendly neighborhood police officers will be showing up sometime soon so we'd best finish this shit up quick."

"We'll be ready. They won't get shit on us."

———

THE TEAM OF EIGHT—FOUR OWENSVILLE COPS, FOUR Indianapolis cops—split up and began to surround the building.

Riley led her crew with Abrams, Decker, and Pruitt. "Okay, we're going to go inside and announce our presence, just like Moody's guys said, okay?"

"You said we were supposed to wait for Ward," Decker replied.

"That was before we saw Virgil Howard roll in."

"Copy that. What if they don't go easy on us?" Abrams asked.

"Then we don't go easy on them." Riley started toward the back entrance of the plant. As they walked through the yard, she spotted the storm shelter. It looked exactly as she remembered.

"Riley, you okay?" Ethan asked.

"Fine. Let's go." She continued toward the loading docks. The large corrugated steel doors were now in place and were open. "We'll go in through here." She signaled her team. "Moody's guys are going in through the front."

Riley was the first to enter, and when all four were inside, she waited for confirmation the other men had entered and now it was about to get messy. "This is the Owensville Police. Put your hands up and step out into the open. Now!"

Virgil looked at Kearns and the others. "Just do as they say, boys. Boss says he's coming. He'll take care of things."

"IMPD. Put your hands up. Now!" Moody's officers pushed through the plant toward the office.

Virgil emerged, hands in the air, and eyed Riley. "You must be Jakey's girl. Or is it, ex-girl? I seen his current squeeze. She is fine."

"Do as she says, man, or I'll take you down," Abrams replied.

"Go ahead. Arrest me. Arrest all of us. You know as well as I do, nothing's going to stick."

Riley caught sight of one of the other men with Virgil. She recognized him, but it took a moment to register. And then it came to her. "It was you. You killed Justin and Chloe."

"How the...?" The man drew his weapon and aimed it at her.

"Whoa, whoa! Let's calm down now, boys," Virgil said. "Little lady, you best wait for the big boys to come. They'll sort this out."

A burst of adrenaline surged through Riley and she willed the gun from the man's hands, ripping it away and cast it a good fifty feet.

"Son of a bitch!" The man's face masked in shock as he looked at Virgil.

"Riley?" Ethan noticed the symptoms. "We got this, Riley. We got this."

A moment later, the man's feet floated up from the floor. With a toss of her head, Riley flung the killer from where he stood, slamming him into the wall. "You killed a pregnant girl and a kid just out of high school."

The thug was pressed up against the wall, terrified and struggling to be freed from her grip. "It was Hammond's fault. He crossed Pryce and that was the price he had to pay."

She dropped him to the ground and shot a look to Ethan before returning her attention to the man. "What did you just say?"

Virgil appeared wide-eyed. "He didn't say nothing. What the fuck is wrong with you, lady?"

"Take a breath, Riley," Ethan said. "We got them."

She ignored his comments and began to step toward the killer.

"It was Captain Pryce with IMPD? He ordered you to kill Chloe and Justin?"

"Yeah." The man trembled as she neared. "Hammond double-crossed him. He was talking to the Feds. He's coming here too and so is the Boss."

"Shut the hell up, man." Virgil's voice cracked as he tried to sound strong.

"That's why they wanted to find him. That's why Jacob was involved. They thought he might know where Hammond was." Riley aimed her weapon on Virgil Howard. "Who do you answer to, Mr. Howard?"

He remained silent, only staring at her in response.

"I can do far worse than throw you across the room, Mr. Howard. You should think about answering my question."

Ethan turned to her again. "Riley, just be careful. Don't let it get away from you again."

She ignored him as though he wasn't standing next to her. She ignored everyone except for Virgil Howard. "That's okay. I think I know the story now. The Feds found something on Hammond and so he made a deal to give them Pryce and Pryce didn't like that. He knew about Chloe Dawson. Maybe he was the one who told Hammond's wife. And she helped him plan how to take Chloe out to bring Hammond back in line. Stop him from cooperating."

Virgil smirked at her. "You have quite the imagination, little lady."

Riley returned a deadly smile. "You have no idea what I can do and what I can see. And I can see everything now." She cocked her weapon.

"Riley, don't!"

Ward and Moody pushed inside. Men in suits trailed behind.

"What the hell is going on?" Moody shouted.

"Lieutenant, it's her." The officer appeared frightened. "She's got some kind of power or something."

Moody creased his brow. "What the hell are you talking about?"

Ward looked at Riley. "Officer Thompson, I need you to stand down. These men here with me are Federal officers. Hammond told them what was going down. They're here to bring in Pryce and every one of these men here." He eyed Ethan, who appeared terrified. "Riley, put down your weapon, now."

"Better do what your daddy says, little girl," Virgil replied. "I knew that son of bitch Hammond wasn't coming."

With a swipe of her arm, Riley flung the man a good ten feet back. He slid to a stop in the middle of the plant.

"Call her off! Call her off!" Virgil demanded.

"Riley!" Ward shouted.

"Pryce ordered the deaths of Chloe Dawson and Justin Rehnquist to get back at George Hammond for cooperating with the FBI."

If we can get proof of that, this'll all be over. I knew Pryce was involved but not to this degree. He played all along like it was the Feds who wouldn't take the case seriously. He was just keeping the heat off him." Moody appeared calm, but his eyes told a different story. "Ward, whatever the hell this is, you have to put an end to it."

"I got this. Just please, let me handle this. She'll listen to me."

"It was all a lie, Lieutenant," Riley said. "Pryce was making sure none of you got too close, making it seem that he'd been working so hard to bring these men to justice. And all it did was get the people I love involved. That's where I draw the line." Riley flicked her leg and Virgil slid another five feet.

"Stop it now, Riley. You have to stop," Ward said. "You've done your job and we can all go home. Jacob is here. He's at the hospital, waiting for you."

Her shoulders dropped and she turned her sights to Ward. "He's here?"

"He's here. It's over now, Riley."

Abrams and Decker had no idea what Riley could do. Only Ethan had known. And this was not something he'd ever seen before. It was worse than the door. Riley was ready to kill Virgil Howard. "Don't do this, Riley. We're going to take these men in. They're going to prison for a long time," Ethan said.

Riley's face reddened and her forehead was drenched in sweat. "And what about Pryce? He tried to get Jacob killed. No. He's going to pay for what he did." She returned her attention to Virgil. "You know he's coming here, don't you?"

"I don't have a damn clue what you're talking about."

"You still don't get it, do you? I see you. I see everything about you." She ripped the gun from Virgil's hands and pushed him against one of the machines. She turned on the conveyor belt and raised him into the air.

"Jesus H. Christ. What the hell is she doing?" Moody said in a panic.

"Ma'am. You need to let us finish this with Hammond and Pryce," one of the agents began. "You don't know me and I don't know you, but I can tell you don't really want harm to come to anyone here."

Ward shot a glance to the agent before returning to Riley. "You disarmed these men. No harm can come to any of us now. You need to stop before you hurt him."

"It's too late," Riley said. "The storm's here."

The building rattled and papers flew wildly about from the desks. The conveyor belt Virgil Howard dangled over was spinning fast.

"For God's sake, do something! Stop her before she kills him." This time, it was Chris Decker who pleaded, a man who had been an ally to Riley, a friend, even. Now he was as afraid as the rest of them.

"Riley!" Ward rushed to her. "Stop! Now! You don't need to do this. This isn't like before. You're not a child anymore. Think about Carl. He needs you and you need him. This has to end now. I can't protect you if you go any further." Her eyes weren't her own. He didn't recognize the woman he saw before him. "Jacob's safe, Riley. He's in the hospital and he's safe. It's over now. These men will go to prison."

"You know what they did to her. What they did to Chloe. And to Justin," Riley said.

"I know. But you can't take justice into your own hands. That's not who you are. I know who you are. I remember the little girl inside the shelter. I know you don't want to hurt these people, even if they deserve it."

She blinked as though battling with the thoughts in her head. Riley began to realize what was happening. They all saw what she had done, what she was doing now. She'd just destroyed her life as she knew it.

Riley collapsed to the ground. The conveyor belt stopped and Virgil Howard fell. The building settled again.

Ethan rushed after her. "It's okay. You're okay."

The other officers and agents took the men into custody, all steering clear of her. She sensed their fear, their confusion. They saw her as a freak.

She dropped her head into her hands and sobbed. "I'm sorry. I'm so sorry."

Ward approached her and looked to Ethan. "Call an ambulance." He turned to Riley. "We're going to get you out of here now. You didn't hurt anyone, Riley. You stopped all of them from hurting us."

———

RILEY WOKE UP IN A HOSPITAL BED. DILLON STOOD NEXT TO her, holding her hand. Ethan stood at the end of the bed.

Ward leaned in the doorway. "Glad to see you're awake." He started inside. "How are you feeling?"

"Better," Riley replied.

"Good."

"Hey, sis. We were all pretty worried about you. Mom's coming down as soon as she finishes her shift at the diner."

"She doesn't have to do that. I'm fine."

"You're not, but you will be," Ethan said.

She looked at Ward. "I don't know what happened to me. Now they all know."

"None of those men in there with you—the officers, the agents —are going to say a damn word about what happened. In fact, I don't think they believe their own eyes anyway. You saved everyone in there from getting hurt, including me. If I'd shown up earlier, before you arrived, who knows what would've happened."

Riley recalled her vision about him. Now it seemed she'd been able to prevent it after all. "What about Pryce? Did he turn up?"

"No. Feds figured he saw the cars out front of the plant and knew things hadn't gone the way he planned. Everyone's on the lookout for him, though."

Riley nodded. "Where's Jacob?"

"Right here."

A nurse wheeled him inside the room. "You can't stay for long, but you can say hello."

Jacob nodded to her and stood up. "Hey, I hear you put on quite a show earlier. Sorry I missed it."

She laughed. "That's not funny. How are you?"

"I'll be fine." He approached her bedside and reached for her hand.

"I'll step out for a moment," Dillon said.

"I'll join you." Ward looked at Ethan.

"Yeah. Right." He eyed Jacob before finally leaving with the others.

"I can't believe what happened," Jacob said.

"Me neither, but I know I don't want it to happen again. I just don't know how to stop it."

"You'll figure it out. You always do." He squeezed her hand. "I called Carl, and after apologizing for taking his car and getting it shot up, I told him what happened."

"That's right, he did." Carl appeared in the doorway. "Kid owes me a lot of money. You know how hard it is to find parts for that old piece of shit?"

"Carl." She smiled.

"Hi, sweetheart." He approached her. "Well, you sure stirred the pot this time, didn't you?"

"I did."

"From what I gather, Ward's gotten everything under control. I knew he'd look after you."

"Dan covered for me," Riley began. "I almost killed someone and he covered for me."

"Believe me, Moody and his men had no problem putting that whole thing in their rear-view. You left a hell of an impression and I don't think they want to get on your bad side," Jacob replied.

"You did your job, kid," Carl said. "Glad you're all right. I'd better get back to the old folks' home. They'll miss me soon."

"You didn't tell them you were coming here?" Riley asked.

"No way. I still have my independence." He leaned in to kiss her cheek. "I don't see any more storms coming, do you?"

She shook her head and smiled.

"Good thing. Don't think my heart could handle it." Carl started to leave but stopped for a moment and regarded Jacob. "You take care of yourself, kid. And I'll be watching out for that check in the mail."

"Yes, sir." He watched as Carl left the room and looked back to Riley. "I'm so grateful you're okay."

"Back at you. What are you going to do now? Go back to the city and look for another job?"

Jacob brushed her hand with his and peered into her eyes. "I was kind of hoping I might stay here for a while. I hear jobs are coming back to town. Maybe an opportunity will present itself."

Ethan appeared in the doorway with a coffee in hand. He stopped short as he listened in on their conversation.

Riley felt his presence and turned in his direction to smile. He returned the smile and walked away.

THE END

ABOUT THE AUTHOR

Robin Mahle lives with her husband and two children in Virginia. She found her passion for writing, which later became her second career, after spending 20 years in the construction industry.

Having always been a lover of books, Robin attributes her creativity to the wonderful overseas adventures she has shared with her husband of 18 years. Traveling throughout Europe and having lived in England opened her mind and with that came a steady stream of story ideas inspired by her author-idols in the mystery/suspense genre.

If you enjoyed Ms. Mahle's work, please share your experience by leaving a review on <u>Amazon</u>.

ALSO BY ROBIN MAHLE

Force of Nature - A Riley Thompson Thriller (Book 0)

All the Shiny Things - A Kate Reid Novel (Book 1)

Law of Five – A Kate Reid Novel (Book 2)

Gone Unnoticed – A Kate Reid Novel (Book 3)

Blackwaters – A Kate Reid Novel (Book 4)

Endangered -A Kate Reid Novel (Book 5)

The Pretty Ones - A Kate Reid Novel (Book 6)

The Last Word – A Kate Reid Novel (Book 7)

Deadly Reckoning – A Kate Reid Novel (Book 8)

Primal Deception - A Lacy Merrick Thriller (Book 1)

Shadow Rising – A Lacy Merrick Thriller (Book 2)

First Target – A Lacy Merrick Thriller (Book 3)

Landslide

Beyond the Clearing

**Sign up to receive Robin's Newsletter so you can stay up to date on her new releases, events, contests and even exclusive new material!

Printed in Great Britain
by Amazon

48632544R00183